Also by Courtney Filigenzi

Let My Colors Out
My Cancer Days

CLOVER DOVES

COURTNEY FILIGENZI

BALBOA
PRESS
A DIVISION OF HAY HOUSE

Copyright © 2013 Courtney Filigenzi.

All rights reserved. No part of this book may be used or reproduced by any means, graphic, electronic, or mechanical, including photocopying, recording, taping or by any information storage retrieval system without the written permission of the publisher except in the case of brief quotations embodied in critical articles and reviews.

Balboa Press books may be ordered through booksellers or by contacting:

Balboa Press
A Division of Hay House
1663 Liberty Drive
Bloomington, IN 47403
www.balboapress.com
1-(877) 407-4847

Because of the dynamic nature of the Internet, any web addresses or links contained in this book may have changed since publication and may no longer be valid. The views expressed in this work are solely those of the author and do not necessarily reflect the views of the publisher, and the publisher hereby disclaims any responsibility for them.

The author of this book does not dispense medical advice or prescribe the use of any technique as a form of treatment for physical, emotional, or medical problems without the advice of a physician, either directly or indirectly. The intent of the author is only to offer information of a general nature to help you in your quest for emotional and spiritual well-being. In the event you use any of the information in this book for yourself, which is your constitutional right, the author and the publisher assume no responsibility for your actions.

Any people depicted in stock imagery provided by Thinkstock are models, and such images are being used for illustrative purposes only. Certain stock imagery © Thinkstock.

ISBN: 978-1-4525-7139-3 (sc)
ISBN: 978-1-4525-7141-6 (hc)
ISBN: 978-1-4525-7140-9 (e)

Library of Congress Control Number: 2013905544

Printed in the United States of America.

Balboa Press rev. date: 04/11/2013

To Anne:
My newest walking buddy!
Love our walks together!
Courtney Filgenzi

For My Soul Family

Acknowledgments

NO MATTER WHAT YOUR SPIRITUAL belief is, there is one absolute truth. Life teaches you lessons and the people that come in and out of your life bring you to these lessons and sometimes help you through them.

I am very fortunate to know so many beautiful souls. I think over the years and remember those who've joined my journey and I honor all the memories and the light you brought to my spirit. You made me who I am today and I love you all.

"Clover Doves" is a work of my soul and at this point in my life, I feel that it is the single most important work I will do in this lifetime. This story is a work of fiction, but Emma's spiritual growth mirrors mine. It is my hope, that those who read this book, read it with an open heart and mind and think about the important people and events in their lives.

It has been nearly six years since I began writing this book, and I would like to thank everyone who has supported me through this journey. First of all, I'd like to thank my Mom and Dad. You sacrificed so much to give me a good life and exposed me to a world of endless possibilities. You allowed me to grow and become the person I am and supported me with this crazy dream of becoming an author. Thank you.

I'd also like to thank the first people who read my book when it was merely a skeleton. Aunt Rita, Uncle Jay, Jack, Tricia and Kate—thank you for your love and support and thank you for dedicating time out of your busy lives to give this work a chance. I treasure all of you more than words can say.

My amazing editor, Evaline Auerbach, spent endless hours polishing this manuscript. Resourceful and thorough, she strengthened my writing and helped me create a story I am proud to present. I also appreciate her son, David Auerbach for helping me with Frederick's accent.

A huge thank you to Len Boswell and Joshua Diddams for helping me with the scenes and information involving Jared's military career and a big hug and thank you to Aime and my Aunt Veronica for taking the time to create beautiful artwork that represents "Clover Doves." Eric Bohacek of the Arizona Paranormal Activity Team also deserves a huge shout out for taking the time to read "Clover Doves" and sharing his thoughts. I greatly appreciate everything he's done.

I would also like to thank my in-laws, Jack and Jean, for their continued support and raising my amazing husband John.

And last but not least . . . my husband, John. John is one of the most incredible souls I know and I am honored to call him my husband and best friend. His love and support and the love and support of my beautiful boys, fill my life with more joy and happiness than I deserve.

Thank you! Thank you!! Thank you!!!

Prologue

THE SHEETS OF RAIN THAT had flowed over the Mustang's foggy windows slowed to a soft patter as the car made its way through the park's now abandoned roads. Mud splattered against the car's fire red paint as it picked its way through the relentless potholes. Emma leaned over and rested her head on Eric's shoulder, feeling for his hand tightly grasping the gear shift. Before they reached the final bend, leaving their secret hiding place for another day, Eric put the car in park, wrapped his arm around Emma and pulled her close. She pressed her body against his, running her fingers along his chest as they sat in silence. The branches of the towering old oak and sycamore trees blew in awkward circles as the wind began to change around them.

Emma raised her chin and pushed her long, dark hair behind her ears. Eric's chocolate eyes searched hers as she leaned over to kiss him. When he pulled himself from her lips, he caught her eyes. "What's up, Pumpkin? What are you thinking about?"

Emma sighed and kissed Eric's cheek, "Do you believe in soul mates?"

Eric smiled and sat back in his seat, "I don't know. What do you mean?"

"I mean reincarnation. Do you think you and I have been together before?"

Chuckling, Eric shook his head and replied, "I don't know . . . maybe?"

Emma pulled her body off his and stretched. Her fingers trailed along the soft, beige ceiling of the mustang as she rolled her shoulders and corrected her posture. "Well, I think we have. I remember the first time you touched me, the first time I looked into your eyes . . ."

"Yeah, I remember that."

Eric took Emma's tiny hand in his, kissed it softly and smiled, "Clumsy girl."

"It wasn't my fault I dropped all those lightbulbs. You bumped into me!"

"I know . . . I know. I'd only been working in that hardware store for a few days, but that's no excuse for running that very full cart right into you at the check-out line."

Emma smiled, "I didn't know a simple trip to the store to buy lightbulbs for my mother was going to be so memorable."

Emma's face grew serious and her eyes met Eric's. "The moment our hands touched, the moment our eyes met, I knew you."

Eric pulled his eyes away from hers, breaking the intensity of her stare and glanced down at their hands, now grasped together on his lap. "Yeah, I kinda know what you mean."

"I can't imagine being with anyone but you. I hope you know, I love you more than anything."

Eric looked into her chestnut brown eyes and all the pain he had felt in his life melted away like the last of the winter snow in the springtime sun. Only her arms could take away the years of pain that filled his soul with sorrow. Up until Emma, he had suffered through so much: his molestation, his parents never believing him, the drugs, the alcohol. It was still very painful and real, but much more bearable now that Emma was in his life. He smiled and leaned in to kiss her, knowing in his heart he would never let her go. "I love you, too."

Part 1
The End

Chapter: Emma

August 1998

Running exhilarates me. There's nothing I love more than feeling my feet pound the pavement. That evening in August was ideal for a run in the park. The sunlight sparkled through the lush tree canopy and the smells of late summer and of fresh cut grass filled the air. A few yellow leaves had already fallen off the tallest poplar trees and I could sense that autumn was near. Crickets called and cicadas sang as I ran further and deeper into the park. I felt at one with the beaten path, full of happiness and peace. Then the peace crashed around me, maybe forever.

Someone I hadn't seen grabbed me from behind and I hit the ground hard.

Pieces of gravel dug into my back as his body weight pushed me harder and harder into the ground. I screamed for help, but my attacker countered with his evil laughter. I punched and kicked, but the pathetic fight I put up against the strength of his body seemed to thrill and encourage him even more. His dark, rough whiskers scratched my face as his stale-beer and cigarette breath enveloped me. I screamed once more, my body throbbing in pain and horror. Then something hit me and everything faded to black.

When light came at last, I first thought I was dead. I was still lying on the ground, but the darkening woods had disappeared and now I was in a warm, bright light. I no longer felt any pain or fear and my attacker was gone. I slowly picked up my head and realized I had to be dreaming because Eric was standing there, and I knew Eric wouldn't be in the afterlife. He stood to the side of me, surrounded in the warm, yellow light that encompassed our surroundings. He held out his arms and I got up from the ground and ran to him. He brushed my debris-covered hair out of my face and looked deep into my eyes.

The powerful energy of the bond we shared flowed through our bodies and to each other. Eric's presence brought even more comfort to my soul. We were instantaneously one. I was his yin. He was my yang. The bond we had as soul mates seemed especially strong in this new ethereal world.

Although I had known Eric for only a year, it felt as though I had known him forever. His perfectly postured, six-foot, two-inch muscular frame and the intensity of his eyes resonated a strength and a consciousness that was far beyond his seventeen years. Eric had already experienced much more than other people his age. The wisdom and depth in his eyes overwhelmed many, but it attracted me full force. Nothing could shake him. The devastation he could laugh off would crumble others.

When he told me about surviving a traumatic childhood, his character fell into perspective. Eric's uncle had started molesting him when he was eight. His parents never believed him so he coped with it alone and by ten he started smoking, drinking and doing pot to numb the pain. By twelve, Eric's parents realized the danger he was in and got him professional help—but it was only for the alcohol and drug addiction. He pulled through, and though he will always be a year behind in school, he's a decent student. Eric's only remaining addiction is cigarettes. He smokes continuously, getting busted in school on more than one occasion.

I treasure every second I have with him, but for some unknown reason, an ache in the pit of my soul tells me that our time together will be short. It's hard for me to imagine anyone who could make me feel more secure or loved than Eric. I can sense his presence before I see him, feeling him deep within my soul. Powers far beyond anything I understand bond us together.

* * *

"Hey, Emma." The sound of Eric's voice comforted me even more. "It's over now. You're safe with me."

I did feel safe and warm in the bright light that surrounded us, in a new place and time, removed instantly from the oppressive horror I had found in the woods. As I glanced at our surroundings, I noticed six shadowy forms encircling us. The shadows were hardly shadows at all. In any other environment, they would have been as bright as a star. Though I should have felt terrified, I felt comforted and relaxed and my eyelids grew heavy. As I drifted off to sleep, voices echoed in my mind.

A woman's voice spoke. "It's not her time yet; she needs to go back."

Someone agreed, "Yes, her journey has just begun. She will grow so much within her lifetime."

Eric's arms tightened around me and I felt the vibration of Eric's chest as he said, "I'll take her back."

* * *

It could have been the light that blinded me, or the pain. I couldn't focus on anything. The comfort I felt moments before had disappeared and pain wracked my body. Voices continued to echo around me, but Eric's was not among them. I couldn't feel him anywhere near me.

A woman's voice called out: "Emma! Emma! Can you hear me?"

I mumbled, "Yes."

"She's coming around! Emma, do you know where you are?"

"No." I whispered as I drifted off again.

"You are at Howard County Medical Center. Do you remember what happened to you?"

Adrenaline pumped through my body and I tried to escape. Cold hands grasped onto my wrist and ankles as my body thrashed around trying to stop him. "Get off me!" I yelled.

"Emma! Emma, stop! It's over now. You are safe! You're in the hospital. We are going to take care of you!"

A needle pierced my upper arm and I suddenly felt calm. Unfamiliar metal, scraping noises echoed around me as nurses and doctors scrambled around the room. Someone called out, "Get me that rape kit, and here's her ID. Contact her parents."

I drifted off again. For how long, I don't know, but I woke with a jolt when a firm hand grasped my shoulder. "Emma, the police are here and need to know who did this to you."

A multitude of faces swam in and out of my line of focus. Cold scissors scraped across my body as my T-shirt was cut off me. Chills ran through me as I lay exposed and naked in the bright, white light.

A petite, blonde nurse in baby blue scrubs threw a scratchy hospital blanket over my chest just as a police officer entered the room.

"Hi, Emma. I'm Officer Cartwright. I need you to tell me who did this to you."

"I don't know . . ." I responded.

"Think Emma. We want to help you. Can you describe the person who hurt you?"

I could see the rapist's face and body clearly in my mind. I shuddered in revulsion as the words struggled to get out of my mouth. "He had really short hair and a goatee. His hair was brown. He had a nose ring and a ring in his eyebrow. He stunk . . . he stunk like beer . . . ."

"Okay, but tell us more about what he looked like." Officer Cartwright encouraged.

"He was big, over six feet tall, and strong . . ." A tear escaped the corner of my eye. I started to drift again. I didn't want to remember.

"What else?" Officer Cartwright demanded, lightly grasping my shoulder again. "Can you tell me more?"

"He smelled like stale cigarettes." I could still smell his stench on me.

"Did he have any tattoos or other markings?" Officer Cartwright continued.

"He had a tattoo on his chest. A dagger with a skull on it . . ."

"Have you ever seen him before?"

"No." I replied. I felt a sudden and unrelenting need to sleep, my body attempting to escape reality once more.

Someone stepped in. A man's voice gently spoke. "That's enough for now. We need to do some tests."

The police officer was ushered out of the room and I felt the doctor place my feet in stirrups as he began to examine me. I felt swabs being brushed across and inside my body and heard vial tops being tightened. "Okay, we got the samples we need. Let's check the wound on her head." My head continued to throb in pain and I kept my eyes clenched shut, trying to prevent it from getting any worse. Silence filled the room as a pair of cold hands pressed against my bruised skull. "Let's get a cat scan on that. I think she's fine, but we better be sure. Rachel, set that up and then clean her up a bit."

I still couldn't open my eyes, but I could hear people shuffling out of the room. Everything went quiet. I jumped when a nurse still at my side suddenly spoke, "Hey, honey. My name is Rachel and I'm going to be cleaning you up before you get your cat scan. Let me know if there is anything I can do to make you more comfortable." Through half-opened eyes I watched Rachel as she gently washed my skin with a thick pile of gauze pads, carefully dabbing at the scrapes and wounds all over my body. Her eyes were caring but her brown hair, the same color brown as the rapist's, brought hatred to a boil within me.

"You're lucky you know." She continued. "I know it doesn't feel like it now, but you could have been hurt much worse than this."

Glaring at her, I wanted to scream, "How dare you! How do you know! Have you ever been raped?" Deep down I wished I were dead. The emotional and physical pain was too much to bear. Exasperated and too tired to say a word, I turned my head and pretended to go to sleep.

Chapter: Eric

MY WORKDAY AT STEWART'S HARDWARE Store had ended uneventfully, but driving home from work I could sense something was wrong. My stomach churned and my legs grew weak and shaky. Even though the warm summer sun was setting behind the trees and the damp humidity was visible in the air, chills embraced my body. Something horrible had happened, but what, I didn't know. Emma's beautiful eyes flashed in my mind.

I called her house on my cell but no one answered. I strummed my fingers on the peeling vinyl steering wheel, desperately trying to grasp where these awful feelings were coming from. My old red mustang puttered to life as I pressed my foot on the accelerator. I needed to find out what was wrong. My cellphone rang, interrupting my racing mind.

"Hello?" I answered. I heard sobbing.

"Eric? It's Mrs. Fiorello. Something horrible has happened."

If I hadn't already sensed that something was terribly wrong, I would have assumed Mrs. Fiorello was on another drunken tirade.

"What?" My heart stopped, "Where's Emma?"

"Eric, we're at HCMC. Emma's been hurt really badly. You need to get here quick."

"What happened?"

"Emma was attacked when she was jogging at the park. She's fine, well, she's alive . . . but pretty messed up." Mrs. Fiorello choked.

I clenched my teeth, "What do you mean she was attacked?" I knew the answer before the words were spoken.

"Oh, Eric, honey . . . she was raped." Sobs erupted from Emma's mom. "She was left for dead. A woman found her and called for help. She's at the hospital. Come to the hospital."

"I'll be right there."

I hung up the phone and did a U-turn in the middle of the road. Stepping on the gas, my tires squealed as I passed the other vehicles in my way. Fury and anger pulsed through my veins. I wanted vengeance. I wanted to kill him. The surrounding homes, businesses and gardens became a colorless blur as I sped toward Emma.

The pleasant face of the hospital's receptionist did little to calm me. I asked for directions and rushed through endless halls to find Emma's room. Two burly, uniformed police officers stood in the hallway outside of her room and they looked at me with curiosity as I peered through the window of her door. Emma's mother cried at her bedside, one hand bracing her forehead, the other holding Emma's hand. Her father paced the room, his footsteps echoing off the barren, white walls, a scowl on his face and a vengeful look in his eyes.

My anger and fury subsided when I saw Emma's face. In sleep, she looked dead. Her face was as pale as her surroundings and deep black circles encompassed her eyes. Scrapes and bruises lined her cheeks and chin and continued down her arms and elbows.

I buckled with the reality that I almost lost the love of my life. I knocked on the door and her parents waved me in.

As usual, I felt uncomfortable near her parents. I knew they didn't like me because of my past, but there was nothing I could do to change that. They felt I brought too much baggage into such a "young relationship." I couldn't change the fact that I had been molested. The emotional pain I carried was something I had to overcome. Counseling had helped me a lot. Lately I had felt that they reluctantly accepted the fact that Emma and I loved each other.

I hesitated in the doorway. I wanted to run to her, to hold her, to touch her, but her parents' presence held me back.

"Eric," Mrs. Fiorello's voice broke the steady rhythm of her father's footsteps, "I'm glad you're here." Surprised at the sincerity in her eyes, I wondered if they might be more understanding towards me now that

Emma was a victim, too. But my gut told me that wasn't so. Mrs. Fiorello continued, "Emma needs you. She keeps calling out for you."

As I walked toward Emma's bed, I asked her father, "Do they know who did this?"

Mr. Fiorello spoke, "They don't know. They have collected a lot of evidence and are working on it. I hope to God they get him before I do."

I nodded, feeling the same way.

"May I?" I tilted my head toward Emma. I desperately needed to touch her.

Mr. Fiorello turned to Mrs. Fiorello. "Why don't we give him some time? We could use a break, get a coffee or something."

Emma's mom growled. I could smell alcohol on her breath. "No! I won't leave her!"

"Come on Cassie, let's take a break." Mr. Fiorello gently took Mrs. Fiorello's arm and coaxed her out of the chair and I watched them walk out the door.

The hard, navy-blue, vinyl seat crackled from age as I sat down next to Emma's bed. I stroked the one soft, unmarked section of her cheek and said, "Emma, Pumpkin, it's Eric. I'm here." She did not respond. Helplessness emptied me as I looked at her frail beaten body. I wanted to do something to fix her, but there was nothing I could do. Frustrated, I leaned down and softly kissed her cheek. I laid my head next to hers and I could smell her sweet, natural scent. I whispered, "Emma, I love you. I am so sorry. Please let me know you're okay."

Emma still didn't respond. "Emma, I could have lost you today. The pain that that thought causes me is too . . . too much . . . . I love you more than anything, please . . . please let me know you can hear me."

I held her hand tightly, hoping she could feel my presence and hear my words, desperate to get a response. Deep inside, I felt nothing but an unrelenting, tumultuous sea of angry emotions pulsating through my body—rage to see Emma hurt like this and guilt for not being able to protect her. Then again, helplessness replaced the anger as I looked at the non-responsive body lying in front of me. Emma's presence was gone—as if her soul had fled and only a shell remained. The sight scared me more than death itself.

Time slipped by and her parents came back. Desperate sadness filled me and I left the room. I rushed past the police officers, found a secluded area and pressed my forehead against the hard, cold wall. For the first time in years, I felt tears flow down my cheeks. An audible noise, like the tender beating of a heart could be heard as the tears dropped to the cold hospital floor.

Chapter: Emma

I WOKE UP TO FIND my parents in the room beside me. My mom sat quietly by the edge of my bed, tears streaming down her cheeks, trying to wipe them away with her hands, ignoring the tissues nearby. My dad paced the room, a dangerous look of vengeance glowing in his eyes.

"Mom, Dad . . . ." I said weakly, my throat sore from screaming during the attack. My head throbbed from being struck.

"Oh, honey!" Mom grabbed my hand. "You're up! I am so sorry! I should've known better! You never should have gone running in that park alone!" I winced as pain shot through my body when she tried to hold me. She sobbed even harder.

"Dad?"

My father's eyes would not meet mine. As he looked out the doorway and into the hallway he stated with a fierce fury, "Emma, we will find out who did this to you. I promise. I will personally find out who did this to you and take care of the bastard myself." He turned to look at me. The look in his eyes was ferocious. For a brief moment, I feared for the rapist.

Still finding it hard to speak, I murmured, "Eric?"

"He's here, honey. He's in the hall. Do you want me to get him?"

Terror filled me, a fear that was almost worse than the rape itself. Questions filled my mind. *Will Eric even be able to look at me? Will he think this is my fault? Will he ever want to be with me again?* The thought of losing Eric was paralyzing.

My dad opened the door and waved him in. Before I knew it, Eric was at my bedside and my parents had left the room. The fear that filled me instantly subsided when I saw him.

Eric still had his work clothes on. The knees of his jeans, starting to form holes, were covered by a light layer of dirt, probably from kneeling as he shelved potting soil or fertilizer. His black T-shirt with the 'Stewart's Hardware' logo looked comfortably worn as well. Small holes were beginning to form around the collar but it hung perfectly on his sculpted body. When he sat down next to me, I brushed the soft brown hair hanging in his face away from his eyes so I could look at him. His red-rimmed eyes and tear-streaked cheeks startled me and he looked away.

"Eric, thank you for coming to get me. You made me feel so safe."

"Oh, Pumpkin," he sighed, "It wasn't me; the EMTs got you into the ambulance and brought you here. I didn't get you. I just wish I had . . ." He took my hand and I suddenly felt intense inner strength. But Eric still avoided my eyes. Looking defeated, his unfocused gaze traveled from my chin to the frame of the hospital bed as he continued, "A woman jogging found you laying on the side of the path and called them."

"But you were there, in the park, holding me."

Eric shook his head, but he still wouldn't look at me. "No, it must have been a dream or something. I have been here at the hospital, though, waiting for you to come back."

Fear enveloped me each time his eyes avoided mine. "I am so sorry." I stuttered as tears began to flow. "If you don't want to be with me anymore, I understand. I tried to fight. I tried so hard, but he was so much stronger than me."

Eric's eyes grew wide with shock and they finally met mine, "Jesus, Emma, this isn't your fault! You should know that, I, of all people would know that! How could you even think I'd want to leave you? I love you. Nothing will ever change the way I feel about you . . . nothing."

He bent over and kissed me gently on the forehead. Peace filled me. My mind flashed to the memory of our first kiss.

In late summer, we had walked down to an old, splintering fishing dock nearby. He gingerly took my hand and pulled me toward him to hold me close. I could feel his warmth against me and I felt sheltered by the size and strength of his body. Eric gently lifted my chin to look me in the eyes. His dark, brown hair blew softly in the breeze and I was amazed at how gorgeous he was. He brushed his lips lightly against mine—his kiss magical and romantic. When he lowered his head to kiss me again, his soft, warm lips pressed harder against mine. In the power flowing between us, I felt our souls combining as one. I felt no doubt that we were supposed to be together; I felt nothing could be more powerful than the love we felt between us. Every kiss felt this way. Every kiss was amazing.

I looked into his eyes. "I hope nothing will change the way you feel about me. I know I will always love you."

Eric smiled. "I love you, too, Pumpkin."

* * *

When that summer ended, I found myself getting ready for the first day of my junior year at Marriottsville High School. Only a few physical scars remained from that horrific evening in the park, but emotionally I felt drained.

During the day, life had continued normally. Home life continued as it always had and Eric and I stayed happy together.

The nights, however, had been the hardest for me. My deepest, darkest fears would escape the protective bondage of my mind, baring and gnashing their putrid yellow teeth in the form of heart-stopping, never-ending, horrendous nightmares. I dreamt that the rapist was always one step behind me, following me everywhere I went, waiting for the perfect moment to attack again. I would run and run, but he stayed dangerously close behind me as I desperately tried to keep myself out of his reach. Too often, he grabbed me and threw me to the ground. I'd see his greedy smile and smell his putrid breath as he'd lower himself onto my body. I woke up screaming, scared and sweaty but fortunately, very much alone.

The police continued their search for the rapist, and I found myself constantly looking over my shoulder. I often felt physically ill just thinking about it, and this morning was no exception.

The smell of eggs and bacon filled the house as another wave of nausea overwhelmed me. I pressed myself against the cool wall, trying to prevent myself from passing out on the floor. Weakness and exhaustion tempted me to bed, but I pulled myself together and walked to the kitchen. Mom looked at me, a worried expression on her face. "Are you all right, honey?" she asked.

"I guess so." I said, sitting down at the kitchen table.

"Are you nervous about the first day back to school?" Mom's back was turned to me. She scraped a pile of scrambled eggs onto a plate and added some bacon.

"Not really." I lied, laying my head down on the table to prevent the nausea from coming again. Actually, I was terrified to face the other kids at school. The news reports and newspapers had never released my name, but in a small town like this, rumors spread rapidly, especially bad ones. Everyone knew what had happened. Facing the stares and whispers in the halls was something I was not looking forward to. At least I had Eric.

"How are you feeling?" My mom looked concerned. "You look gray."

"Not that great." I replied, trying to lift my head off the table. "I had another dream last night. I feel really weak and tired today."

"Oh . . ." My mother's face blanched and the frying pans clanged as she dropped them into the sink. Confused by her reaction, I changed the subject. "I have biology with Mr. Peterson this year. That will be great!" Mom smiled and I struggled to respond in kind.

I loved biology. I worked part time at a veterinary office and was considering becoming a veterinarian. I loved spending time in nature hiking, biking and kayaking. Of course now, I was terrified of being in nature alone.

As Mom placed the plate of eggs and bacon in front of me, I noticed it was time to leave, so quickly ate a few bites, grabbed my bags and headed toward the door. "Thanks for the eggs! See you after school!" I said as positively as I could.

"Okay, honey. See you then." Mom's face still looked ashen. I assumed her worry about my first day of school had gotten the best of her.

Eric pulled up in his old red, 1978 Cobra Ford Mustang. He and his father had rebuilt the entire engine together. Then he used some of the money he earned at the hardware store to get it a new paint job. It looked fantastic.

As we drove to school, Eric smiled and assured me everything would be fine. His presence relaxed me. Whenever Eric was around, I felt like everything would be fine.

The stares and whispers were not nearly as bad as I had thought they would be. Most people avoided me. While this would usually bother me, it filled me with relief. I had learned that most people avoid situations that make them feel uncomfortable. You could figure out who were your true friends when they showed up to be with you in the toughest times. Apparently, my girl friends weren't truly friends at all. Every one of them disappeared into thin air after the rape.

Eric knew I was nervous so he made sure he could walk me to every class. Just one look into his eyes and the warmth of his hand sustained me through the hours we were apart. Before I knew it, the day was over.

Driving home, Eric smiled and said, "That wasn't so bad was it?"

"No," I smiled. "Much better than I thought. Thank you so much for being there. It really helped to have you with me between classes."

Pulling into the driveway, he replied, "I loved to do it. You know I will always be there for you." He leaned over to kiss me goodbye. "Love you. I'll call you after work." I watched as Eric drove off to Stewart's hardware store to stock more shelves and smiled.

Mom met me at the door with a very anxious look on her face. "How'd it go?"

"Fine." I said. She still looked gray. I couldn't ignore it any longer. "Mom, what's wrong?"

"I got something for you." She handed me a brown paper bag. I opened it and the fear that overtook me caused me to drop the bag onto the floor. It was a pregnancy test.

My mom grasped my arm. "Oh, honey, I didn't mean to upset you. It's just that I noticed you haven't started yet and I'm worried about your symptoms." Biting her lip she continued, "I know all your initial STD tests came back negative, but this couldn't be checked that early, and, well, I think we better check."

Shocked and terrified, I didn't know what to think. It never occurred to me that I could have gotten pregnant from the rape.

My hands shook uncontrollably. I bent down to pick up the bag and nearly passed out. But then, with a deep breath, I grabbed it and walked steadily to the bathroom. After carefully reading the instructions, I took the test. My mind became vacant with panic as I waited the longest two minutes of my life.

I tried to focus on something positive, but there was nothing to grasp onto. I checked my watch and turned to look at the results. Pregnant. I was pregnant. Grasping the edge of the sink, I sunk to the floor and sobbed.

I heard a soft knock on the door. My mother entered. I could barely see her through the tears, but I could tell she was holding something. I focused on her eyes and she looked at me with a resolve I didn't understand. "This will be taken care of," she said.

She thumbed through the item she was holding-a phone book. I heard her dial a number, but I don't remember a word she spoke. After hanging up the phone, she told me I had an appointment tomorrow, Tuesday, and it would all be over soon. The reality of what she had done hit me like a boulder. She had called an abortion clinic. Guttural wails escaped from the tortured pit of my soul. My body thrashed in the agony that enveloped my every cell. I wanted to die. All I wanted to do was die.

Looking blankly in my direction then turning to leave the room, my mother said calmly, "This is for the best."

The only response I could muster were sobs of pain. My mind shut down. My only coherent thoughts were, "I want it out of me now. I want it over."

I lay alone on the cold bathroom floor for almost an hour. By the time I stopped crying, I couldn't think, I couldn't move. I could hardly even breathe.

I don't remember finding enough strength to pull myself up from the floor, but eventually, I must have stumbled to my bedroom, collapsed on my bed, and fallen into a restless sleep.

Images of Eric flashed in my mind. A beautiful baby bounced happily in his arms. The baby looked at me with deep brown eyes,

Eric's eyes, and he smiled at me. Shock and fear consumed me. I woke up, ran to the bathroom and puked.

I braced myself against the sink as I splashed ice cold water on my face and slowly patted it dry with a towel. I stared blankly into the vacant face reflected in the mirror and wondered, "Could it be true? Could this baby be Eric's?" Vomit burned my throat again.

I dreamt of being pregnant with Eric's baby, but I always envisioned my first pregnancy as being a proper one: after a beautiful wedding and after being settled down a few years. I never envisioned the nightmare I was in now.

Trying to think clearly, I thought about the timing. The last time Eric and I had sex was before my last period. It couldn't be our baby. It must be that bastard's.

I took a deep breath and steadied myself. Looking into the mirror, I stared at my hollow eyes and tried to convince myself, "It's not our baby. It's his . . . I need to get it out of me, now!" I barely made it to the toilet in time to throw up again.

Chapter: Eric

Knowing Emma had been raped distressed me in many ways. First and foremost, I hated to see the woman I loved physically hurt and in pain. The bruises and scrapes slowly faded over time, but I could clearly see the emotional struggle she faced within. I knew what she was feeling. I had experienced it myself.

It was this second truth that tore at my soul. The swirling clouds of torment and pain in her eyes mirrored a perfect reflection of my former self. To see the pain I had felt in someone I loved so much was too much to bear. I tried to stay strong for Emma, but I could feel myself slipping back into that deep dark well that took years to climb out of.

Echoes of my past continuously filled my mind. Images that I had long ago suppressed appeared and once again ripped me apart.

When I was eight, my mom's brother, Uncle Tim, had started casually touching me in places I knew he shouldn't. As months passed, the touching became more and more physical, culminating in rape. He made me promise to never tell anyone. The molestation had been going on for over nine months when I had turned nine.

Knowing he had done something wrong to me, I finally mustered up enough strength to tell my parents the truth. I remember being terrified. I can still hear my soft footsteps on the hardwood floor as I walked into the kitchen. The smell of the fried eggs and sausage my mother cooked smelled, not appetizing but nauseating. My father sat at our old, kitchen table reading the local newspaper, sipping a cup of coffee. Moments passed before either of them realized I was there.

"Oh, hi honey! I didn't know you were up yet!" My mother said. "You look cute today!" She straightened the collar of my favorite blue shirt and kissed me on the forehead. I started to cry.

"Eric, what's wrong?" My mom asked. Dad sat the paper down and for the first time looked in my direction.

Clenching my fists, and holding myself as erect as I could, I said, "Uncle Tim has been hurting me." Tears of relief flowed from me. I had finally told someone the horrible secret I had been hiding.

"How does Uncle Tim hurt you?" My mother asked, surprised.

Feeling stronger, I replied with the response I had practiced over and over again in front of the mirror, "He touches my privates and puts his near mine." I released my clenched hands in relief.

I saw anger flare into my mom's eyes and I thought to myself, "Oh, thank god, she's going to help me!"

She dropped her spatula, glared at me and then at my father. "How dare you!" she spit. "How dare you say something so awful about your Uncle Timmy! If you ever say anything like that again, I will beat your ass silly and throw you out on the street you ungrateful little bastard! Go to your room." My father shook his head in disappointment and never said a word.

I ran to my room and hid in the dark corner of my closet, scared that my parents would punish me for what I had said. I was completely, and totally confused. My parents didn't believe me, abandoning me instead of protecting me-threatening me instead of my asshole Uncle Tim. I never expected to be left alone to deal with this pain. The two people I adored more than anyone actually thought I was lying. I remember thinking, "If they don't believe me, no one else will." I silently sobbed in the dark, alone and scared.

By the time I was ten, I was in an emotional hole I never thought I could escape. Uncle Tim had moved out of state, but the memories of his abuse still tormented me. I started to smoke cigarettes. Then I started sneaking booze out of my parents' cabinets. By eleven, I was smoking pot daily. The tranquility I felt from the drugs and alcohol momentarily soothed my pain, but when their effects wore off, I would emotionally crumble, desperately needing another fix again. Eventually, my parents noticed my bad habits and got me help to overcome my symptoms, but to this day, they still don't believe I was molested. Thank god my counselor did.

Seeing Emma violated the way I was burnt a hole in my soul. As the memories of my past resurfaced, I craved the drugs that helped me through those times. Eventually, I succumbed and a few months after her rape, I bought some pot and started smoking again. I told myself that doing it was no big deal, especially if it helped me help Emma. Knowing I was there to help her through this difficult time empowered me. I may have had to suffer alone, but at least Emma didn't. Everyone knew about Emma's rape. There were no secrets, just absolute truth. Emma was raped and no one could contradict that. She had me and anyone else who was willing to be there for her.

I was thrilled that the first day of school had gone so well. I noticed a few whispers in the hallways when I walked Emma to class, but nothing more. The nervous air around her disappeared as the day went on. When I dropped her off at home, she was actually smiling. Things were starting to look better.

Emma and I spent hours talking about her rape as well as mine. I watched her grow stronger day by day, but hid the fact that I was falling apart inside. I had never lied to her about anything and this charade made me feel guilt on top of everything else. To myself, I justified the drugs because they enabled me to be Emma's "Knight in shining armor." I didn't want to fail her. I wanted to be her counselor, her unconditional support. I felt that as long as I could be there for her, she would be fine and so would I.

Then, my cell phone rang.

"Eric, It's Mrs. Fiorello."

"Oh, Hey!" I replied, surprised to hear her voice instead of Emma's.

"Emma doesn't know that I am calling you, but I think there is something you need to know."

"Okay, so, what do I need to know?"

Mrs. Fiorello sighed. "Emma's pregnant."

"What?" I never expected to hear this.

"Emma has been a little ill lately, so when she got home from school, I gave her a pregnancy test. She took it. She's pregnant." She didn't wait for me to respond. "I set up an appointment at the clinic tomorrow. She will be having an abortion." Mrs. Fiorello's voice sounded unusual, almost cocky.

"Can I, can I talk to her?"

"No. As I'm sure you understand, she was very upset with this news. She's had a rough afternoon and is sleeping right now. I have turned off the ringer on the phone in her room so she won't be disturbed. She will not be going to school tomorrow so there is no need to pick her up."

"Oh, okay. I will try to call her tomorrow then."

"Thanks, Eric. Goodbye."

I listened as she hung up the phone.

I felt sick. Emma was pregnant, presumably from the rape. As soon as I got home, I checked a calendar. I knew when her last period was. The last time we made love was two days before it. It was technically impossible that the baby could be ours. Technically. I recalculated the timing and came up with the same conclusion. The baby had to have been conceived by the rape. The abortion would be for the best. Regardless, it was Emma's decision.

Waiting all night to talk to Emma nearly killed me. When I woke up the next morning, I tried to reach her, but no one answered. Disappointed, I figured either her ringer was still off or they must have already left for the appointment at the clinic. I reluctantly drove to school, desperately wishing I could be there for Emma. I could not get her out of my mind. I needed to be there for her.

The first few hours of school crept by, and when lunch finally arrived, I frantically dialed Emma's number again. No one answered.

Anxiety and fear filled me as the day dragged on. I desperately needed to talk to Emma. I needed to know that she was okay.

Once school ended, I tried to call her again. Still no answer, but this time I left a message.

"Emma, hey, it's Eric. I'm worried about you. Give me a call."

Minute after minute, hour after hour passed and no call came. I wondered where she was and if she was avoiding me. I felt completely strung out. After dinner, I picked up the phone and tried to reach her again. Still, no one answered. By 9:00, the desire to be near her persuaded me to walk to her house. A cold, biting wind, out of season for the time of year, whipped me as I walked down the wood-lined streets. The sound of the wind blowing through the trees reminded me of hiking with Emma and I couldn't help but smile at the past.

The house looked dark and abandoned when I arrived there. The screen door was swinging on its hinge, hitting the house every time a chilling, stiff breeze came through. The cars were parked in the driveway, but nobody was up. I stood on the front curb and stared up at Emma's bedroom window, hoping she'd sense me and look out like she has done so many times before. She never came

I lit a cigarette, and whispered, "Come on Emma, I'm here," but I couldn't feel her presence. I wondered if she couldn't feel mine, or if she was ignoring me. Over an hour passed as I sat on the curb and waited for something to happen. I lit my last cigarette and inhaled deeply. The smoke burning in my chest comforted me. I stared at her window, praying to catch just one glimpse of her. As time passed, I realized there was nothing I could do. Knowing she was safe in bed, I left.

Not being able to reach Emma and knowing what she must be going through frustrated me. I needed a smoke, but this time, a cigarette wouldn't do. I changed course, deciding not to walk home but to go to Tristan's. I knew he'd have what I needed and he did.

* * *

The next morning, I was pretty fucked up. My head was pounding and I felt like I had a hole in my heart. I managed to get up in time for school and tried calling Emma again, but no one answered. They were avoiding me. I wondered if this avoidance was coming from Emma or her parents. Maybe she was too emotional to care. There was no way for me to know.

I drove by her house on the way to school. The front screen door still swung on its hinge and all the cars still sat in the driveway. Frustrated, I drove to school.

With little hope, I tried to call Emma again at lunch. This time someone answered.

"Hello?" Mrs. Fiorello said.

Shocked I replied, "Finally, Hi Mrs. F. It's Eric. Can I please talk to Emma?"

Mrs. Fiorello answered. "I'm sorry, no, Eric. She's sleeping right now. Can I give her a message?"

Frustration shook me. I replied through gritted teeth, "Please tell her to call me. I really need to talk to her."

"I will, but don't be surprised if you don't hear from her." Mrs. Fiorello's voice sounded unusually peppy under the circumstances. I wondered if she had been drinking again. She continued, "She's exhausted and stressed. All she wants to do is sleep. She's having the abortion first thing tomorrow morning. She doesn't seem to want anyone near her."

"Well, let her know I am here if she needs me." I wanted so much for her to need me.

Mrs. Fiorello snorted, "Okay, Bye."

"Bye." I hung up, pissed off at Mrs. F's attitude. Frustrated, I punched a nearby locker. A couple students, startled from the noise, quickly moved away as my social studies teacher grabbed me by the shoulder, glared at me and said, "Eric, cool it down. Behavior like that can get you suspended."

"Whatever," I murmured, pulling myself from his grip. I sneered as he continued down the hallway, then turned and rubbed the broken skin on my knuckles. I didn't give a shit what he thought, what anybody thought. The rest of the school day dragged on. I went to work after school, and then went to hang out with Tristan again. I hated not being with Emma. I wanted to help her through this. The pain from not being able to see Emma coupled with the pain from my past started to tear at my soul. I needed drugs to avoid it and drugs I got.

Chapter: Emma

THE ABORTION WAS SCHEDULED FOR Thursday. On Thursday morning, my mother and father both drove me to the clinic. Numbness filled my bones as I sat in the waiting room. I remember looking at all the women waiting—their faces blank, their eyes empty, as their babies faced the same fate as mine. I wondered if those children were conceived in an act of love, or if they were conceived in horror like mine. Regardless, they all faced the same end.

I heard a nurse call my name. She lead me through a maze of stark white hallways to the room where the abortion was to be performed. Blinded by the brightness of my surroundings, I secretly laughed at the irony. The shining, tiled floor, the blank white walls and the painted, white ceiling mocked me. I wrapped my arms around myself, trying to hide the filthiness inside of me. Such purity—such clean, total whiteness enveloping this painful dark experience. It was unbearable. I got undressed, put on a white hospital gown, and lay down on the table as instructed.

A nurse came in and hooked me up to a heart monitor. My heartbeat echoed throughout the room. I couldn't escape the sound. The pounding in my head made me feel as though I was going to pass out. In a strange state of consciousness, I became confused. Was the heartbeat mine or the baby's? A tear rolled down my cheek.

Trying to focus on anything but the heartbeat, I searched my surroundings. A poster on the ceiling above me had five penguins on it. All of them looked exactly alike except the one in the middle who had on a top hat and a colorful Hawaiian shirt. The poster read "You're one in a million!" I found myself internally, insanely laughing again. I thought about how terrified I had been that the rapist would find me and hurt me again. Constantly looking over my shoulder, it never occurred to me that he didn't need to be present to torture me again. The night he raped me, not only had he raped me physically and emotionally, but a month later, the remains of his evil attack would succeed in tearing out the last small piece of innocence in my soul. The white vacuum surrounding me sucked that one minuscule remaining light of innocence from me. In my heart and soul, I knew I could never get back what the rapist took from me that night. That Emma was forever, permanently gone.

After an eternity, a doctor came in. He smiled and asked how old I was. "Seventeen," I replied.

"Let's see," he smiled. He looked over my records, and with a new understanding, his almond eyes stopped smiling at me. He pushed up the sleeves of his white jacket, called in his nurses, and as they started to put me under anesthesia he said with a new sense of urgency, "Don't worry, this will be all over soon."

"Yeah, right." I thought as the anesthesia blissfully sent me to sleep.

*   *   *

I slowly began to wake up as the anesthesia wore off. Disoriented, I became nervous at the unfamiliar surroundings, but a sudden onset of horrible abdominal cramps reminded me of where I was. On my side of the room, chairs and beds lined the wall and cheap white cabinets lined the opposite wall. A woman sitting in a chair directly next to my bed threw up in a bedpan. I could smell vomit and antiseptic. I looked around and noticed my mother speaking quietly to the doctor in the corner of the room.

During my pre-surgical counseling, I had decided to start taking birth control pills. I realized I had no control whether a man raped me, but I could control whether or not I got pregnant. I never wanted to be in this horrific position again. I listened as the doctor gave my mother instructions on when to begin the pills and watched as he handed her a prescription. When he was through, he looked up and glanced in my direction. He smiled as he walked over to the bed and said, "How's our girl doing? It's all over now." I couldn't respond. I felt sick. I needed to puke.

    I don't remember getting to the car. I don't remember the ride home, but I do remember getting home and going straight to the bathroom. In a daze, I stripped off all my clothes and stepped into the shower. I let the warm water splash over me. I grabbed a washcloth, covered it with soap and started to frantically scrub my entire body. I scrubbed so hard I turned red, but I couldn't get the disgusting feeling off me. I silently, desperately sobbed while I scrubbed at the evil on my body, but no matter how hard I tried, I couldn't get it off me.

Chapter: Eric

I DIDN'T EVEN BOTHER TRYING to call on Thursday, the day of the abortion. I couldn't understand why Emma avoided me. I would have done anything to have someone by my side, but of course, this was entirely different. Emma was not alone. She had her parents, but deep down inside, I knew they couldn't possibly understand her pain the way I did. I desperately wanted to be with her. I hoped that Emma realized, somewhere inside of her, that I was there if she needed me. Apparently, she didn't. After school, I got high again.

Emma didn't need me on Friday either. The question "Why?" kept reverberating in my mind and I wondered if the question reverberated in Emma's mind as well. It probably did, but for entirely different reasons: *Why did this happen to her? Why did she have to get pregnant?*

I decided that on Saturday I would see her no matter what. I would make her see me, make her talk to me. But, disappointed in my drug use and myself, I realized that Emma deserved better than I had become. I knew I had to stop the drugs and alcohol. I didn't do any pot Friday. I wanted to be clean and strong when I finally saw Emma on Saturday.

Chapter: Emma

SLEEP QUICKLY BECAME MY DEAREST friend, my only place of safety. Dreams of the warm, beautiful light and Eric holding me replaced the nightmares that had haunted me. I couldn't identify the six shadows that surrounded us in a shield of strength, but they did not scare me. Occasionally, I caught a glimpse of the most beautiful blue eyes, but they disappeared as quickly as I saw them. Eric held me close to his strong, warm body. The sound of his heartbeat drummed in perfect synchrony with mine. The six shadows surrounding us silently communicated, their presence exuding a peace and love that I couldn't even begin to imagine when awake. I wished I could sleep forever.

My alarm clock jolted me awake. All the peace I felt subsided and the holes it left filled with an anxious combination of pain and dread. It was Saturday, two days after the abortion. I decided I could no longer hide in my room, away from life. I needed to get back to my regular schedule. I hoped that routine would distract me from the endless waves of emotional pain.

My shift at the veterinary office started at 8:00. Dragging myself out of bed and into the bathroom, I looked in the mirror and empty eyes stared back. I washed my face, brushed my teeth and slowly got into a pair of purple scrubs.

A soft knock at the door preceded my mom's entrance. She looked beautiful in a delicate pink nightgown as she stretched a refreshing night of sleep away. Her long brown hair was pulled up into a tight bun and her make-up was already perfect. "Are you sure you want to go, honey? I could call in sick for you?"

"No, I mean yes . . . I am going . . . I want to go." Overwhelmed, I turned my head so she couldn't see how hard it was for me to try to go on. I wanted to exude strength. This situation had already caused enough pain for all of us.

"Okay then," she replied. "Please call me if you need anything. I packed you a lunch. Make sure you eat it."

"Thanks." Grabbing the bagged lunch, I bolted out the door. Tears rolled down my cheeks as anxiety gripped me. I sat in my car for a brief moment trying to collect myself. Realizing my mom watched from the window, I fumbled for the keys, turned on the car and drove to the vet clinic. I arrived fifteen minutes early. "Good," I thought, "time to pull myself together."

I took a deep breath and closed my eyes. Suddenly, I felt stronger. I felt peace. I couldn't see him, but I could sense he'd be here soon. I felt Eric's strength and love. Comfort enveloped me. This happened all the time. At first I thought I imagined these feelings, but I soon realized it was real. I could feel Eric's presence before I saw him. He felt mine, too. Our souls spoke to each other before our minds even knew we were together again.

I watched as Eric's mustang pulled into the parking lot and parked next to me. He smiled, but the smile did not reach his eyes. Concerned, he searched my face for a sign. I wondered what he saw. I slowly got out of the car and he rushed over to me. Taking my chin in his hand, he held my face so his soul could look directly at mine. "Are you okay?"

I couldn't hide the truth from him. I didn't need to speak for him to know how I felt. I lowered my gaze from the intensity of his eyes, but our souls were locked. No way to avoid the truth, I responded in the most realistic, but not completely honest way I could to minimize the pain I felt inside. "I'm alive."

"Well," Eric shuddered, "thank god for that!" My words settled him slightly and he drew me close. A small part of me felt peace in his arms.

I hadn't seen him since I found out I was pregnant. In fact, I had avoided him. Eric had tried to call me but I hadn't wanted to face him with the truth. My mother, however, filled him in on everything, which distressed me intensely. That strange feeling that told me our time together was short, kept creeping back and I didn't think my mother informing him helped our situation at all. Deep inside, I thought he'd be disgusted with me. How could he want to be with someone like me? The evil and dirt that touched my physical body now tore at my soul. No one, not even Eric, would want someone damaged like me.

As if he read my mind, Eric pushed my body from his so he could look me in the eyes again. "Why didn't you talk to me? I wanted to be there for you."

"Why would you?" I smirked, adverting my eyes from his.

"I love you. Don't you realize that?"

"How? How can you love me? How can you want to be with me? I'm dirty. I'm disgusting. And, now I'm a murderer . . ." My knees buckled at these words of my newfound reality escaped with my breath. Regardless of the fact that I got pregnant from a rape, I found the guilt from the abortion one of the most difficult things for me to handle. I never would kill anything intentionally, but I had an abortion without ever giving it a second thought. Doing something like this was not in my nature, not in my soul. Now, guilt topped the overwhelming flow of emotions I felt, and it was drowning me.

"Emma, you are not a murderer. You are a victim. This was for the best."

I shook my head, "In my mind I know that, but in my soul . . . it hurts . . ." My voice trailed off. "Regardless, you deserve someone better, someone less . . . damaged."

"Don't you realize I only want you? I almost had to face losing you, forever, and it nearly killed me. I hate what happened to you. If I could take it back, I would, but never, never will I ever hold you to blame for this! Nothing will ever change the way I feel about you! Nothing!"

I looked deeply in his eyes and saw the truth there, but I didn't want to believe it. *"Yeah right,"* I thought to myself.

Eric smiled at me. "I can tell you don't believe me, but it's true. You'll see." He kissed me on the forehead and I couldn't help but smile. At that moment, having him near me and having the hope that what he spoke was the truth, was good enough for me—for now.

Realizing it was 8:00, I started to walk toward the door of the vet clinic. Eric stopped me, "One more thing. Don't ever leave me out of your life again. I want to be there for you. I wanted to be there for you on Thursday." He stumbled for words. "I hated not being there . . . please . . . never again . . ."

"Okay," I replied, "I promise." I couldn't imagine anything else that could possibly happen to drive us apart again. Waving goodbye, I turned to walk into the office. Flyers were posted along the storefront. The evil eyes and menacing tattoo on the sketches of my assailant stared back at me. I shuddered as I walk through the door and wondered if he would ever be caught.

Work went well that day. All my negative thoughts were pushed aside as I worked alongside the doctor. I loved working with the animals and they liked me too and I found comfort in knowing that, at least, I could help ease their pain. Before I knew it, it was 3:30 and time to go home.

Eric had to work at the hardware store that night and all the next day so I spent my time sleeping as much as possible. By Monday morning, I found myself well rested and ready to face school. Fortunately, the latest terrible episode in my life, the abortion, wouldn't headline the evening newspaper or make it to the evening news, so no one paid much attention to me. I liked it that way.

Chapter: Eric

AFTER SEEING EMMA ON SATURDAY, I felt a lot better. I worked through the rest of the weekend, excited for Monday to come.

When I picked up Emma, she was smiling. School went really well that day. Things were practically normal.

After school, I drove Emma home, gave her a huge kiss and went back to my house. Filled with relief and happiness, I burst through the front door, dropped my backpack on the floor and looked up. Uncle Tim was standing there.

"Hi Eric! How have you been?" He sauntered toward me and tried to give me a hug.

I backed away and demanded, "What are you doing here?"

"I thought I'd stop by for a visit," he smiled. "Aren't you happy to see me?"

Panic flowed through every cell in my body. I knew I was stronger now, but the fear I felt as a child embraced me completely. "Where are my parents?"

"They went out to the store to pick up a few things for dinner. They weren't expecting me." Uncle Tim tilted his head as he stepped closer and stroked my cheek with his baby soft, perfectly manicured fingers. "You don't know how much I've missed you."

My heart pounding, adrenaline pumping, I stepped back and tripped over my backpack and fell to the floor. Uncle Tim stepped closer, his blue eyes absorbing me. "You have grown into a beautiful young man . . ."

"You know I haven't missed you." I spit, scrambling to my feet and finding myself still way to close to him.

"Oh, yes you have. I know you don't want to admit it." He reached for my arms to pull me closer to him.

I pulled my fist back and punched him as hard as I could. Shocked, he stumbled backwards, and rubbed his face where I hit him. Anger filled his eyes. "So you're going to put up a fight this time!" Uncle Tim lunged toward me again and tried to grab me.

"Yeah." I growled.

After the first punch, I knew I had the upper hand. I may have been younger, but now I was stronger. I jumped forward, repeatedly punching him in the stomach then in his face. Uncle Tim toppled over in pain. I pushed him to the floor and started to kick him. I couldn't stop myself. I didn't want to stop myself. Years of pain turned to rage. I wanted to kill him.

Bloodied and bruised, Uncle Tim, cowered in fear. Suddenly, the front door opened.

"What the hell is going on here?" My father yelled as he grabbed me by the arms to pull me off Uncle Tim. My mother walked through the door and screamed. She ran to Uncle Tim's side and tried to help him up, her black wavy hair sticking to the tears that streamed down her cheeks.

"How dare you let this bastard into our house after what he has done!" I yelled at my parents.

"Stop it Eric! Stop it right now! You know nothing ever happened!" My mom demanded.

"YES, IT DID YOU FUCK HEADS! How? How can you not believe me?" Shaking with anger, I wished for proof.

My parents looked at me with disgust. My father let me go and I punched a hole in the wall.

I concentrated on the blood seeping from my busted knuckles, and realized I did have proof. I grabbed my father by his arm and pulled him to the security system. My parents had recently put in the security system, along with a camera, due to an increase of burglaries in the area. I never prayed for anything, but now I prayed it had been on.

It was. I rewound the tape and pressed play, watching in relief as my parents viewed the confrontation between Uncle Tim and me.

My mom covered her mouth in disbelief. Her legs buckled and she tumbled to the floor.

"It . . . it . . . it's not what you think . . ." Uncle Tim stammered "I . . . I . . . ."

Grasping onto the nearest table to restrain himself, my father turned to Uncle Tim and growled, "Get out of my house you perverted bastard! How dare you do this to our son!" Dad's face grew increasingly red with anger and then he lost control. He jerked forward, grabbed my uncle and threw him against the wall. Uncle Tim crumbled to the floor, only to be dragged back up by his shirt as Dad pressed him against the wall, "You better get out of here before I take care of you permanently." Uncle Tim pissed his pants. Then he stumbled to his feet and ran, tripping over his own feet, out of the house.

My parents turned to me. The anger that had flared in their eyes turned to sadness and grief. Mom ran to me and pulled me into her arms, "Oh my god, Eric, I'm so sorry." Huge tears spilled from her eyes. She held me so tightly I could barely move, "Oh, Baby, my poor little baby . . . I am so sorry . . . why didn't we believe you?" I was twice her size but she held me like a child, stroking my hair as she sobbed.

I tried to push her away, but she wouldn't let me go. I didn't want her to touch me. The adrenaline pulsing through me veins wasn't nearly as powerful as the words I longed to speak. I wanted to scream, "Bitch! I told you this years ago and it had to come to this! THIS!!!!"

When I finally pulled from her grasp, my eyes met my mother's and for a brief moment, my anger gave way to sadness and understanding. For years I had waited for this moment. For years, I had prayed that they would believe me. I could see the sorrow in her eyes, but my forgiveness only lasted a few seconds before the anger of the knowledge that their inaction led to more sexual abuse enveloped me. I didn't even need to think about the horrible emotional pain I felt from their abandonment in my greatest time of need. For whatever sick reason they didn't believe me before, they knew now. I pushed down the anger I felt, camouflaged the words I longed to speak, and growled, "It's okay, mom. You know now. It only took eight or nine lonely years . . . of hell, but we all know you just always try to see the best in people." More sobs erupted from my mother.

I felt a little guilty for being so hard, so I gave her a quick hug, but that was all I could do.

My dad let out a horrible wail that resembled a injured dog. He picked up the phone. My mom asked, "Who are you calling?"

"The police. That animal is going to jail."

My mom stammered, "But . . . he's . . ."

My father slammed down the phone. "I don't care if he's the god damn pope. So what, *"He's your brother."* I don't give a shit about your god damn brother. I knew it . . ."

My father looked at me, shaking his head. He looked like he was going to throw up. He stumbled forward and grabbed my shoulder, then fell to his knees.

Tears flowed from his eyes. "I knew it." He grabbed for my hand. "I knew you wouldn't make this up. I am so sorry."

"What?" I cried, confused and devastated. "But why?"

My father pulled himself off the ground, ran his hands across his head and headed to the phone. "He was fucking weird. I knew he was fucking weird. But, your mother . . ."

She shook her head and started to sob, "It wasn't my fault!"

"No, but we should have trusted our son! But it's over now. I'm ending this right now!"

Dad dialed the phone and within minutes, the police were at my house. My parents couldn't even look at each other, but they explained everything to the police and showed them the video. The police immediately dispatched Uncle Tim's description and his car's description, and then asked me a ton of questions. Uncle Tim was captured within the hour. My parents pressed charges. I worried Uncle Tim would press charges against me for beating the shit out of him, but he never did.

When it was all said and done, the three of us remained in stoic silence. My father sat in his leather recliner with his head in his hands. My mother sat on the couch, tears streaming down her face and I paced the room. Even though we were together, we were all on our own desolate islands of tumultuous emotions.

I had never felt so overwhelmed. I was relieved that my parents finally believed me and delighted that I had the chance to beat the shit out of Uncle Tim. I felt guilt because I had wanted to kill him and I still felt sorrow from the pain of the abuse even though I was elated about Uncle Tim's arrest. I even had some anxiety that I may be charged for assault. However, most of all, I had a deep-seated feeling of anger and a lingering sense of betrayal bubbling within me. I couldn't understand why it had to come to this for my parents to finally believe me and I didn't know what else to say. I was pissed.

My parents had to work through their pain now, and I didn't want to be there to help. I also didn't want to face feeling anything more tonight. I had already felt my share of pain for years. I needed to get away, so without a word, I stormed out the door and walked to Tristan's.

* * *

"Oh my god, Eric, why didn't you call me last night?" Emma demanded after I told her what had happened. She clenched the steering wheel tightly as she drove to school.

"I was pretty stressed out . . . *you* should understand." I said curtly, still hurt by all the times I wanted to be there for Emma when she left me hanging. My head pounded from a hangover.

"Well, I guess I do . . . but . . . anyway, I'm happy to know your parents finally believe you and that Uncle Tim's behind bars." Emma reached out to hold my hand but I pulled mine away. Seeing the shock and hurt in her eyes, I put my arm around her and pulled myself closer to her.

"I'm sorry," I said. "You know, it's all been so much to go through."

"I know. Tell me about it. Maybe this is the end."

I kissed her on the forehead and replied, "Maybe . . ."

We got to school and I walked Emma to class. I wanted to skip school for the day—take some time to think about all that had happened, but I decided to stay, for Emma.

By Wednesday, I couldn't take it anymore, so I skipped first period and hid behind the back of the building to have a smoke. The fresh air felt good. The sunshine was warm and not having to listen to a teacher drone on and on about something I couldn't care less about was a relief. I smiled. Things were definitely starting to look better.

"Well, what do we have here?" Vice Principal Story sneered as he walked around the corner.

"*Shit*," I thought to myself, "*There goes my happy feeling.*" Busted, I took one more long drag on my cigarette then slowly mashed it with my foot. "Hey, Mr. Story." I said coolly.

"Okay, Eric, come with me . . . hooking class, smoking . . . looks like a suspension to me."

Exhaling what remained of the smoke, I followed him to the principal's office.

Within hours, I was suspended and sent home. I even convinced myself that Emma would be fine without me. The last few days had passed without any issues for her. Her life had returned to normal. When I got home, I grabbed the stash that Tristan gave me and got high, but guilt washed over me.

Chapter: Emma

ON WEDNESDAY, I NOTICED GROUPS of students gawking at me as I walked by. No one pretended I didn't exist anymore and no one attempted to hide their looks of shock and disgust. Unsure of the sudden increase in attention, I waited anxiously for Eric to meet me between first to second period. He never showed up. Each class dragged on and on and my anxiety grew stronger with every tick of the clock. Each time the bell rang, I bolted to the hallway, desperate to find Eric in the crowd, but he never appeared. He was gone.

Lunch absolutely sucked. Groups of students stared at me as I stood in line waiting to buy stale tacos and chocolate milk. They talked in hushed voices amongst themselves and kept peering at me like I was a circus freak. I made eye contact with one of my old girlfriends and tried to smile, but she ducked her head and turned away. It hurt. Without Eric, I felt vulnerable and scared. I wondered if I was just being paranoid, but something didn't seem right. Desperation filled me. *Where was Eric?* I tucked my chin and made my way to an empty table in the corner of the cafeteria. It felt like everyone's eyes were following me. I tried to eat, but I couldn't.

As soon as the bell rang, I threw away my tray and dashed to my art class. My heart reached a crescendo I'd never experienced before and I started to shake. I accidentally stumbled into Eric's friend Steve, who also tried to avoid me, but I grabbed his arm and demanded to know where Eric was. Steve pulled his arm away and quickly looked around to see if anybody noticed. I wondered why he'd be so embarrassed to be seen with me. Steve answered my question before ducking his head and rushing away, "Eric was busted for hooking and smoking again. I think he was suspended. Sorry."

The fear that raged in me quickly turned to anger and it pulsed through my veins. I prayed Steve was lying, but I knew he wasn't. Without Eric by my side, school had become hell. People watched my every move and whispered. Why? I did not know, but without Eric, everything got weird. Eric always had a friendly but intimidating manner so no one would mess with him. Now that he was gone, I had suddenly become fair game.

I walked past a group of girls and heard someone whisper, "Whore." I turned in their direction, wondering if they were talking about me. Giggles filled the air, then I heard, "No, she's a murderer . . ."

Desperation and panic enveloped me. My stomach clenched tightly and I leaned on the wall for support. *How did they know?*

When the final bell rang, I bolted to my car, avoiding the stares and sidelong glances, coming even from those who had been at least polite before. Desperately trying to get away as fast as I could, I struggled to get my key in the door, threw my backpack in the passenger seat, slammed the door shut, started the ignition and drove home.

When I turned into my driveway, I had to slam on the brakes. Eric stood there, casually leaning on his car, smoking a cigarette. The smile that met my glare quickly diminished to a look of concern.

"Hey Pumpkin!" He said as he reached for me.

I pulled away. "What the hell were you thinking!"

Eric dropped his cigarette to the ground and stomped it out. "Oh, come on. You know I hate going to class . . . It's no big deal."

"No big deal . . . NO BIG DEAL! Eric, you've been suspended . . . SUSPENDED! How do you think my parents are going to take this? It was hard enough before, for my parents to let us be together, now this? How are your parents going to take this? How am I . . . ." I couldn't hold back any longer. Tears began to flow.

"Pumpkin, I'm telling you. It's no big thing. I'll be back on Tuesday. Everything is going to be fine." Eric laughed and I looked at him. I noticed his gorgeous brown eyes were bloodshot and the rims were red. He was high. As he moved closer, I could smell the pot on him.

Shocked, I backed away. *He was doing drugs again.* Devastated, I struggled to catch my breath. "Everything will not be fine. It's not fine . . ."

"It will be" Eric sauntered toward me, reached up and twirled a strand of my hair. I crumbled.

"They know . . ."

"They know what?" Eric replied.

The words flowed from me quickly "You weren't there and they weren't holding back. They were staring at me, glaring at me. They called me a whore and a . . . a . . . a . . . murderer . . ."

As those words hit me, I became hysterical. Tears flowed from my eyes so that I couldn't see anything. I wiped at them . . . I struggled to keep myself from wildly hitting out, punching anything near me. I needed to scream. Eric grabbed me and guided me toward the front door. My mom met us and helped him get me inside. "Oh my god, what happened?" she demanded, her mouth opened in shock.

Eric tried to explain, but all attention went back to me. I fell to the floor. The emotional pain felt like a knife cutting through my skin. I screamed and thrashed. Eric got on top of me to prevent me from hurting myself. I wanted him to go away. Not even he could stop this spiral into hell. I slipped into a deep dark well, unaware then of the years it would take me to climb out. I wanted my life to end. I wanted it over, now. Regardless of the words I spoke, no matter how hateful I became, Eric stayed there, holding me. He pressed his body tightly against mine and restrained my arms and legs to prevent me from punching and kicking everything near me. There was nothing I wanted more than to hurt everyone around me, including myself. Eric calmly spoke to me, words I don't remember, but his voice and presence helped me come up through the pain. The warm pressure and scent of his body eventually comforted me and after what seemed like hours, I finally calmed down, my body limp against his.

Physical exhaustion drained Eric. His forehead glistened with sweat and his arms shook from restraining me for so long. Still, he managed to pick me up and lay me carefully on the bed. Kissing me softly on the forehead, he said, "I love you, Emma." I curled up into a ball and cried. Only then did Eric feel safe to let go of me.

My mom stood in the doorway, staring at me in shock. Her perfectly painted face remained sweat and tear-free; her hair sleek and perfect in a French knot. She pressed her manicured fingers against her lips. She looked like a wealthy spectator, watching a freak show, rather than a mother watching the dissolution of her daughter. Not once did she try to reach out to me. Not once did she try to help Eric.

Eric met her at my bedroom door. "What happened?" she whispered.

"The kids at school found out. They called her names . . . whore . . . murderer. I don't know how they could've figured it out."

I could see my mom's reaction out of the corner of my eye. She turned pale white. "Oh shit," she said, clenching her hands in front of her face. "Oh shit."

Eric looked at her, "I know. It's bad."

"No, Eric. It's my fault." She gasped, "Oh my God, it's my fault."

I sat up and looked at her. Eric turned to me and then looked at her again. Anger radiated from him. "What?"

"Oh, well . . . you know how it is." My mom chuckled nervously as she averted her glance from Eric's. "I had a few too many when I went out with Stacy and well . . . I told her . . . everything . . ."

I barely made it to the bathroom in time to throw up. My mother betrayed me. In a drunken stupor, she told Stacy, who apparently told her daughter Hannah, and now the entire school knew.

Eric tore into her. "What the hell were you thinking?" He yelled. "This is your daughter, YOUR DAUGHTER you're talking about. How the fuck could you do something like this to her?"

Death looked beautiful to me. "How could you? Why?" I screamed as I braced myself against the bathroom sink. My voice echoed through the house. I heard a door slam, and a car squeal out of the driveway. Eric yelled, "That's right, bitch. Run! Run, you fucking loser!"

Eric stormed into the bathroom and held me. The anger he felt toward my mom, palpable. Not only did she let the secret out, she was now too guilt ridden to help me. She left the house, leaving me sobbing in pain and Eric disgusted. He pulled me into his arms and we sunk to the bathroom floor. As Eric stroked my hair, he desperately tried to find the words he wanted to say to comfort me, but he couldn't. I could hear the frustration and conflict in his voice. A part of me felt the need to comfort him, to tell him that him being there was enough, but I didn't have the strength to try and honestly, I just didn't care anymore.

Eric stayed with me until my dad got home. He met my father at the door and I could hear their voices murmuring in the next room. Eric gave me a huge hug before he left. "I gotta go, Pumpkin. I love you. Please call me if you need anything."

I couldn't respond. I knew he faced his own hell when he got home, but facing his parents about a suspension seemed minuscule compared to the nightmare of my world. Unlike me, it was his choices that got him where he was. I had no control over what had happened to me. Now people with no understanding—people with easy, happy lives that never faced the pain I went through stood in judgment of my very soul. No argument could change their minds. I knew how close-minded they truly were. Their world was black and white—no shades of gray. I was doomed to live in their judgment forever.

Going back to my room, I lay on my bed and curled up in a ball. Running my fingers along the seam of my purple pillow, I heard a car pull into the driveway and the front door screech open and slam shut. Whispers floated in the hallway before my mom finally walked into my room. I turned to look at her disheveled clothes and hair. She finally looked how I felt and it made me feel good. I couldn't imagine treating a child the way she treated me. Her eyes, which refused to meet mine, were bloodshot and mascara streaked her cheeks. She also reeked of alcohol. "Emma, I'm sorry this happened. I should have kept my mouth shut."

The telephone rang, interrupting her apology. Distracted, she forced a smile, then patted my back. "I'm sure you'll be fine soon enough." She hiccuped as she left the room and shut the door quietly behind her.

A few minutes later, my dad opened the door and came in. He stood there in shock for a couple seconds before saying, "They found him."

I jumped up, "Who-oh, now?" Did they take him to jail, or . . ."

Dad shook his head. "He's dead . . . found him behind a dumpster a week and a half ago. They wouldn't have known it was him if it wasn't for the tattoo. A DNA test proved it was him . . . It's over now, we can move on."

I looked at my dad with disbelief—not only because the rapist was found, but also because my father seemed to think that all the pain and horror I felt would just dissipate into thin air because he was dead. True, the nagging worry that the rapist would come back to get me was gone, but that didn't erase the past. I never expected it to end this way. I feared he would never get caught or that he would get caught and I would have to face him in court. Luck, it seemed, was on my side for once. He was dead.

"What's his name? How did he die?" Questions rushed out of me.

My father's eyes bothered me. He looked distressed, or maybe he was relieved. I couldn't tell, but whatever it was soon disappeared and he smiled at me. "His name was Matt Johansen. He was shot in the head. Looks like a drug related murder."

"Oh . . ." I started to cry again, but this time, they were tears of relief. Three statements revolved in my mind: They found him. He's dead. I'll never have to face him again.

That evening, I watched the local news with my parents. A beautiful blonde reporter stated publicly the words that filled me with so much relief. "The Waverly Park Rapist has been identified. Matt Johansen, of 6253 Pulmer Street, was found dead over a week ago by local business owner Stephen Rex. Initially identified by the tattoo on his chest, DNA test confirmed he was the park rapist. Police believe his murder to be drug related. More information will be provided after further investigation."

Not realizing I had held my breath through the entire report, I gasped for air when it was over. It was true. Matt Johansen was dead and I didn't need to worry about him any more.

Chapter: Cassie

THE RAPIST WAS FINALLY FOUND, and shot dead, too. After James got the call, I snuck into the living room to pour myself a celebratory drink, toasting the end of a nightmare. It was time to move on.

I had grown sick of worrying about it. I couldn't stand watching Emma cry and couldn't understand why she just couldn't get over it. Her father insisted I stay home, night after night, to be there for her, but what the hell could I do? I wanted to party with my friends. Instead, I got stuck at home looking at my boring, distant husband and an emotionally distraught daughter. Fun. Real fun.

James would say, "Can't you be a mother for once? Is it so damn hard for you to be there for your little girl when she needs you?" I'd scoff and roll my eyes. I told him, "She doesn't need me, and even if she did, she'd get over it. Emma's practically an adult and smart enough to work through it herself." He glared at me in disgust, just like that Eric kid. Who the hell do they think they are and what the hell is so special about Emma?

No—now that she's older, it's *my* time and I resented being held hostage in my own home. I had played the motherly game long enough. I changed her diapers, let her suckle me and fed her that disgusting, slimy baby food. That alone was enough. Now, it's my turn. I only have one life to live and I wanted to have fun. Enough of my life had been wasted on trying to be a good mother and a wife. I wanted to party and experience everything I could, and I didn't want anything or anyone to bring me down, and Emma was, most certainly, bringing me down.

I stood quietly in the hallway, sipping my cocktail as I listened to Emma and her father talk in her room. Their voices echoed relief and happiness—*Yay! The rapist had been found dead.* Hearing them bond like that filled me with disgust.

In a fit of jealousy, I slammed my glass down on the table and rushed out the door. A visit to a bar would do me some good.

Chapter: Emma

HAVING TO FACE TWO MORE days of school before the weekend darkened what little I felt in relief and happiness, especially knowing Eric wouldn't be there. I prayed that now my rapist was dead, the other students would be more understanding of all I had been through. On Thursday, their eyes and whispers still followed my every move, but by Friday, most people seemed to lose interest.

Before my final class began, I went to the bathroom. Fortunately, it was empty. As I washed my hands, I heard the door creak open and watched in the mirror as a group of girls entered behind me. I didn't like the thrill that flashed across one girl's face. Her name was Shannon, a beefy, lump of a girl who seemed to control every move of her four clone sidekicks.

"Well, look who've we got here!" Shannon crooned, nodding her head of greasy blond curls in my direction. "It's the whore, Emma. Tell me, how's it feel now that two lives have ended because of you?"

My body shook with anger. I knew I was outnumbered, but I didn't care if I lived or died anymore. I rolled my eyes and turned to face them. "How could I possibly be to blame for his death? He made his choices. He faced the consequences."

"Yeah," Shannon taunted, "his choice . . . I bet you were tempting him with your cute little running shorts. I've seen you jogging. If you weren't flaunting yourself so much, he wouldn't have wanted you. You asked for it!" The girls behind her nodded their heads in agreement and glared at me with the exact fake disgusted look plastered on their leader's face.

Fury enveloped me. No one asked to be raped and the outfit I wore was an oversized T-shirt and running shorts-no more tempting than a baggy pair of pajamas.

Clenching my fists, I looked her in the eyes. "NO. ONE. EVER. ASKS. TO. BE. RAPED." The girls behind her laughed at my anger.

Shannon backed off a bit as the door opened behind us. It wasn't a teacher, so she turned to me and continued. "Well, even so, it was certainly your choice to kill the baby."

I glared at her. How could this be so blatantly held against me too?

Why was it so hard for these Neanderthals to see it from my point of view?

Just then, a girl with long, blonde hair, dark mascara and a leather jacket pushed through the group and stood between Shannon and me. She put her face right up to Shannon's face—her ocean blue eyes pierced Shannon's empty black ones. "How dare you treat Emma this way! Keep your mouths shut until you've walked even a quarter of a mile in her shoes. You have no right to judge her or what she has been through!"

Shannon laughed. "I'll judge anyone I want to—bitch."

"Sounds to me like your trying to justify your lowly existence by knocking down everyone around you. Get a fucking life!"

Shannon moved forward to attack the girl. We both lunged forward to protect ourselves, but before things got too out of hand, two teachers burst into the bathroom. "What's going on here?" they demanded.

Instantly backing away from each other, we all mumbled "Nothing."

"Good, then get to class!" The teachers watched us until we dispersed.

Shannon and the gang glared at the blonde girl and me as we exited the bathroom. My new friend glared back and stuck her tongue out at them.

I turned to her, "Thank you so much for standing up for me like that. I can't believe you would do that for a stranger"

The girl's long hair fell over her eyes as she searched through her purse for something. "No problem. I was happy to do it."

"What's your name?" I asked.

Giving up on her search, she replied, "I'm Beth."

"I'm Emma."

"Yeah, I know." She laughed.

We walked down the hallway together. She didn't try to avoid being seen with me.

"Well, I'd better get to class." I said, wishing I could express in words the gratitude I had for this girl.

"Okay," she replied. "I'll see you later."

"Thanks again!"

"No problem!" Beth smiled.

I was thankful for Beth's defense, but also crushed by the words spoken to me in the bathroom. I knew nothing could change what people thought of me, especially if they couldn't understand what I'd been through. Yet, I couldn't imagine any circumstances that would ever make me treat people with the downright disrespect and ignorance that these girls showed. I figured some people are just too stupid and close-minded to accept anyone other than their tight little group of "friends."

* * *

Eric had been grounded for the weekend because of his suspension. Since I didn't have to work at the veterinarian office until Sunday, I tried to keep myself as busy as I could. I worked on a few homework assignments, started to clean my room and even pulled out my guitar and played a few chords, but nothing could keep my mind from wandering back to the incident in the ladies room. Anger filled me; anger at my mom for unintentionally letting the news of my abortion out, anger at the girls at school for completely failing to see my side and anger at Eric for being stupid enough to get suspended again. I felt alone and frustrated. Nothing I could do would fix any of this and the lack of control made me panic. Tears started to flow and the pain of everything I went through came to the surface again. I laid down on my bed and tried to control the sobbing surging from me, but my father had already heard it. He walked into my room and looked at me.

First his eyes showed concern. "What's going on?" He asked.

Not knowing how to respond, I asked, "Why? Why?"

He glared at me then grabbed me tightly by the shoulders. Looking me straight in the eyes, he said, "Emma, its over. Everything is now in the past. Let it go. I never want to see you crying about any of this, ever again!"

Shocked at the intensity of my father's glare and the finality of his words, I stopped crying at once. My father had never spoken to me like that and he had never once laid a hand on me, not even for a spanking. The way he had grabbed my shoulders was fierce and intense, but it was his eyes that terrified me. Within seconds, he let go of my shoulders and turned to leave the room. Getting up and closing the door behind him, I fell to my knees, and pressed my head against the cool, hard wood of the door. I felt even more alone than I had moments before; however, this time, no tears fell. I could no longer cry. The pain inside had nowhere left to go, so I buried it deep within my soul.

By Sunday morning, the spiral downward was complete. I had again fallen to the bottom of the deep, dark well. The well was so deep, no light could be seen above me; the walls so slippery—no way to climb out of it. I became darkness: a shadow of my former self. Every waking moment, pain bubbled through my veins. Nothing brought me joy anymore, not even Eric.

Suicide began to seduce me, caressing my every thought, promising an end to my pain. By Sunday morning, its seduction was complete. I filled a bathtub full of hot water. Steam filled the entire room, its humidity condensing on every cool surface. I climbed into the scalding water. My skin burned, but the physical pain was a welcomed distraction from the emotions I felt inside. Grabbing a razor blade, I slowly brushed the blunt side against my wrist, contemplating the best way to cut myself. The ice, cold metal of the blade burned my skin. A desperate pull to end the pain enveloped me, and I sliced open my wrist. I leaned back into the tub and watched as my blood diffused through the water, drifting like smoke rising from a candle.

A calm voice echoed in my head. "No, not this time. Not again."

Ignoring the voice, I insanely chuckled to myself. I soon realized that the cut wasn't deep enough, but the physical pain was a sweet release from the emotions I had buried deep inside. I turned the blade vertical to the cut I had made before and sliced again, unintentionally making a cross on my arm. The voice spoke again, "Not again, Emma. Not again."

Chapter: Emma

A SUDDEN KNOCK ON THE door shocked me out of my suicidal haze. Blood was everywhere-red rivers streamed from where my wrist had come to rest on the side of the tub and flowed into the hazy, red water I was soaking in. I grasped onto the side of the tub and pulled myself out of the water. Drops of muted red splattered across the linoleum floor. I grabbed a towel and examined my wrist. I realized I hadn't cut deep enough. From working at the vet's office, I knew a little blood went a long way.

Nauseous from the sight of what I had done, I collapsed on the floor.

"Emma, are you okay in there?" my mother asked.

"Yes, I'm fine . . ." I answered weakly, as more water diluted blood spread across the floor.

"Okay, just wanted to check. You've been in there for quite a while."

I called out, "No worries! I'll be out soon!" After holding toilet paper tight to my wrist for a while, the bleeding had finally stopped. I drained the water out of the tub, rinsed it out, wiped everything down and flushed the evidence down the toilet.

After putting a large bandage on my wrist, I went to my room to get dressed for work. A voice in my head kept repeating, "No, not this time." I couldn't shake it. It wouldn't shut up.

For some reason, I felt functional and alive again. I put on my scrubs and prepared to go to work just like any other normal day. Not wanting my parents to notice my arm, I rushed into the kitchen to grab my lunch and ran out the door. I heard my mom call, "Don't you want any breakfast?"

"No thanks!" I answered as I closed the door.

I got into my car and smiled. I even giggled. "I must be going crazy." I thought to myself, but I liked it. My wrist throbbed in pain—but that pain I could handle. Physical pain was so much easier to deal with than emotional. Every time my wrist throbbed, I could focus on that and nothing else—an unexpected reprieve from my unending emotional turmoil.

As I drove my car out of the neighborhood, I heard the voice again. "Not this time. Not this time."

"Okay," I answered to the voice in my head. "Not this time."

The voice went silent.

* * *

Work went well and left me with a very good cover up story for the bandage on my wrist. Cats scratched me all the time during their exams and it wouldn't be difficult to convince anyone that this scratch came from a cat, as long as I kept it covered.

The cover up worked well. As soon as I walked through the door, my dad noticed the bandage and asked me about it. I nonchalantly responded that a cat got me again and the subject was dropped. Relieved, I ate my dinner then went to my room to finish my physics homework.

I opened my physics book to the first law of thermodynamics, the conservation of energy: the book read, "Energy cannot be created or destroyed, only transferred or converted from one form to another." I read this sentence repeatedly, but I couldn't grasp its meaning. I stared blankly at the book, my mind a million lightyears away.

I winced in pain as I struck a match to light a vanilla-scented candle on my desk. My wrist throbbed every time I moved it in the wrong direction, but I didn't mind. I breathed deeply, enjoying the warm vanilla scent as it filled me up. The deep breathing and the wonderful smell relaxed me.

Smells had always been important to me. So many of my childhood memories were linked to smells. A scent could transport me to another time or place instantaneously. I closed my eyes as my mind began to wander.

I thought of my grandmother who had died three years before. She was such a lovely woman. Her smile was like the moon, reflecting the sun that was in her heart. The wrinkles on her skin showed a lifetime of trials and hard work, but also laughter. She was a joy to be around and she always told the best stories. I could listen to her for hours. The other grandkids grew sick of her stories and would leave to play, but I cherished the time we spent together. I would stay and listen to any story she told.

After years of storytelling and creating special memories, my grandmother died. Shortly before her death, she requested that she'd be cremated without having any type of a ceremony. She didn't want a "big hoopla" over her death. Because my family was not very religious or spiritual, her request was respected, but this left all of us with no way to say goodbye. This was the first time I felt true emotional pain in my life. Facing death with no spiritual belief is difficult, especially as a child. You're left with so many unanswered questions.

My grandmother did leave me a beautiful jewelry box filled with several pieces of jewelry that she had worn throughout her life. Since it remained in her room until the end, I could still smell her sweet perfume whenever I opened the box. However, as days passed and then weeks, my grandmother's smell slowly disappeared from the box. Remembering it that night upset me somehow. It had been weeks since she had died, but there I was, crying in my room, remembering the time we had together.

All of a sudden, a feeling of peace enveloped me and my entire room filled with the smell of my grandmother. I wondered if I was imagining things, but I couldn't avoid it. The smell was everywhere. I buried my head into my pillow trying to get away form the smell, but it was there too. Taking a deep breath, I sat up in the silent room, smelling the person I missed so much.

"Grandma?" I called out. There was no reply.

I hesitated, feeling slightly silly, but then went on, "I love you and I miss you." The smell grew stronger, and then disappeared as fast as it came. I was sure she had been there, saying goodbye, reaching out to me the only way she could.

Staring into the candle, my mind continued to float in and out of my memories.

The mysterious voice echoed in my mind again. "Not this time. Not this time." The wound on my wrist suddenly throbbed in pain and a puzzle started to sort out in my mind. I remembered, after that horrid attack, Eric holding me in the light, dark shadows surrounding us. That voice had come then:

"It's not her time yet. She needs to go back."

"Her journey has just begun. She will grow so much in this lifetime."

Then Eric's reply, "I'll take her back."

Did I die? No one seemed to think I did, but then again, no one knew exactly how long I was lying on the path before someone found me.

The memories of the light left no doubt in my mind that Eric was my soul mate and that the presence of the other spirits comforted me. They expected me to achieve more, and those spirits sent me back. If souls and reincarnation did exist, maybe these ghostly figures were my soul family? But why was Eric there? He wasn't dead.

I closed my eyes and took a deep breath.

"Not this time! Not this time!" the inner voice echoed in my mind.

What did that mean? Where did that come from?

Could I have possibly committed suicide in a past life? Was this voice warning me not to do it again? If so, why? Did I have to face this adversity again to overcome it because I wimped out and succumbed to it before? Is that what it meant?

"Maybe," I said aloud, then laughed to myself, "or maybe I'm losing it and going over the edge now." If God existed, why would he cause such suffering, not only to myself, but also to so many innocent people around the world? *What is the purpose of that?*

Maybe there is no purpose, My thoughts continued. *Shit happens and then you die. When it's over, it's over and that's that.* Deep within, I hoped there was more, but scientifically it just never made sense to me. I knew my mother felt the same way. She always said religion was nothing more than a way for power hungry assholes to gain control over the masses. She believed we were born to live, and then we died and that was it. We turned to dust and dust we remained for eternity.

> *But what about my feelings for Eric and the connection there? What about looking at people, babies even, complete strangers and feeling you have known them before, or feeling like they have been here before because of the wisdom in their eyes? Could it be soul connections? Could it be that Eric and I are truly soul mates and we have been together for God knows how many lifetimes?*

It started to make sense in my mind. The words in my physics book stared back at me: energy cannot be created or destroyed, only transformed. Could that energy within us, our soul, our life's energy, transform and continue on?

> *But what would the purpose of suffering be?*

That unfamiliar voice in my mind spoke again, "To remember what it is like to know God. You are a part of God, and without your soul experiencing what it is to be empty, to lose out, to suffer pain, you cannot fully realize the magnificence of being who you truly are. As you achieve many lifetimes of learning, you grow closer and closer to remembering the absolute truth, that you are, and have always been—a part of God."

I had no idea where these thoughts were coming from, but they comforted me. Feeling as if I finally understood the basic purpose of life, I felt refreshed and renewed. This understanding brought me strength and courage. At the same time that I knew I could face life, I felt less need to be in control.

Though the memory of my rape and abortion still hurt me greatly, I no longer asked "why?" I now looked at my suffering as a mountain I had to climb successfully, to achieve a greater understanding. I knew I could face years of rocky talus slopes and boulders as I climbed this mountain, but I knew I could climb it, steadily, day by day. I had to, if I didn't want to do this all over again.

I don't know where the voice came from, but I knew it came from deep within. It almost felt as if a guardian angel had spoken to me, helping me through my pain so I could finally move on. Regardless of its origin, I found my new spirituality extremely personal and private and never shared it with anyone.

Though no homework got finished that night, I had learned a lot. I slowly drifted to sleep and dreamed of Eric holding me in the light, safe and calm.

* * *

The sun glared into my bedroom waking me early Monday morning. Swiftly, the dread of facing another day greeted me, but I felt stronger. I dragged myself out of bed and got ready for school. I had to face only one more day without Eric. The next day, his suspension would be over and he would finally be back.

When I got to school, I refused to make eye contact with anyone and tried my best to avoid everyone around me. I sat on a bench, slightly hidden from view, hoping no one would notice me. I closed my eyes and waited for the bell to ring. I must have started to drift off to sleep because I was shocked at the light tap on my shoulder. I jumped in confusion and turned to see Beth standing there, a beautiful smile on her face.

"Hey!" she said. "I'm sorry if I scared you!"

"Oh," I muttered, speechless again. "That's okay. I just didn't expected anyone . . ."

She cocked her head to the side and asked, "How are you doing? You holding up okay?" I looked at her as if she had gone crazy. I wondered why in the hell she cared. No one else seemed to. She stepped back and started to turn away. "I'm sorry. I shouldn't have bothered you."

Guilt washed over me. Deep down I knew she was just trying to be nice. Not wanting to push her away, I smiled weakly and said, "No, it's okay. It's just that I'm sort of shocked that you are here talking to me." I shifted my gaze to the ground. "You know, everyone else avoids me. I didn't mean to offend you."

I looked at her and tried to smile again. This time it was much easier. I continued, "Anyway, I am okay. Feeling much better now, thanks!"

Beth smiled back.

I liked Beth. She was one of the most sincere people I had met in a long time.

"You know," she said, sitting down next to me. "Most of the people avoid you because they just don't know what to say or do in a situation like this."

"Yeah? I was wondering that. Kind of funny because I don't know what to say or do, either." I replied.

Beth smiled, "Yeah, but you're doing okay. Honestly, a lot of them are just really ignorant."

I remembered the confrontation in the bathroom and how she had stood up for me. "Thanks again, you know, for the other day."

I don't know what came over me but the floodgates opened and I started to talk about everything that had been on my mind. "I can't believe they can be so harsh. Like I chose this! They actually think it is my fault!"

"They're just stupid. Some people live such self-centered lives they can't see beyond the nose on their faces, let alone put themselves in anyone else's shoes. They only see things in black and white, right and wrong, no areas of gray."

"Yeah, I know."

The bell rang and we got up to walk to class. "Hey," Beth said, "you have lunch sixth period, right?"

"Yeah, I do."

"Come eat with me."

"Okay," I smiled. "I'll see you then."

A small light of hope glowed within me. Today, things were a little better than yesterday. Maybe someday soon, things would be right again.

"Whore," some guy whispered as he brushed passed me. His girlfriend started laughing.

"*Okay, maybe not.*" I said to myself.

* * *

Beth and I became close friends, spending time together both in and out of school. She was a blast to be around. We constantly laughed and had a wonderful time. Every few days after school, we'd take a walk up to the corner coffee shop. I always bought tea. She always bought hot chocolate. We'd enjoy our drinks, and walk for hours. One time I heard a strange noise coming from her. I turned to see what was wrong and she was using her mouth to hold the empty cup up around her nose. Her fingers were curled like ears on her head and she was snorting like a pig. I was so shocked at what I saw, the tea in my mouth sprayed all over the sidewalk and we both started laughing hysterically. I quickly emptied my cup and joined her. We marched along the streets, oinking at all the people who passed by us. Some laughed, some thought we were crazy-we probably were—but regardless, it was fun!

By the time red and yellow leaves covered the sidewalks and the smell of chimney smoke filled the air, talk of my ordeal became yesterday's news and I had blended into the crowd again.

I still struggled with the memories of my rape and abortion. A glimpse of a tattoo could cause sheer panic; A baby's cry could cause a stream of tears to flow from my eyes. Overall, I had lost my faith that there was goodness in everybody and I had lost my trust as well. For the longest time, I feared I would be scared of Eric, but the overwhelming comfort his presence brought was stronger than the fear and pain I felt inside. I thrived in his presence. I wanted him near me more than anything else in the world.

Eric and I spent hours together every week. Our favorite place to hang out was his backyard, which at the height of the summer, flowered in a rainbow of color.

Eric's mother loved to garden and their backyard was a botanical paradise. Rose arbors marked the entrances to winding paths throughout the backyard, themselves lined with hundreds of flowers. In the spring, the gardens were filled with every color of pansies, hyacinths, crocuses and narcissus. Forsythia and azaleas standing higher behind these added to the beauty. In the summer, these gave way to luscious hydrangea, lilac and butterfly bushes, which accented the daisies, roses, impatiens, purple cosmos, yellow and orange marigolds and lavender along all the pathways. The miniature Japanese maples provided shady hideouts for the squirrels and rabbits in the yard. Feathery ferns lined the dark edge of the property that continued into a stand of trees.

A large oak tree marked the center of the yard, and under the shade of its majestic branches was a beautiful koi pond. The relaxing sound of water bubbling over stones rose from its small waterfall. Lily pads covered the pond and frogs would sit on their smooth green leaves waiting patiently for a meal to fly by, occasionally croaking in the evening light.

Though the colors had started to fade and leaves littered the ground, the magic remained for me. As the sunset cast a purple glow through the air and across the pond, Eric and I sat on a wrought iron bench beside the purple water. I sat sideways on his lap, my head pressed against his chest. I listen to his heartbeat, still in perfect synchrony with mine. We didn't speak a word as we held each other, absorbed in the beauty of our surroundings and the comfort we shared with each other.

Eric took a sudden deep breath and blew it out slowly. He had been deep in thought and softly whispered, "Oh, Emma."

Taking my chin in his hand, he tilted my face up to his. His lips pressed softly against mine, his smooth tongue passing over mine. The gentle caress of his lips became more urgent, as his muscular arms carefully and quickly pulled my body up and around to face him. We continued to kiss passionately. Eric's one hand softly traced the contour of my neck and shoulders, while the other pressed firmly against the small of my back, pulling me closer to him. Intensity radiated from him. I could tell he desperately wanted me, but I could also tell he was terrified of going too far for my sake. I pressed myself against his body, signaling that I wanted more. He hesitated, looked at me intensely and whispered, "Emma, I want you so much. I need you."

I wanted him too. I put my fingers up to his lips then bent forward to passionately kiss him again. He picked me up, and carried me through the maze of beautiful flowers into his house, and up to his bedroom.

"But, your parents," I said.

"They won't be home for another hour." Laying me down on his bed, he began to undress me and I followed. We made love so passionately, I cried. I cried because of the love between us. I cried because it was the first time we had made love since the rape. I cried because of how lucky I felt to be with Eric. I surrendered myself completely to him and I shuddered in delight.

I had been terrified of this moment, but the magic I felt with Eric erased my mind of all the pain I had endured. The love between us was incredibly strong, and I melted in the safety of his arms.

We stayed in bed as long as we could, then got dressed and went to sit by the pond again. It was dark and the light of the full moon glittered on the rippling water as crickets sang songs of love around us. It felt like heaven.

All of a sudden, Eric pulled away and stood at the edge of the pond. The moon light accentuated his muscular shoulders and highlighted his dark brown hair.

His abrupt move worried me. "Eric? Is something wrong?" I asked.

"No, Emma. Absolutely nothing is wrong." He turned to look at me and I noticed his eyes were glistening.

Eric walked back and kneeled at my feet. He laid his head in my lap and I ran my fingers through his hair. I started to worry. "No, something's wrong. What is it?"

He remained silent and after a few moments, he lifted his head and looked me deeply in the eyes. Then he took my hands into his and holding them up to his lips he softly kissed them and whispered, "Emma, I can't believe the love I feel for you. You are the best thing that has ever happened to me and I never want to lose you. Will you marry me?"

My heart stopped. I couldn't believe my ears.

"Yes. Yes, Eric. Of course I will marry you." We kissed and we held on to each other. I can still feel the light breeze that rustled the leaves of the oak tree. I can still see the moonlight glittering on the water. I can still smell the sweet scent of his body and the smell of the autumn leaves and I can still feel the warmth of his body as he held me. I never wanted that night to end.

Pulling away from me, Eric smiled, "I better walk you home." Taking my hand, he led me through the leaf covered garden. Slowly we strolled back to my house under the twinkling autumn stars.

* * *

It didn't matter that we were only juniors in high school. We didn't care what other people would think. No practical means passed through our minds. We knew we were meant to be together, forever, and that was all that mattered. We didn't intend for it to be a secret, but that's how our engagement stayed. We told no one. It was a secret bond between the two of us. We knew a "marriage" would not happen for years, but in our hearts and minds we were fully committed. We simply spoke what our souls already knew. There was a bond between us that could never be broken.

Eric went to the beach with his parents the weekend before homecoming, leaving Beth and me plenty of time to shop for our homecoming gowns. After going to the Columbia Mall, we ended up in downtown Ellicott City, where we found a quaint little shop with the cutest dresses. After trying on several gowns, Beth decided on a beautiful maroon gown that was perfect for her coloring. I picked out a black gown that was trimmed in black lace. We felt and looked fabulous!

When Eric arrived home from the beach Sunday night, he stopped by my house to see me. As we sat on the front porch, he handed me an envelope. Inside of it was a photograph of a huge heart drawn in the sand with the words, "I love you, Pumpkin!" written inside it. Bubbles from the edge of a wave kissed the side of the heart and a couple of seashells were strategically placed in the sand. It looked absolutely beautiful, too perfect to be real. I wondered if there was anything he wasn't good at.

On the back of the photograph, a note read, "I missed you Emma. You are always in my heart and mind. Love, forever, Eric."

* * *

Before we knew it, it was Friday night, time for Eric, Beth, her boyfriend Scott and I to go to the Homecoming game at the high school. Still paranoid, I thought I caught a few people looking at me strangely as we climbed the steps of the stadium, but no one ever said anything with Eric around. They wouldn't mess with Beth either. The story of how she stood up for me in the bathroom quickly traveled around the school and people backed off. The Marriottsville High Vikings beat the Patapsco High Pirates 21 to 17. It was a great game!

On Saturday, Beth and I got ready for the homecoming dance together. Eric and Scott surprised us by picking us up in a black Lincoln Town Car and taking us to dinner at Maria's, a quaint Italian restaurant in downtown Ellicott City. Maria's was my favorite restaurant, one my parents took me to on special occasions like my birthday. We made our way back to the high school gymnasium for the dance. Eric and I got lost in our own little world together. We danced to every song. I can still see him smiling at me as he sang "Brown-eyed girl," and I can still feel the contours of his muscular chest and the warmth of his body as we slow danced to "Everything I Do, I Do It For You." Eric's breath caressed my neck as he sang along with Bryan Adams. It felt as though every word was meant for me. At the end of the song, he softly kissed me on my neck and whispered, "I love you, future Mrs. Florentino." He winked at me as he walked off to get us a drink. I smiled to myself, "Mrs. Florentino sounds perfect."

Chapter: Eric

LIFE WAS GOOD. NO, IT was fucking incredible! Emma and I couldn't have been better. We thrived together.

The night we got engaged was a turning point for me. When I looked into those beautiful brown eyes and asked her to marry me I could see our future, our life together. I envisioned us finishing high school, going to college, getting married. I saw our children. These visions made me stronger than ever. I wanted to succeed for us and for our kids. Drugs became a thing of the past. I didn't need them anymore. I had Emma and the love we shared was the greatest drug I could imagine.

My grades improved. I even stopped smoking cigarettes. I didn't want anything to stand in our way, *anything*. I loved Emma and I wanted to ensure we would be together, forever.

My uncle's trial began in late January. Until then, I had endured tons of interviews from the police and the prosecuting attorney. Every last detail of my uncle's abuse was painfully pulled from the recesses of my mind, but I survived, drug free. I embraced my past; realizing it made me the person I had become and I grew from it. I was actually proud of myself.

I didn't realize how easy it was to take a stand against someone you didn't have to face. A completely different story unfolds when you have to be in the same room and look them in the eyes when you take the stand during a trial.

"I'd like to call witness, Eric Nathaniel Florentino, to the stand."

Taking a deep breath, I walked up to the stand and took my seat. Initially, I felt ready—ready to have closure on the pain I had been through because of this man. As I looked around the courtroom, I saw my parents looking back at me with worried anticipation. Emma was there, her beautiful brown eyes focused on mine. I knew I had support now. I knew I'd be okay.

My uncle's defense lawyer cleared his throat. I turned to look in his direction. That's when I saw Uncle Tim, his head in his hands, his elbows propped on the table. He was dressed in a navy blue suit and looked as if he had aged twenty years. His hair had grayed and had been left uncut for months. His beard was salt and pepper and shaggy. Big, swollen rings hung under his closed eyes. He must have sensed me looking at him because he opened his eyes and looked directly into mine. He glared at me—his eyes on fire, full of anger and hatred. Panic filled me. I tried not to buckle under the pressure.

The prosecuting attorney approached the stand.

"Hi, Eric. Thank you for coming today."

Pulling my eyes from my uncle's stare, I searched for Emma. She gave me a reassuring smile and I felt a little better.

"No problem." I responded.

"Eric, could you state your full name for the court."

"Eric Nathaniel Florentino."

"Thank you. Eric, is the person who molested you as a child sitting in this courtroom today?"

"Yes," I replied.

"Could you please point him out for the jury?"

Becoming nervous, I reluctantly pointed in my uncle's direction. I refused to look at him.

"Is it true that this man, Mr. Timothy Faulkner, molested and raped you multiple times between the ages of eight and ten?"

"Yes, it is." I answered quietly.

"How many times did this occur?"

"About twenty times, sir."

"Torturous, unimaginable pain for anyone to survive, Eric. Is there anything you would like to tell the jury about the emotional and physical pain you suffered as a child?"

Could I do it? Until this point, I thought I could, but now that he was staring at me, I wavered. I could feel my uncle's glare, as well as

Emma's gaze. My eyes met Emma's, our souls connected and I found strength.

"Yes," I stated. Taking a deep breath I spoke the words I had been practicing for today. "Fortunately, many of you don't know what it is like to be raped. For those of us that do, it's a painful experience, both physically and emotionally. I have been permanently scarred by the events of my past. I have lost the ability to trust, and don't think I will ever regain it. Though I will never forget what has happened, I am finding a way to put it behind me. Some victims are not this strong. Many victims crumble from a lack of support, turn to drugs and commit suicide. Please don't let this man out on the street again. Please don't let him hurt anyone else."

"Thank you, Eric. Prosecution rests."

I noticed my uncle turn to his lawyer and whisper something in his ear.

My uncle's lawyer cleared his throat again and stood up. Panic enveloped me, but I was ready for the attack. I had prepared for the worst. Our attorney had drilled me repeatedly. I was prepared for any slimy defense tactics he might use.

"Defense rests. Thank you."

I couldn't believe my ears. No questions? It was over? I looked at my uncle. Instead of anger, there were tears in his eyes and a look of remorse.

"Prosecution rests. Eric, you may leave the stand."

In a daze, I walked out of the courtroom. Emma came out and held me. "It's almost over," she whispered.

At the sentencing, my uncle received fifteen years with no parole. The remorse in his eyes turned to anger. He glared at me one last time as he was taken from the courtroom. All I could think was "Yeah, fuck you, too, you bastard. Have a good life." I pulled Emma to my side and we left the courtroom.

* * *

February came and went. March roared in like a lion dumping more than one foot of snow on us in the first week. By the time April arrived, we were more than ready for spring. Emma, Beth, Scott and I were enjoying our school lunch break out in the sun when a group of guys walked by. I heard one of them say under his breath, "Hey, check out the whore and her rape victim society." A couple of the other guys laughed.

I turned around, "Excuse me?"

Emma pleaded under her breath, "Eric . . . don't."

"Oh, look," said the gaunt, long nosed leader of the group. "Prince Eric is going to stand up for her. I guess he can relate, being he was his Uncle's bitch."

I tackled that asshole to the ground, and punched his face. His enormous nose swelled and blood flowed down his lips and chin. His friends jumped on me, but I pushed them to the ground, kicked them in their sides then went for their heads.

By the time Scott, two teachers and Principal Woodworth, pulled me away, I managed to knock the air out of all three of them, and gave each a bloody nose and one or two black eyes. Not one put a scratch on me.

"What the hell is going on here? Eric, get control of yourself!" One of the teachers exclaimed.

Adrenaline still pumping, I tried to catch my breath.

"Eric, you didn't have to do that!" Emma cried.

"Yes, I did. YES, I DID!!! They have disrespected you and me enough! ENOUGH!" I yelled.

Scott let me go, but the teachers and Mr. Woodworth held on strong.

"Get those three kids to the nurse's office," Mr. Woodworth said to several teachers standing by. "We'll take Eric to the office."

Chapter: Emma

"Expelled? You were expelled?" I yelled

"Yes."

"But you were provoked! You were doing so well!"

"I ran out of chances. I can't go back."

"Eric!"

"And that's not the worst of it. To be able to attend another county school, I have to complete a residential anger management treatment program."

"Well, that won't be so bad."

"For three weeks, in Pennsylvania."

"What?" I exclaimed.

"And that's not even the worst of it." Eric's stoic voice continued.

I couldn't respond. What could possibly be worse than that?

"My dad got transferred to Colorado. We're moving there at the end of the month."

I crumbled, "What? But what about . . . what about us?"

The strength Eric exuded quickly diminished and he sat down, defeated and deflated on my front steps. A tear crept down the beautiful contours of his face and he swept it away. Looking into the distance, he murmured, "I don't know. Maybe there shouldn't be any more 'us.'"

Shocked, I roared, "How can you say that? After all we have been through?"

"You know it kills me to say it. I don't want it this way! We have been through so much . . . so much . . ." Eric's voice trailed off. "We've made it through hell together. Nobody understands this but us."

"Who needs to understand?" I asked. "It's none of their business. It's between us!"

"Except for the fact that our parents think our 'baggage' is too much and they think we'd all be better off away from each other." Eric stated.

"Who said that? I know my parents thought that before I was raped, but they got over it! Well, at least my dad did," I corrected myself knowing my mother felt threatened by Eric because he was one of the only people in the world who saw through her act. "I think my dad really likes you now."

"*My parents*," he interrupted, "are embarrassed by the whole incident with my uncle. When they look at you, I think they feel even more guilty about not believing me when it started to happen. I can't explain it. Anyway, they decided to move sometime during the trial. It's been planned for quite some time now. They've already rented out the house and bought a new one out west. They wanted a new start, for all of us."

"We can make it! A long distance relationship will be hard, but we can do it. I know we can!" I cried desperately. "We love each other!"

"I hope so." Eric replied. Embracing one another, we tried to figure a path out of this mess, but could imagine none.

A day ago, Eric and I had thought we had a lifetime in front of us. Now, we only had five days left together. In five days, Eric would leave for anger management treatment, which he still had to complete to go to public school in Colorado. Immediately after the class, he would fly to Colorado to live with his family.

I felt sick when Eric left for the evening. Crawling into my bed, I laid awake all night, realizing that the inevitable end I feared had finally arrived. No matter how much love we felt for each other, we weren't meant to last. I knew that. For some bizarre reason, I felt I had always known that.

When the first light of dawn crept into my room, I buried myself deeper under the covers. Knowing about Eric's leaving was too much for me to bear. I loved Eric more than life itself, and couldn't imagine life without him, but life without him was what I had to face. He was going away forever. My body felt lifeless—my heart, crushed.

The sleepless night made me realize a long good-bye would kill me. Dragging out the inevitable was something I couldn't do. I decided to end our relationship that night. I knew it was the only way I could survive the pain. Swallowing my love and emotions, I drove myself to become cold.

Chapter: Eric

LIFE IS A FUCKING BITCH!

I slammed the front door as I left to pick Emma up for school. I dared anyone to stop me. I may have been expelled but I planned to be there for Emma as long as I could. Anger embraced me as I screamed, "Yeah, these last four fucking days I can be with her!" Slamming the car in reverse, I backed out of the driveway and squealed off to Emma's house.

When I got to her house, I jumped out of the car and paced up and down the driveway. I couldn't calm down. The life I had worked so hard to achieve was crumbling around me. Sitting on the rear bumper of my car, I put my head in my hands and tried not to cry. "Four days, only four more days . . . FUCK!"

Standing up abruptly, I almost knocked Emma over. "Oh, hey Pumpkin. I didn't know you were there."

"What are you doing here?" she asked coolly.

"Picking you up for school. What do you think I'm doing here?" I replied.

"You're not taking me to school."

"Yes, I am."

"No, your not." Emma said. "You've been expelled."

"I don't give a shit. I am taking you to school and I will pick you up. I am going to be there for you."

"No, Eric. You're not."

I stopped and looked Emma directly in the eyes for the first time that morning. Her glare was ice cold.

"Come on, Emma! Why are you being like this?"

"Eric, I can't take it anymore."

"Well, shit! Neither can I!" I growled.

"Eric, look at me."

My heart clutched in fear. For the first time since I've known Emma, I didn't want to look into her eyes, those gorgeous, intense, chocolate brown eyes. I turned away.

"Eric, turn around and look at me," she demanded.

I inhaled deeply and turned to her. Her eyes remained cold and empty. All I could think was, "*Oh, God no . . . . Emma . . .*"

"Eric, it's over."

I shook my head, "No . . . no."

"It is, Eric. It was over before it had begun. We always knew that."

"No, it wasn't, Emma."

"Eric, I love you. I will always love you, but it's time. You know it." Emma's cold façade slipped, with a tear from her eye.

"No, Emma, please . . . ."

"We weren't meant to be together."

"But what about . . ."

Emma interrupted me. "No, Eric. I'm sorry. It's over."

She stood there, stone faced, as if there had never been anything between us. I searched her eyes but the only evidence of emotion she showed was the one moist tear streak on her cheek.

I got down on my knees, "We can make it, Emma. We can work this out."

"No, Eric. There is nothing left to work for."

Intense pain filled me. Desperate to release it, I turned and punched the door of my car, leaving a small dent.

"Eric!" Emma yelled.

I couldn't respond. Jumping into my car, I left as fast as I could. I had to get far, far away.

* * *

So, it was over. Just like that. The love, the pain, the honesty, the incredible bond we had was over, but not gone. It would never, ever be fully gone.

I parked in my driveway and sat in my mustang for hours. I needed a smoke, but I didn't cave in. A voice in my mind kept repeating, "You're not turning to drugs again. You're beyond that now."

"True," I responded, "but I could sure use a cigarette."

I drove up to the corner drug store and bought a pack of cigarettes. The smoke burned my throat, but it felt so good. I hadn't smoked in months.

I sat on the cold concrete curb in the parking lot, in a trance, watching life pass by. Mothers were loading groceries into their cars while their children bounced in the shopping carts, dogs and cats were being carried into the vet for their yearly vaccinations and friends were meeting for lunch. Life continued on, but I felt alone and extremely hollow.

Eventually, I went back to my house and started to pack my things as tears silently flowed down my face. I packed one suitcase for anger management therapy. The rest was packed in boxes for Colorado. Pain tore my heart as I packed the few gifts I had from Emma. There was a teddy bear she had won for me at our high school's Fall Festival and a necklace she had given me for Christmas. I broke it long ago and I should have thrown it away, but I couldn't do it. It was a part of us, a part of Emma.

"Emma . . ." I whispered to myself.

Eventually, the sun began to set. I had only three days left in Maryland. After visiting a couple friends to say goodbye, I decided to walk to Emma's house. I wanted to be near her, even if she no longer wanted me.

I sat on the curb outside of her house for hours, staring up at her window as I had so many nights before, but now with a sad and heavy heart. I smoked a couple of cigarettes and remembered the good times. Tears flowed—I felt so weak, so hollow. I loved her so much. I wished I could see her one last time to hold her and to tell her how much she would always mean to me. I took one last drag on my last cigarette then turned to walk home.

The following night, I found myself outside of Emma's house again. I watched the light go off in her room when she went to bed and prayed she would sense me and come out to see me one last time, but she never did.

Chapter: Emma

I NEVER INTENDED TO END our relationship the way it did, but it was over none-the-less. I had to constantly clear my mind of my feelings for Eric. I loved him so much. I felt we were cursed and feared—that as long as we were together, our lives would be in constant turmoil. I truly believed it would be a waste for us to continue living in the constant hell we had been through together and accepted the fact that maybe our time apart would help us to both grow. In what ways, I didn't know. I just knew this vicious cycle had to be broken. "Maybe someday . . ." I started to say to myself, but I stopped, knowing I couldn't go there.

The days slowly passed by. Before I knew it, Eric would be in town only one more night. I desperately wanted to see him again, but I feared the pain would be too much to bear. Saying goodbye once was hard enough.

After barely touching my dinner, I went to my room for the remainder of the evening. Panic filled me as I thought, *Oh my God, what have I done! Eric's my soul mate! I ended it horribly, and I'll never see him again.* My heart pounded as I paced the floor. My head throbbed. Every sound seemed to magnify the pain and the light stabbed at my brain. Turning off my lamp, I lay down on my bed to calm myself and relax. Tears started to flow. I lay as quietly as I could so as not to attract my parents' attention. Breathing deeply, I started to calm myself, but a more overwhelming peacefulness settled my soul. I could feel Eric.

Jumping up, I ran to my window and looked into the dark street. Beneath the tree shadows, along the curb of the road, I could see the outline of Eric's figure and the faint red glow of the bud of his cigarette. I stood there entranced; looking at the ghostly figure of the man I loved with my entire heart and soul. I watched as he put out his cigarette and turned to walk slowly down the street.

Without a moment's hesitation, I threw my bedroom door open, slammed it against the wall and leaped down the staircase two steps at a time. I ran out the front door and into the cold damp, air, feeling the moist grass and dirt under my bare feet.

"Eric!" I called, but he was no longer there.

Desperately, I ran into the street, searching for him. I saw him walking underneath a street lamp down the road. "Eric!" I yelled again, but he still didn't hear me.

I ran, stubbing my toes on rocks and scraping my feet on the rough gravel of the road, but I didn't care. I needed him.

"Eric! Please Stop!" I screamed, one more time. This time he heard me.

He turned and looked at me with disbelief, but happiness glowed in his eyes. I ran into his arms and he held me silently, underneath the yellow glow of the lamplight, our hearts beating in synchrony again—our love at peace, at home. No words were spoken. Nothing could be said that we didn't already know.

Eventually, Eric slowly pulled himself away from me. Without a word, he softly stroked my cheek and leaned down to kiss me one last time. The soft caress of his lips took me back to the night he asked me to marry him. When he pulled away, the corner of his mouth curled up into a sad smile. Tears welled in his eyes. After looking at me one last time, he turned and silently walked away.

I watched Eric disappear into the dark night, with the undying hope that someday we'd be together again.

Part 2

Chapter: Emma

YEARS LATER, I HAD FINALLY begun to look at those horrible experiences in high school as an essential evil in my life. Sure it was hell, and I hated the anguish and fear I felt, but through that pain, I learned who I was and found a belief system outside of myself. I finally realized there was more to life than any of us knew. I started to believe in a God and a greater purpose, as well as reincarnation and soul mates. I believed, without a shadow of a doubt, that Eric was my "ultimate soulmate" and that we were brought together in this lifetime to remember that we all had a greater purpose here, even if we didn't know what it was. From the very beginning of our relationship, I always knew we weren't meant to be together, and that was painful to accept. In fact, I could hardly accept it at all. Eventually, I learned to get over the pain of losing Eric like I learned to get over the pain of my past—one day at a time.

The last I heard from him was one week after he left for the anger management class. I arrived home from school to find an envelope addressed to me sitting on the kitchen table. It looked odd: My name and address had been typed and there was no return address. Curious, I opened it and unfolded the crisp white paper. I was shocked to find a letter from Eric. Unlike the envelope, it was written in his very familiar longhand:

Dear Emma,

Hey, Pumpkin! Well, I arrived at Fresh Start Anger Management. My address for the next three weeks will be P.O. Box 2398, Scranton, PA. I'm hoping to hear from you. I'm

> also hoping I can get my life straight so something like this doesn't happen again—not with you, but with me. I hate the fact that we won't be together. I really wish it could've worked out. I'll never forget about you, not in a million years. I can't get you out of my mind. No matter where I am, or what I see, something always reminds me of you.
>
> I'm hoping that you'll think of me as I will be thinking of you.
>
> Well, I got to go. Please take care and please remember that I still love you and always will. Nothing will ever change the way I feel about you. NOTHING.
>
> Love, Eric

Tears streaming down my face, I snatched up some paper to write back. I don't remember exactly what I wrote, but I know I told Eric I would wait for him—forever if I had to. I told him how I couldn't stand us being apart and that I would love him until the day I died. I apologized for ending the relationship the way I did, and told him how I wished I could take it all back. I asked him to let me know how to reach him after the anger management treatment. When I was done, I folded the letter, copied his address on the envelope and immediately took it out to the mailbox.

Days passed by, then weeks. A response never came. Every day, I prayed for a letter, but we got only bills and junk mail. Eventually I started to assume he had decided to let me go so he could move on with his life. When the twelfth week went by with no word, I gave up, devastated. I no longer even cared what came in the mailbox. As time passed, thoughts of Eric became less and less frequent, decreasing from every minute, to every hour, then eventually to every day. But there I was stuck: Eric never crossed my mind less than once a day and he often visited my dreams at night.

Beth and I became very close as we completed our one remaining year of high school together. We hung out constantly and shared a ton of laughter. She kept my spirits up. It was impossible to be depressed when she was around.

It helped to find that the gossip that had centered on me for so long disappeared. The kids at school stopped focusing on my life, which had become quite boring, and focused on who was wearing what brand of jeans and carrying what type of purse. Shallow, but I didn't care. The spotlight was off me. My father also made sure I got the counseling I needed, helping me on my journey out of the slippery well I had fallen into.

Everyday, I grew stronger. My doctor spent hours with me discussing all the pain, fear and horror that harbored inside me from the events of the past couple years. For the most part, we focused on the rape. I confided in him how vulnerable I felt when I was alone and how scared I was when I met new people. It's not that I knew the rapist—I didn't, but that fact didn't help me overcome trusting anyone I met or ran into. Not only did I fear for my physical well-being, I also feared that if people knew my past, they would blame me, use it against me or maybe even dislike me because of the choices I made—especially that of the abortion. I was ashamed of the skeletons in my closet, so I found it hard to open up to anyone. In retrospect, maybe I just didn't think anyone was worthy enough to open up to. Nobody was Eric.

My doctor gave me coping mechanisms for the unexpected times when the pain would tear at my soul. Meditation became routine in my life. I'd clear my mind of the demons that haunted me and learned to focus on the here and now. If I couldn't sit down and meditate, I learned to take a deep breath and really evaluate my situation. *Was I in immediate danger? Did it really matter what strangers thought?* I eventually learned that my past had a place—in my past and I worked everyday to let it go.

Learning to deal with the emotional pain was very healing. Over time, life became mundane and mechanical, but it was easier. I'd wake up, meditate, go to school or work, come home and then go to bed. My mom encouraged me to go out more, and when I'd refuse she'd slur, "God, you're boring and pathetic. You should really get a life."

I'd roll my eyes and watch as she sauntered through the house in a drunken stupor. I was proud to be different than her and I certainly didn't need any more excitement. I felt comfortable, safe and free, and that was more important to me than what she perceived I was missing in my life—parties and boyfriends. I was happy just as I was. The only downside that remained was the hollow feeling inside that echoed Eric's name.

After high school, I continued to work at the veterinary hospital while attending Howard Community College. I carried a full load of courses and diligently worked towards an associate's degree. I wanted to become a teacher and dreamed of the day I'd make a difference in a child's life. My grade point average was stellar, only missing 4.0 when I made a stupid mistake on my phys ed, bowling test. I knew that my success was due to two things: first, my inner drive to disprove people's notion that I was worthless; second, my lack of a social life.

I certainly missed Beth and Scott who had left town to attend Penn State University together. Befriending new people became difficult for me because I believed that any relationship would be superficial unless I told them about my past, and as I discussed with my therapist, I feared my past would scare them away. However, being alone, without superficial "friends" hovering around had never bothered me.

Life continued to be dull and mundane until my sophomore year at the community college. That's when life as I knew it, as the world knew it, changed.

My memory of September 11, 2001, is as crisp as the bright morning sun that fateful day. I missed my 8:00 Calculus I class, because I was home in bed, sick with a cold. My head ached as I listened to the clicks and clinks of my mom putting dishes away in the kitchen. The smell of freshly brewed coffee filled the air and jingles of commercials played softly on the television.

I crawled deeper under the covers allowing the hum of my surroundings to lull me back to sleep.

Startled by the sudden noise of an avalanche of pans falling to the floor in the kitchen, I jumped.

"Emma!" My mom yelled. "Emma, come quick! Something horrible's happened!"

I pulled myself out of bed. My head spun from the pressure in my sinuses as I stumbled down the hall.

"What? What is it?" I groaned.

"Look at the T.V.!"

We watched in horror as the reporters tried to make sense of what was happening. Airplanes had flown into the World Trade Center and the Pentagon and one crashed in Pennsylvania. After some time, the first of the grand towers started to collapse. Then, the second. We silently observed, our mouths drying out as we held them open, wiping the tears streaming down our faces as thousands of people died before our eyes. The images were repeated over and over again on the television, forever imprinting on my mind.

As sadness filled me, I closed my eyes to find that familiar pair of beautiful blue eyes piercing my thoughts. But this time, tears flowed from those eyes and fell into oblivion. The pain and horror reflected in those eyes broke my heart wider apart.

* * *

In early March, my sophomore year at the community college, my life changed even more. I had just finished a grueling organic chemistry lab. It sucked. Not only was organic chemistry difficult, the chemistry laboratory at HCC was as hot as the inside of a furnace. The temperature outside had broken a record high, reaching 85 degrees. The school had not turned off the heaters, because technically it was still winter, so between the heat produced from them, the sun streaming through the windows and about sixteen Bunsen burners firing away, we were all exhausted and drenched in sweat by the end of our four hour lab.

My lab partner, Judy, and I decided to go to the cafeteria for a cold drink. Judy, an adorable petite girl with shoulder-length, black hair and gorgeous almond-shaped eyes had a bubbly personality and a contagious smile. As we walked down the hallway, Judy rolled her eyes and exclaimed, "Well, that sucked!"

"Tell me about it!" I replied. "And only eight more left to go! I can't wait 'til this class is over!"

Judy laughed, "Me, too. So what are you going to be doing next year?"

"I just finished sending in my application to Towson. I want to major in some sort of education. I still can't figure out whether I want to teach high school biology or elementary school."

"Hmm, that's a hard choice, but either one would be great!" she smiled. "I can see it now, Emma, the teacher . . ."

I laughed, "So, what are you going to do?"

Judy replied, "I'm going to major in English."

"What? Giving up the whole biology major thing?" I asked.

We had reached the crowded cafeteria and grabbed a couple of drinks from the cooler. Getting in line to pay, Judy answered, "Yeah, weird, huh? Biology is fun stuff, but my heart's not in it. I'd much rather spend my time reading or writing. My parents aren't too thrilled about it. They don't think a degree in English can get you anywhere, but the truth is, a degree in biology can't get you very far either unless you go on to med school or vet school or something, and I really don't want to do that. So, I promised them if I majored in English, I would get a teaching degree as well. I'm hoping to get into Maryland next year."

"That sounds great! I hope you find out soon!"

"Yeah, me too. I hate all this waiting."

The cafeteria line stopped moving forward and I maneuvered myself to look at the front of the line. The cashier was having problems with the register. Everyone in line was eager to pay and the question "What's going on?" echoed all around. The cashier slammed the drawer shut and started to dig at the receipt paper which had gotten jammed.

Embittered, the cashier called out, "I'm sorry everyone. This lane is closed." She threw up the closed sign and a groan of disappointment resonated through the line. As I started to back up to move toward another register, I bumped into someone.

I turned to apologize, "Oh sorry, I didn't mean to . . ." but stopped in mid-sentence.

I had backed into the most gorgeous guy I had seen in years. His familiar blue eyes smiled down at me through long locks of blond hair, and his smile took my breath away. "No problem," he replied. "Need a new checkout line?"

"Uh, yeah . . ." I replied nervously biting my lip. My mind went blank. I hadn't noticed any one of the opposite sex since Eric. He invited Judy and me to join him in line, letting us cut in front of him.

"My name is Jared Stafford." Jared reached out his hand to shake mine. My hand felt tiny and cold in his firm grip. I smiled, "I'm Emma . . . Emma Fiorello."

Jared turned to Judy, "And you are?"

She shook his hand, "I'm Judy."

"It's nice to meet you both!" He smiled. His eyes lingered on mine for an extra second. A girl in front of Judy tapped her on the shoulder and she excused herself to join her friend.

Jared looked at me again and continued, "I've seen you around quite a bit, but I never had a chance to introduce myself."

I smiled, feeling slightly uncomfortable. I knew I had never seen him before—I would have remembered it.

"What year are you in?"

"Sophomore," I answered.

"That's great! So, you'll be graduating in May, too?"

"Yep, I will." I replied, still in shock and at a complete loss for words. This gorgeous guy was speaking to ME.

"Are you going anywhere next year?"

"I'm hoping to get into Towson to study education. How about you?"

"I just applied for an ROTC scholarship and I'm hoping to get into UVA. I want to major in computer science there."

"Wow, the ROTC? That's the military, isn't it?" I asked.

"Yeah, they will pay for my final two years of schooling if I promise to work for them for eight years, four of which will be active duty. My parents have paid for my first two years and can't afford much more. I already live out on my own, and work as a waiter to pay for my condo, so, to be honest, I can't really afford it either. I thought this would work out well. I can finish my degree, and I'll already have a job lined up. My father is thrilled."

"Wow! You've planned it all out, haven't you?" I smiled. "You'll have to chop off that hair though."

Jared laughed, "Yeah, I thought of that."

Judy reached the cashier and paid for her drink. After getting her change, she signaled that she was going to go find a table. I motioned that I would meet up with her.

As the cashier rung me up, Jared said, "Hey, I don't usually do this, but it's taken me quite a long time to finally meet you. Would you like to go out and get some coffee sometime?"

A date? Was this gorgeous guy asking ME out on a date? I glanced at the cashier and she smiled.

"Um," I hesitated. An image of Eric's face passed through my mind. I hadn't been asked out on a date since Eric. The cashier raised her eyebrows at me as if to say *"You're kidding me! You're gonna say no?"*

I turned to look at Jared and noticed he looked worried. He said, "I'm sorry. I shouldn't have been so forward," and took a step back.

"No . . . no . . ." I smiled, shocked at how nervous, yet comfortable I felt with him. "I would really like that!"

"Great! That's great!" Jared sighed in relief. "Let me give you my number."

Jared finished paying for his drink then dropped his backpack on the nearest table. He grabbed a piece of scrap paper out of his bag and scribbled his name and number on it.

After he handed it to me, I tore off a piece and said, "Here, let me give you mine." Taking his pen, I wrote down my name and number.

"Great!" he smiled. I noticed a dimple on his left cheek. "Talk to you soon!"

"Okay, bye!" I smiled back. Excitement began to build in me. I had to keep myself from running to the table where Judy was waiting for me.

Sliding into my seat, I burst, "You are never going to believe what just happened!"

Judy laughed, "I don't know, but by the look on your face something had to have happened with that guy."

"HE ASKED ME OUT!" I squealed!

Judy squealed and grabbed my hand. "That's fantastic! He is so hot!"

"I know." Biting my lip nervously, I thought of Eric and reveled in the excitement and trepidation of being with someone new. Realizing I hadn't bought any new clothes in years, I gasped, "Oh, God . . ." I turned to Judy, "What am I going to wear? I haven't been on a date in years!"

Judy's smile widened, "Well, you have happened to luck out, Miss Emma. Shopping happens to be one of my specialties! Let's go!"

"Now?"

"Yes, now! It'll be fun!"

Laughing, we grabbed our things and headed to the parking lot. I followed Judy's white Chevy pick-up truck to the mall which had expanded significantly since the last time I visited. New parking garages and restaurants surrounded the sprawling shopping center, while new clothes stores, shoe stores and boutiques lined hallways that didn't exist five years ago.

Overwhelmed, I asked Judy, "Where should we start?"

She grabbed me by the arm, "Don't you worry, honey! Just come with me!"

Judy sent me to the dressing room with all the latest styles. I think I tried on more clothes in one hour than I'd owned in my lifetime. We laughed at the absurdity of some of the styles while striking poses and pretending to strut on catwalks. It felt good. I hadn't laughed like that in the longest time. By the end of the day, I had three large bags full of new clothes, earrings, necklaces, belts and shoes.

Later that night, Jared called. Our conversation felt natural, easy and before I knew it, two hours had passed. His voice reflected his radiant personality and I could hear the smile in his voice and see the sparkle in his eyes.

Eventually, I had to hang up the phone, needing to complete the labs and papers waiting in stacks on my desk.

"Jared, I have to go. I need to get some work done."

"Yeah, you're right." He replied.

"Well, I guess I'll . . ."

"Emma, why don't we meet tomorrow night? Get some coffee?"

"Don't you have to work?" I asked.

"No, I usually do, but I'm off tomorrow night. I switched with a friend who needed Monday off. So, you wanna go?"

A nervous dread passed over me. I didn't know if I was ready to be alone with this guy no matter how charming or gorgeous he may be. I felt rushed and overwhelmed.

"Uh, well . . ." I started.

"Wait! I got a better idea! Let's not wait that long!"

"What?" I laughed. "It's only tomorrow night!"

"True . . . true . . . but why don't we meet for lunch tomorrow in the cafeteria?"

The pleading sound in his voice was palpable.

"Okay," I agreed, relieved that our first "date" would be in the school cafeteria. I didn't have to ride alone with him or be taken someplace new and unknown yet.

"That would be nice."

Hanging up the phone, I wondered if I would ever feel safe with a man other than Eric. The sad, hollow feeling that accompanied thoughts of him silently gripped my soul but for the first time ever, they were eclipsed by an intense feeling of excitement. I couldn't wait to get to school the next day.

* * *

The next morning, I spent a little extra time getting myself ready for school. I slipped on a new pair of blue jeans and a black, button-down, collared shirt, then put on my new boots and belt. After brushing my hair, I put on a little make-up—something I hadn't done in a long time. When I looked at the finished product in the mirror, I caught myself by surprise. I actually looked good.

A flashback of the rape seized me and my knees buckled. My counselor's voice echoed in my head, "It wasn't your fault. It wasn't what you were wearing or how you looked that made him do it. It was the evil inside of him."

I pulled myself together and looked deeply into my own eyes and saw a beautiful, strong woman staring back; a woman that had overcome so much and whose life was worth more than solitude and fear.

An inner voice spoke, "It's okay. It's time to move on."

I smiled to myself and answered, "Why, yes it is!" but my smile wavered as a flash of Eric's face crept into my mind.

* * *

"Wow! You look fantastic!" Judy said when we met in the hallway.

"You should really consider going into fashion design." I winked. "You're a natural fashionista, baby!"

Judy laughed, "It was fun!"

"Yeah, it was." I agreed. "Thank you so much! I feel like a completely different person today."

"We should do it again sometime!"

"Definitely!"

"Soooo, what's going on?" Judy asked.

"Not too much. How about . . ."

"Oh come on!" Judy interrupted. "Don't make me pull it out of you! What's going on with Jared?"

"Oh, with *Jared* . . ." I smiled. "Well, we talked on the phone for almost two hours last night and we are meeting for lunch in the cafeteria today."

"Get out!" She exclaimed as she pushed me back a little with both hands.

"Okay, Elaine!" I laughed remembering an old Seinfeld episode.

Judy burst out laughing. "So, you're meeting for lunch today?"

"Yep, 12:30."

"In the *cafeteria*? You go girl—but that's not so romantic for the first date!"

I shrugged, "It doesn't bother me at all. In fact, I think it's perfect."

"Oh, come on! Going out for dinner or a drink or coffee or something would be a little more romantic, don't you think?"

"Well, he originally wanted to take me out for coffee tonight, but said he couldn't wait that long. So then he asked me if we could meet for lunch. I didn't care either way. Actually, I feel a lot safer this way." I replied.

"Safer? Who gives a shit about being safer? I wouldn't mind if he jumped me in a dark alleyway!" Judy giggled and glanced in my direction. She froze when she looked at my face.

"Apparently, you haven't been in my shoes." I retorted and turned to walk away.

Judy caught up with me, "Oh my God, Emma. I'm sorry. Did I say something?"

I took a deep breath to prevent myself from saying all I wanted to. How was she to know?

"Yes, Judy. What you said really bothered me."

"I'm sorry."

Her apology was sincere, but I still felt angry.

Judy hesitated, then touched my arm. "Do you mind me asking you why?"

"Why?" I snapped, pulling my arm away. "Because rape isn't something to joke about. It sucks."

"Oh," she gasped, her eyes bulging when her mind put the pieces together.

I had never told Judy anything about my past, but now I was sure she could figure out why I hadn't dated anyone for years and avoided most men like the plague.

"Oh, Emma! I'm so sorry! I had no idea."

I shook my head, "It's okay. It's not something I talk about. You didn't know."

"But still, I am so sorry. That was a really stupid thing to say either way."

I smiled weakly, "It's really okay. Forget about it!"

"Are you sure?" she asked.

"Yeah."

"Well, if you ever need to talk about anything, I hope you know I'm here and I consider you a good friend."

Smiling more easily this time, I said, "Thanks, Judy. I really appreciate it."

Relieved, she turned to walk away. "Well, have a great lunch! Call me!"

"I will."

Even though I was excited about my lunch date, I lost myself in my own little world during American Literature class. Literature and music always transported me to another world, and my professor, Dr. Clyburn was one of the most interesting lecturers I ever listened to. His talks about Edgar Allan Poe's "The Raven" sparked my imagination, while Bryant's "Thanatopsis" and Emerson's "Self-Reliance" peaked my spiritual curiosity. I'll never forget Emerson's words, "A man should learn to detect and watch that gleam of light which flashes across his mind from within, more than the lustre of the firmament of bards and sages. Yet he dismisses without notice his thoughts, because it is his."

During Dr. Clyburn's discussion of Robert Frost's "The Road Not Taken" and "For Once, Then, Something." the poems sang to my soul, and I found my mind drifting into a world of its own. Dr. Clyburn's voice became a comforting hum in the background.

I was looking into a well of water. Something white was laying near the bottom of the well under the ripples of my reflection. I tried to focus on it, but it disappeared into the depths. A soft voice behind me whispered, "Emma." I turned to face the edge of a forest. Two paths stretched into the darkness of the woods. On the left path stood Eric, holding a small, white object emanating its own light. He slowly walked up to me and with a stoic face, looked deeply in my eyes and placed the small white light in my hand. It was beautiful and warm. I turned to Eric to ask him what it was, but he was already walking down the path, disappearing into the forest. I called for him and he turned to me and winked before merging into darkness.

Another whisper called my name, but this time it was on the path to the right. I turned and saw Jared standing there. He held out his hand requesting me to go with him. Eric's voice echoed through the woods, "Go."

Dr. Clyburn called my name, bringing my focus back to the classroom. "Emma, what do you think the whiteness at the bottom of the well represents?"

Without a second thought, I replied, "A soul." Students chuckled around me but I reacted only to my own vision, feeling a chill run through my body—a combination of sadness and excitement.

"Very interesting." He smiled. "Anyone else?"

Nobody replied.

"We will continue this discussion on Friday. Class dismissed."

I quickly collected my things and walked to the cafeteria. My mind was still mulling over the vision I had in American Lit, but it went blank when I saw Jared standing there. Leaning casually in the doorway, he looked like he just stepped out of a GQ magazine. The black sweater, layered on top of a white t-shirt accented his broad shoulders and he was wearing jeans. His gorgeous blue eyes searched the crowd of students filing past him and when they focused on me, he smiled.

Chapter: Jared

I COULDN'T WAIT ANY LONGER. I had to see Emma again. She was the most beautiful woman I had ever seen. Not only did her physical beauty entranced me, but she radiated a tantalizing mysterious pull. She was irresistible.

Our two-hour conversation on the phone the night before left me wanting so much more. I felt like we were old friends finally finding each other again. Incredibly bright and sophisticated, Emma possessed a deepness that intrigued me.

As soon as we hung up the phone, I realized we forgot to pick a meeting place for lunch. So I was there a half hour early. Not wanting to get lost in the bustling crowd of the cafeteria, I waited for her by the doorway. I scanned the crowd, anxiously waiting for her arrival. I checked my watch for the umpteenth time, then saw her walking down the hallway.

Students and faculty branched in every direction as she carefully picked her way through the crowd. Her gorgeous brown hair shielded her face from me, but then she shook it back from her face and our eyes met. My chin dropped—she literally took my breath away. Embarrassed by my reaction, I cleared my throat and looked toward the floor. I hadn't felt this nervous and excited since high school. In fact, I don't think I had ever felt like this about anyone. I took a deep breath and lifted my eyes back to hers. She smiled at me.

"Hey Emma!" I couldn't contain myself—I smiled ear to ear.

"Hey Jared!" she blushed.

God she is beautiful. I lost my breath again. Clearing my throat, I asked, "So, uh, hungry?"

Emma said, "Yes, actually I am. It's been a long, long morning."

"Tell me about it!"

She smiled at me with that gorgeous, beautiful, sparkling smile.

We both spoke, "I thought lunch . . ."

Laughing nervously, I said, "Go on."

"No, you go on."

I ran my hand through my hair, "Oh-well, I thought lunch . . ."

"Would never get here." She finished. She blushed again and bit her lip.

"Exactly." I wanted those lips so badly.

We walked into the cafeteria and picked out our food, then made our way to a table in the back corner of the room.

As we sat down, I said, "I really enjoyed talking to you last night."

"Me too." She replied.

"So, how have your classes been today?"

"Good. Long." She said. "And you?"

"Good. Long." I chuckled.

Emma grabbed the ketchup bottle and poured a huge pile on her plate for her fries, then smothered her burger with it.

"Like ketchup?" I laughed.

Embarrassed, she hid her face behind her hair and answered, "Yeah, I love ketchup. It's quite a family joke. I eat it on everything, eggs, steak . . ."

"You're kidding! Me too!"

She laughed, "Really?"

"Yeah."

She smiled, "Well, I guess that's something else we have in common."

"We are quite similar, aren't we?" I reached and ran my fingers along her hand. She didn't pull it away so I took it in mine. It was tiny and soft. She even felt amazing.

Emma blushed and pulled her hand away to pick up her burger. I hoped I hadn't been too forward. It took everything within me not to sweep this girl off her feet and kiss her right there. My body craved to be near her.

"I'm sorry, I . . ." I felt so conflicted. I wanted to be near her so badly. It had been so easy to talk to her on the phone last night, but now, in her presence, I felt too awkward to know what to say.

"Don't be." She said. "It felt nice."

Relief filled me.

A couple guys ran by passing a football and hollering through the cafeteria. A girl shrieked as the ball skimmed past her head. Laughter broke out.

"Emma? Would you let me take you out for a real dinner, maybe Friday night if I can work it out with my boss?"

"What? You and me away from this?" She teased, watching the chaos in the cafeteria, and looking more comfortable. "Yeah, I'd like that."

"Great, you like Italian?"

A look of sadness crossed Emma's face but it was quickly erased by a smile.

"Yes, I like Italian."

"How about Maria's?"

"That would be wonderful," she smiled, but sadness filled her eyes.

"Is everything okay?"

"Yep, everything's fine." Emma grabbed a French fry and said, "So, do you do this often?"

"Do what?"

"Pick up strange girls and sweep them off their feet?"

I blushed, "Is that what I'm doing? Sweeping you off your feet?"

"Maybe." Emma replied.

"No, Emma. This is a first for me." I looked out the window. "There's something about you. I can't help it."

"I can't imagine what that could be!" She laughed. "I haven't been out on a date for years!"

"You're kidding!"

"Nope."

"Well, those guys don't know what they're missing."

Emma snickered, "Yeah right."

"They don't. Not only are you gorgeous, you are intelligent and . . ."

"And what?" she laughed.

"Well, there's something really intriguing about you . . . it's sexy. I can see it in your eyes."

Now she burst out laughing even harder. "Oh yeah, and what is that?"

"You have a deep side about you . . . a past."

Emma stopped laughing and glared at me. "What is that supposed to mean?"

Shocked by her response, I tried to recover. "Nothing—nothing bad, just, you're more deep than most girls; more in tuned to life or something. Your eyes say so much."

I reached out and touched her cheek and lost myself in her eyes. There was so much there: excitement, pain, sadness, intelligence. Her eyes were gorgeous, intriguing.

"Oh." She looked at me suspiciously then glanced down to her lap to avoid my gaze.

Pulling my hand away, I continued, "Really, it's not a bad thing. In fact, I really, really like that about you."

"Well," Emma smiled weakly. "I guess that can be a good thing."

"Really, it is." I reassured her.

We finished our lunch and it was time to go to our afternoon classes. I cleared the table and watched Emma as she started to gather her things. She seemed so sad and so anxious. *What could it be?*

Emma thanked me for lunch and started to leave the cafeteria. I grabbed her hand, "No problem. Can we do it again tomorrow?"

"Yes." She nodded her head tentatively.

"I'll call you tonight."

"I'll be waiting." She smiled coyly and walked away.

As I watched her walk down the hall, I thought to myself, "*Damn, that is one stunning, intriguing woman.*"

Emma didn't leave my mind for the remainder of the day.

Chapter: Emma

As I walked to class, my mind raced.

Lunch with Jared had been interesting. He was absolutely gorgeous and smart, but in all honesty, the idea of him terrified me. He seemed completely and totally head over heels infatuated with me and I wasn't sure why. It's not like I didn't enjoy the attention. I did, but it was going too fast. He didn't know anything about me or my past. If Jared knew the truth, would he still like me as much as he did now? I doubted it.

I missed Eric. He loved me for me and already knew everything. I couldn't imagine anyone else could love me so completely. I hoped I was wrong, especially since Eric had disappeared for good.

Then, Jared asked me to go to Maria's—our Maria's. I remembered homecoming dinner there with Eric, Beth and Scott. Memories of the dance filled my mind and I remembered how Eric held me close and sang softly in my ear. I'd never forget the look in his eyes when he said, "I love you, future Mrs. Florentino."

It was useless—the memories still took my breath away. Forgetting Eric and all we went through was never going to happen, but I knew it was time to put the past in the past and explore new possibilities in life. Was Jared the man to help me do this? I didn't know.

So far with Jared, one moment had been foreign and uncomfortable, while the next seemed exciting and wonderful. *One step at a time, Emma,* I said to myself. I took a deep breath. I knew I really liked Jared; He was smart and fun. I was just scared. I felt like a fake—a charade: a beautiful, smart girl on the outside hiding a deep, dark truth within.

I believed nobody could truly love me unless he embraced that truth, and I wouldn't share my past with just anyone. It was a part of me:

the deepest, darkest part of me. Eric embraced it, but now he was gone. Could anyone else love me for all I was, all I've been? Could Jared?

Thoughts of Eric and Jared plagued my mind through Western Civilization. I was mentally exhausted by the end of class.

The ominous clouds in the sky reflected my mood, and I dragged myself to my car so I could drive home. I turned on the radio searching for a song to free my mind from the torrent of questions that had plagued me all afternoon. Commercials played on every station. Frustrated, I stopped switching the stations and left it on 106.5. An obnoxious ad for a car dealership played. "Ugh!" I sighed. *Why is there never any good music on when you need it?*

My mind drifted again. I remembered watching Eric walking away from me the last night we were together. I could still see the outline of his body in the lamplight, fading slowly into darkness. I thought of Jared looking at me at lunch. I saw the smile in his eyes and remembered his gentle touch. I thought about how kind and attentive he seemed.

I said out loud, "What now? What do I do? Can I move on? *Should* I move on?"

A song started playing on the radio. Green Day's "Good Riddance" came on. The lyrics sang to my soul and perfectly described my dilemma. Tears streamed down my face. I *was* facing a fork in the road. This song on the radio and the poems in class were forcing me to face the truth and were answering my deepest, most sincere question. It was time to switch course, and it was okay. My vision in American Lit may have been a daydream, but its symbolism was clear as well.

Deep, painful sobs erupted from me. I had to let him go. Eric was gone. It was over and it had been for a long time. I now needed to take the new fork in the road, the new path—and see where it would lead me. I cried out loud, "Eric, I hope you know, wherever you are, that I will always love you and I will never forget you. Please, never forget me."

I knew Eric couldn't hear me, but finally saying the words I wished I had said during our last moments together brought me peace. I whispered, "Goodbye, Eric," as cold tears streamed down my cheeks.

My cell phone rang. Swallowing my emotions, I answered, "Hello?"

"Hey Emma, it's Jared."

I felt a smile spread ear to ear. I took a deep breath and fully embraced the diverging paths in my life. I envisioned Eric walking down one path as I turned toward the new one.

I said, "Hi Jared! I'm happy you called," and I meant it with all of my heart.

"Is everything okay? I've been a little worried about you since lunch. You seemed upset or something."

"I'm sorry." I explained. "It's just that . . . I had to work through a few things."

"Okay. Do you need to talk about anything?"

"No, I'm fine now. I worked it all out."

"Is there anything I can do?" Jared asked.

"Yes, meet me for coffee."

I could hear the excitement in his voice. "You got it! Joe's?"

"Yep, Joe's."

"Be there in five minutes."

"See you then." I smiled.

As I drove to Joe's the churning clouds overhead suddenly released torrents of rain. Traffic slowed and my windshield wipers could barely keep up with the unrelenting downpour. It took over fifteen minutes to complete the usual five minute drive to the coffee shop. By the time I got there, Jared was standing out front under a huge black umbrella. When I pulled in, he ran up to my car to help me out. His strong arms pulled me close to his body as we ran through the rain under his umbrella. The warmth of his skin and the musky smell of his body enveloped me and I didn't want to let go.

Once we reached the front of Joe's Coffee Shop and sheltered underneath the blue and white awning, we finally spoke.

"Jesus, where did that rain come from!" Jared said as he closed and shook out his umbrella with the one hand that wasn't holding me tightly against him.

"I don't know." I replied. "I certainly wasn't expecting it. Sorry I'm a little late. Traffic practically stopped out there!"

I started to pull away but Jared pulled me closer. He dropped his umbrella to the ground and turned me toward him. Taking my chin in his hand, he tilted my face so he could look me straight in the eyes. "Emma, don't apologize. I've waited to find you my entire life. Waiting for you an extra ten minutes at the coffee shop is nothing compared to that."

Blood rushed to my cheeks. I couldn't help but blush. *This guy sure knows how to talk to a girl.* I bit my lip and tried to turn away. *How could this gorgeous guy like me so much?*

Jared's smile faded a little and his eyes filled with sincerity. "I'm sorry Emma. I hope I'm not scaring you. It's just that since the first time I saw you, you've been the only thing I can think about. I'm just so happy to be with you again."

To reassure him, I said, "You're not scaring me. I like being with you, too. Everything has just taken me by surprise."

Jared smiled. "Let's get some coffee." He took my hand and led me into Joe's. The small brick building was filled with the warm smell of fresh coffee and pastries. The dull lighting gave even the busiest table a feeling of privacy, but we hid ourselves at a small two-person table in the back corner of the coffee shop. The romantic sound of jazz music played in the background.

As we drank our cappuccinos, we talked about all kinds of things; our favorite movies, drinks, music and trips we'd taken. We had so much in common. We both loved Star Wars, and Empire Strikes Back was our favorite of the trilogy. Both of our families visited Ocean City in the summer and Shenandoah National Park in the Fall. Our music preferences did vary a bit. While I preferred to listen to Top 40 music, he listened to Metallica, Green Day and Linkin Park, but I did know and love some of their songs as well. Even though we had just met each other, I felt we had known each other for years. We were like long lost friends who had finally found each other again. I started to feel extremely comfortable and safe with Jared. As I looked into his eyes, I knew I could easily fall in love with this man.

Before we knew it, several hours had passed and we were both hungry for dinner.

"Why don't we go to Maria's tonight?" Jared suggested.

"Really?" I asked, my stomach grumbling.

"Yeah, why not? I'm starving. You hungry, too?"

"Yeah."

"Then let's go! I'll drive."

Jared paid the bill then led me to his car. The rain had finally stopped and the clouds had started to part. The low-setting sun cast an orange glow in the sky. Jared opened the door of his black Pontiac Firebird and let me in. We rolled down the windows and he started the ignition. The radio blared the UB40 cover of "Fools Rush In."

Jared smiled at me and started to sing along with the music as he pulled out of the parking lot. He had a beautiful, strong voice.

I laughed as people walking along the road stared at us in disbelief. I started to sing along, too. As we drove down the road, singing at the top of our lungs, the warm wind blew through my hair and the fresh moist smell of the spring rain enveloped me. I felt so free and alive! I knew this was the beginning of something magical. I hoped this feeling would last forever.

Chapter: Jared

THE DÉCOR HAD CHANGED SINCE the last time I was in Maria's. Pillars were added between the booths giving it a more ethnic look and oil paintings of the Italian countryside covered the walls. Plain white tablecloths were replaced by deep red ones and three candles glowed in the center of each table.

Emma looked gorgeous. I watched the reflection of the candlelight dance in her eyes and admired how the light and shadows enhanced the delicate contours of her face.

The car ride to Maria's was incredible. Being with Emma, singing and laughing and seeing the wind whip through her hair filled me with an electricity I couldn't explain. I was falling for this woman, fast.

I reached across the table for her hand and held it tight in mine. Emma smiled at me. Filled with emotion, I said, "Emma I think I'm in love with you."

Emma's smile faded and panic filled her eyes. "Jared, I . . ."

"Welcome to Maria's!" interrupted an excessively cheerful waitress. The lines on her face drew a picture of a difficult life. Reaching into her apron to grab a pen, she continued, "Would you like to hear our specials today?"

I hesitated and looked at Emma. I wondered if I had pushed it too far this time. Turning back to the waitress I said, "Sure."

As she rattled off the specials of the day, I studied Emma's face. She pretended to listen to the waitress, but I could tell her mind was somewhere else. She looked pale, almost lifeless. I felt my heart slowly breaking. This incredible girl didn't feel even half of what I felt for her. I let out an audible sigh.

"So, what can I get you this evening?" asked the waitress.

Emma replied, "I'll take the spinach cannelloni and an ice tea, please."

I told the waitress, "I'll take the lasagna and a coke, thanks."

"Okay, thanks kids. I'll be back with your drinks in a minute."

As soon as she walked away I started, "Emma . . ."

Emma interrupted me sharply, "Jared, there is no way you can love me already."

"But . . ."

"No, Jared, there's something you need to know. You need to know the truth about me. If you can still love me after that, then I will believe you." She sighed, "Right now, you just think you're in love with me, but you don't even know who I am and what I've been through."

"Okay." I wondered what she could possibly tell me that would be so bad that I couldn't love her. It's not like she could have killed someone. "So, can you tell me now?"

Emma glanced around the half empty restaurant then looked at me, "Jared, I really like you a lot. There is no doubt in my mind that I could fall in love with you." She bit her lip and looked down at her lap and whispered, "I may have fallen in love with you already."

I smiled and reached for her, but she pulled away.

"But, before this goes any further, you need to know a little more about me. If you want to end things, I'll understand. I can't stay in a relationship where my past is not known or respected. I can't live a lie."

Growing anxious, I asked, "Okay, so what happened?"

Emma leaned forward, placed her elbows on the table and propped her chin on her clenched hands. I reached for her hands again, but she still pulled away. Fire burned in her eyes. I could see purpose and strength in her soul. Emma was on a mission. She was testing me. I started to wonder if I would pass. Could I accept what she was about to tell me?

"When I was sixteen years old, I was raped by a man named Matt Johansen. He was found dead a few months later. His murderer has never been found, but the police suspect that it was a drug related murder."

My mouth dropped open. I certainly didn't expect this. "Wow, Emma. That's horrible. Thank God you're okay."

"Wait." Emma interrupted, "That's not everything."

The waitress brought the drinks to our table and told us our meals would be coming out soon. While the waitress stood there, Emma's eyes penetrated me. She seemed to be searching for something.

As soon as the waitress left, I said, "Go on."

"A month after the rape, I found out I was pregnant. I had an abortion."

I couldn't speak.

Tears welled up in Emma's eyes. "Honestly," she said, "that was almost as hard as the rape. I ended up getting so depressed I almost killed myself." She showed me a light cross-shaped scar on her wrist.

"Wow." I couldn't think of anything else to say. And to think I had been just joking to myself about the fact that she couldn't have killed anyone. My stomach turned. I felt nauseous, but the truth was, I wasn't upset about the abortion. I got that. It was the fact that she almost killed herself that upset me the most. I had only known her a couple days and I already couldn't imagine a world without her. I was speechless.

Tears rolled down Emma's cheeks. She mumbled, "I understand Jared, it's okay." She reached for her purse and got up to leave.

Jumping up, I grabbed her hand and pulled her back to the table. "Don't leave Emma. It's not what you think."

She took a deep breath and sat down. She grabbed a napkin and dabbed at her tears.

"Truth is, I don't know what to say or where to begin." I watched as more tears streamed down her face, "Please don't . . . . I . . . I . . . ." I stumbled over my words, then gave up. I was at a loss. Wanting nothing more than to hold her, I got up and moved to the seat next to her. I pulled her close to me and held her as I tried to formulate the right words to say.

"God, Emma—you have been through a lot. Nobody deserves that. I am so, so sorry you had to go through all that. It wasn't your fault. None of it was your fault."

She sat quietly, leaning against me. I could tell she was bracing herself, waiting for the other shoe to drop.

"I'm not angry, well . . . I'm angry at the bastard who did that to you. I'm glad he's dead, and I'm relieved that you are alive and okay."

Softly, she asked, "But what about the abortion?"

I took a deep breath, "In my mind, that was a necessary evil. I couldn't imagine you having to carry a child of a rapist for nine months. Frankly, I wouldn't want the genes of a bastard like that to continue on in society. It was for the best."

She choked, "Some people don't see it that way. You should hear what they've said to me."

"I heard some of that 'crap' from so-called religious people, but I'm not 'those' people. I care about you and you made the best decision you could in the horrific situation you were in."

Emma sat up and looked me in the eyes, "So, you're okay with it? You're okay with me?"

"Yes."

The waitress brought the food to our table. Emma hid her tear-stained face behind her hair as she pretended to search for something in her purse. "I see we had a change in seating arrangements," the waitress smiled. "Is there anything else I can get you?"

"No, thanks." I replied.

As soon as the waitress left, Emma turned to look at me, "You know, when I first told you and saw the look on your face, I thought you were going to walk out."

"No." I replied. "To be completely honest with you, the thing that bothered me the most was the fact that you tried to kill yourself. The thought of never knowing you made me sick."

"You're kidding."

"Nope. That's the absolute truth."

"So, we're definitely okay then?"

"Yeah, we're okay." I said and meant it with my entire body and soul.

Chapter: Emma

RELIEF. THAT'S WHAT I FELT—RELIEF. Jared knew the truth and seemed okay with it.

The conversation during dinner quickly went from deep hidden truths to our usual fun banter. By the time Jared and I left the restaurant, we were back to laughing and having a great time. Jared refused to leave my side. His arm remained around me through dinner and instead of growing dark and distant as I feared, those gorgeous, blue eyes sparkled even brighter when they looked at me. He didn't hate me. If anything, he liked me even more.

Jared put his arm around me and pulled me close as we left Maria's. A full moon was shining above downtown Ellicott City. Most of the antique stores and specialty shops that lined Main Street had closed for the night, so the only other pedestrians were a few women window shopping, a group of friends laughing as they walked into a bar and a few couples walking hand in hand on the cobbled streets.

Jared turned to me and said, "Let's walk." Taking my hand, we strolled up and down the street in comfortable silence. Eventually, we stopped near a stone wall that overlooked part of the Patapsco River. The bare branches of the oak trees above us shown in the moonlight and stars began to show their sparkling glow one at a time.

Jared stood behind me as we watched the moonlight glitter on the cascading, gurgling water. His arms were loosely wrapped around me as we stood in silence, enjoying the beauty of the night. Leaning down, Jared pressed his face gently against the back of my head and whispered, "I love you, Emma."

I broke out of his embrace and turned to him. The moonlight intensified the strong lines of his face and the graceful beauty of his eyes. I reached up and ran my hand along his chin. "I love you, too." I said.

Jared moved a long strand of hair out of my face and smiled at me. Gently pulling me closer, he leaned down to kiss me. The touch of his lips stirred me. I kissed back and our bodies pressed closer together. The intensity I felt for Jared was something I had not felt in a long time; something, I thought I would never feel again.

As our kissing grew more intense, Jared's hands found the small of my back and he pulled me tightly against his body. "Want to go back to my place?"

"Uh-huh," was the only response I could make before Jared was passionately kissing me again. Inhaling deeply, he pulled away and we quickly walked toward his car. Still holding me close, he leaned over and kissed my cheek.

He fumbled to unlock the car door with his keys, but before he opened it, he pressed me against the car and kissed me again. I didn't want him to stop.

When he finally pulled away, we got into the car.

Starting the ignition, Jared said, "Wow, Emma. You're incredible."

"You're not so bad yourself!" I leaned over, grabbed his hand then kissed his cheek. He caught my chin, kissed me again then whispered, "No, Emma. You're incredible. Everything about you is unbelievable. You amaze me, even more now that I know what you've been through. I have no words to explain it . . ."

All I could say was, "Thanks."

As he drove toward his home, Jared said, "Can I ask you something?"

"Sure." I replied.

"How did you do it?" Jared asked.

"Do what?"

"How did you go through all that hell and turn out the way you are now?"

"Oh." My heart stopped as a picture of Eric passed through my mind. "I didn't do it alone."

"Do you mind if I ask who helped you?"

I hesitated, "Well, counseling, lots of counseling, my Dad, but mostly, Eric." I couldn't look at Jared's face.

"Who's Eric?"

I felt a lump in my throat. *Did I really want to go there?*

I paused. *It's only fair to be honest. Lies are never a good thing.*

"Eric was my boyfriend. We had both been through so much. Let's just say, he understood what I was going through. He was my strength."

An uncontrollable tear rolled down my cheek. It hurt to think of Eric, but it was even worse to explain who he was and what he meant to me now that I had given up on him.

Jared said, "He obviously means a lot to you. Do you mind me asking what happened between the two of you?"

"We just weren't meant to be together. Life kept throwing us curve balls. He moved to Colorado. I haven't heard from him since."

"Wow." Jared stopped his car outside his condo building. It was a large, old three-story brick building with green shutters and well manicured gardens.

Jared's voice shook slightly as he asked, "So, do you still have feelings for him?"

Nobody had ever asked me this before. Now, I had to voice something so painful, I could barely breath. *Be honest.* I said to myself. *If this relationship is going to work, it has to be built on honesty.* But how honest should I be?

I picked my words carefully. "There will always, *always* be a special place in my heart for Eric. He and I went through so much together. If it weren't for him, I probably wouldn't be sitting here right now."

I couldn't continue.

Jared turned my face towards his. "I understand." The pained look in his eyes broke my heart.

Hoping to prevent him from hurting anymore, I said, "Jared, I want you to know that no matter what, Eric and I weren't meant to be. It's been over for many years now."

He looked deeply in my eyes, searching for a hidden meaning behind the words I spoke.

"So, Eric is what you had to work through before we got together?" He pried.

"Yes."

Jared adverted his eyes from mine. "Are you ready now?"

I smiled, "More than you'll ever know." I leaned forward to kiss him. A deep groan resonated through his body.

We got out of the car. Jared met me at my door and I reached up and ran my fingers along the contour of his cheek. I said, "You're the first guy I've noticed or wanted to be with in the longest of times." I kissed him again. "You're incredible and I couldn't want anyone more." I pressed my body firmly against his. I could feel how much he wanted me, too.

Jared grabbed my hand and pulled me towards the front door of the building. He led me to Suite 109 and gave me a quick tour of his apartment.

I was surprised by how clean it was inside. It was a two-bedroom apartment. The living room had a green couch and side chair facing a rather large television. On top of the rectangular oak coffee table lay several books, and a large peace lily blossomed in the corner of the room. The kitchen was nondescript and had a small round wooden table and two chairs. The first bedroom had been turned into a gym, and the second bedroom had a full sized bed, a dresser and was cluttered with clothes, CD cases and even more books.

Walking back into the living room, I said, "Wow, this is really nice! And to think, I'm still living at home with my mom and dad."

Jared smiled and he sat down on the couch, pulling me onto him. "Living alone does have its advantages!"

His lips tenderly traced the side of my neck but when they found their way back to mine, they were no longer gentle, but eager and hungry. As he quickly unbuttoned my shirt, removed my bra and continued to kiss every square inch of me, I took off his shirt and ran my hands along the hard lines of his muscular chest. My hands made their way down to his jeans and I unzipped them. The obvious intensity he felt melted me and neither of us could wait any longer. In one swift movement, Jared lifted me off the couch to carry me to his bedroom, but the passion that had been building up inside us was so intense that we didn't get that far.

Laying me softly on the floor, he quickly finished undressing me. As soon as I felt him enter me, I exploded. The feeling of his strong body pressing rhythmically against mine was amazing. I never wanted him to stop.

Neither of us could get enough of each other that night. We made love for hours and could barely pull ourselves away from each other even when he drove me back to my car, still parked in Joe's now vacant parking lot.

Chapter: Jared

EMMA FREAKIN' ROCKS. THIS GIRL makes me feel things I have never felt before. She has an irresistible charm and passion that keeps me coming back for more. I cannot get enough of her mentally or physically. We barely know each other and I already know I never want us to be apart.

Our time at the community college was quickly ending. Every afternoon, we studied and worked on homework together. Wednesday through Saturday nights, I had to work from four to one a.m. at Le Garde-Manger, to maintain the income I needed to continue paying for my condo and my living expenses. The nights I had to work late were the worse, but the evenings I had off were unimaginable. The time Emma and I spent apart fueled the intensity we felt for each other and we more than made up for our time apart when we were together again.

Emma received her acceptance to Towson one day before I received the two-year, ROTC scholarship to University of Virginia. My parents were thrilled and I could see a sense of pride every time I looked into my father's eyes. My father had received a Bronze Star and a Purple Heart in Vietnam, and he had always dreamed I would follow in his footsteps. "There's nothing more honorable than serving the country," he'd say. After I was accepted to the ROTC program, he'd puff up his chest and tell everyone who would listen, "My son's going to be a Marine. By the time he's done at UVA, he'll be a second lieutenant in the United States Marine Corps." Seeing the pride in his eyes made me proud, but there was an underlying sadness knowing how long I'd be away from Emma. OCS would start soon, and I would be at Quantico for six and one-half weeks, this coming summer.

Emma showed me nothing but support, but I could tell she dreaded our separation too, for more reasons than the time apart. She was sure I was going to be shipped off to Afghanistan or Iraq, and she didn't like that one bit. Personally, I believed the war would be over by the time I would have to go. We discussed my reasons for going into the military: the ROTC was paying for my tuition, fees and books for the last two years of college and I was ensured a good job when I graduated. Emma and I both agreed that this was a large, positive step toward a good, secure future together. After acknowledging the sacrifices we knew we had to make, we embraced our decision and looked ahead. I truly felt blessed having Emma by my side. I knew we were going to have a good life.

* * *

After seeing each other for a month, Emma took me to meet her parents. As I walked into her house, they didn't hide their shocked expressions when they saw me. It must have been my long hair that threw them off.

Mr. Fiorello walked toward me to shake my hand. His hair was short, mostly gray, with the memory of black from his younger years. The lines carved on his face made him look tired and distressed, and he seemed gruff.

"Hi, Jared! It's nice to meet you." Mr. Fiorello shook my hand an eyed me closely. His eyes penetrated mine. "I thought Emma said you were going into the Marines?"

Looking him straight in the eyes, without blinking, I replied, "Yes, sir. This summer. I have been accepted to an ROTC program at UVA where I will be studying computer science."

Tilting his head back and looking down his angular nose at me he snarled, "I see their standards have fallen. I didn't think they'd allow hippies to join, but with the obvious need . . ."

"Dad!" Emma exclaimed, her cheeks bright red with embarrassment.

"They'll be cutting off my hair this summer, Sir. No worries there. Apparently my grade point average and work ethic enabled them to overlook my other downfalls. Sir, hopefully you will do the same."

I held my breath as Mr. Fiorello and I stared each other down. Suddenly, he broke into a smile and laughed, "I think you'll fit in just fine here, son. Welcome."

I felt as if I had passed some sort of test.

Mrs. Fiorello smiled and rushed up to me, "I'm so happy to finally meet you, Jared! We've heard so much about you!" Mrs. Fiorello's smile did not reach her eyes, giving her a very superficial look. I noticed she also reeked of alcohol.

Hiding my shock I responded, "Good things, I hope."

"Of course," Mrs. Fiorello blushed and she winked at me.

"But she did leave out the bit about your hair," Mr. Fiorello smiled.

"Well, I'm always one to surprise."

"I can see that." Mr. Fiorello's eyes examined me closely. I wondered what was he searching for. He continued, "Why don't we go have a drink and talk."

"I'd like that." I said. I followed Mr. Fiorello through the back of the house, toward the deck. I glanced back at Emma who looked extremely happy, but shell-shocked. She called out, "I'll bring out some tea!"

"That'll be fine, Em." Her dad responded.

Mr. Fiorello opened the sliding screen door to the deck and motioned me to sit in one of the two rocking chairs. On the deck, there were three freshly planted flower boxes, a propane grill, and a wrought iron table set, decorated with two half-melted burgundy candles, sitting on antiqued brass candle holders. I sat down in one of the rockers as he pulled the other forward and sat down next to me.

We sat in silence as Emma brought out our drinks then excused herself to make dinner. I could smell her cherry blossom hair as she walked by. She squeezed my shoulder as she passed.

Mr. Fiorello spoke, "So, I understand that you and Emma are quite serious."

"Yes, we are. I think the world of your daughter, sir."

"You should." Mr. Fiorello turned to look me straight in the eyes. "That girl has been through a lot. I don't want to see her hurt anymore."

"I know, sir. Neither do I."

"You know?" His eyes bore into mine. I stared back.

"Yes, sir. I know." I answered, trying to make sure my voice didn't break or show any sign of weakness. The intensity that radiated off the man who sat before me set me on edge. This was someone you did not want to piss off.

His gaze finally broke from mine. "She has a strong heart and a good soul. I expect you to protect her."

"I will." I responded, confused as to what he was trying to say. I hadn't asked him for her hand in marriage, yet, but the lecture I was getting made me feel like I had.

He looked at me again, shook his head, then turned and looked vacantly out across the yard. "I failed her. You know that? I failed her. Her father . . . I should have protected her, but I didn't." Mr. Fiorello's aged hands grasped onto the handles of the rocker as he continued, "But I made up for it . . . I did! She just doesn't know it yet . . ."

I didn't know what to say, but I had to say something. "I think she knows it, sir. If it weren't for you sending her to counseling, she'd be a lot worse off right now."

Mr. Fiorello chuckled, a distant look in his eyes. "Yeah, that's true." His eyes glazed over as his mind seemed to wander. He sat quietly for several seconds before he spoke again, "Just treat her right. She thinks the world of you."

"I will. I can guarantee you that."

"Good. I believe you. I can see it in your eyes."

Our eyes met when I said, "Thanks."

Mr. Fiorello and I went on to talk about fishing and baseball, all the normal things you'd expect to talk about when meeting your girlfriend's father for the first time. It felt good and we really got along well.

Mrs. Fiorello and Emma cooked a fantastic dinner. We had steak, boiled red potatoes with butter and dill, fresh green beans and the flakiest, buttery rolls. We had a thoroughly enjoyable night. From then on the Fiorello's, Emma and I spent every Tuesday night together, having dinner and visiting.

My parents loved Emma as well, but they were often out of town on business, so we could visit with them only occasionally. Nevertheless, by the time graduation arrived, we were all very close, like a large happy family.

The love Emma and I felt for each other grew stronger every day. I never imagined loving anyone as much as I loved her and I dreaded our time apart as OCS time got closer.

Late one night, when our warm, naked bodies were holding each other close, we lay quietly on my bed, listening to the rain overflowing from the upstairs gutters splashing on the ground outside my window. A cold drop fell on my chest. Emma was crying.

"What's wrong, Em?" I asked.

"I'm really going to miss being here with you."

"I know. I'm going to miss it, too." I ran my fingers through her bed-teased hair. "You know, I was thinking. What would you think about moving in here while I'm gone? You could watch the place."

"Really?" Emma propped herself up on her elbows. "That is such a great idea! I would love that!"

". . . And maybe, when I get back, you won't have to leave."

Her eyes grew wide and she laughed, "You mean, move in with you? Permanently?"

"Well, yeah . . . sort of. I'll be back for a couple of weeks before I have to go to UVA. Then, I'll have to live at the dorm in Charlottesville during the week, but I could come back almost every weekend and you could live here while you go to school."

"Wow! I don't know what to say, except it won't be the same without you here and . . ."

"Em, I'd really feel good knowing you were here. It's our place now. You belong here."

"Okay." She hesitated. "Okay, I'll be here."

"Waiting for me?"

"Of course. I'll be here waiting for you."

"Love you."

"Love you, too, baby."

* * *

Emma's parents were a little shocked that their baby girl was moving out, but I think they thought it would be good for her. A week before I had to leave for OCS, Emma moved in with me. I loved having her in my house. I loved smelling her shampoo and body wash when it filled the air after she showered, I loved hearing her sigh when she slept, I loved it when she hung up her underwear to dry on laundry day, and I loved hearing her sing softly in the kitchen while she made breakfast and dinner. I loved everything about her. I had never felt so whole in my life.

Two days before I left, Emma decided she wanted to shave my head.

"No, Em. They'll do it." I insisted.

"Oh, come on! I know they'll do it, but I want to! Let me do it! They don't love that hair the way I do!"

Her pleading eyes convinced me and she led me to the bathroom. After getting out the clippers, and plugging them in, she said, "Kneel down, honey."

I took off my shirt, but left my jeans on. Getting down on my knees, I kneeled before her. My eyes were level with her perfect body. The curve of her breasts and the flair of her hips entranced me. When she walked behind me, her thighs pressed softly against me. I could feel my body react strongly to her presence. Emma lovingly brushed my hair back and put it in a ponytail, then trimmed right above the band so she could keep it. She kissed me softly on the neck, picked up the clippers and tenderly started to shave the rest of my head. Strands of what was left of my blonde hair started to cover the floor but it didn't bother me a bit. All I wanted was for Emma to finish so I could go to her. After she finished the back, she came around to finish up the front. I couldn't control myself anymore. I pulled her body to my face, lifted her shirt and started to kiss her perfect stomach. She groaned and giggled.

"Wait, Jared. I'm almost done."

"No leave it." I started to unbutton her shorts.

"Hold still." She demanded.

While she made the last few runs over my now bald head, I caressed and kissed her body. Her smell enveloped me. I didn't want to wait any longer. As soon as the razor went off, I slipped the rest of her clothes off, sat her on the edge of the sink and made love to her. We both shuddered in ecstasy.

*   *   *

"Nice hair cut." Mr. Fiorello smiled. "You're starting to look like a Marine."

I laughed. "Thanks. Emma gave it to me." I winked at her.

It was the day before I had to leave for OCS at Quantico and Emma and I were making our rounds to say goodbye.

Mrs. Fiorello made my favorite homemade lasagna, accompanied by a salad and fresh bread. We all sat around the candlelit, oak dining room table talking late into the evening. When it was time for us to leave, Mr. Fiorello shook my hand and said, "Good luck, son. I know you'll make us proud."

I responded, "Thank you, sir."

Tears were forming in Mrs. Fiorello's eyes and she walked up and gave me a hug. "Take care of yourself! Make sure you eat well!"

"Thank you, I will Mrs. Fiorello."

Emma's eyes were full of tears as we walked out the door. "They really, really like you!" she smiled.

"Yeah, I think they do!"

Our last night together was intense. We made love, we cried, but excitement roiled all around it. I kept in mind that the next six weeks apart would help prepare an exciting, secure future for the two of us. There was nothing I wanted more than to finish my education, get a good job and live with Emma for the rest of my life. When I looked in her eyes, I saw my future, my children and my dreams. I loved her more than anything. It was 10:30 p.m. when I decided we had to go out.

"Emma, get dressed. I need to take you somewhere."

"Now?" Emma groaned. "It's late!"

"Yes. Get dressed." I said pulling back the covers and pulling her out of bed. "Let's go, now."

She laughed. "Okay. Okay. Where are we going?"

"It's a surprise!"

We quickly got dressed. Emma wore her favorite pair of jeans and a black tank top. I wore jeans and a T-shirt. We jumped into the car and I sped off. It was a beautiful night. The moon hung in the sky, surrounded by stars glistening in the night. The roads were empty. Occasionally, my headlights would reflect in deers' eyes as they carefully watched my car speeding past them. I drove into old downtown Ellicott City and parked my car in the empty parking lot, near the small overlook of the Patapsco River.

I opened her door, took her hand and led her to the place we had our first kiss. I held her close as we watched the moonlight dancing on the river again.

"Do you remember?" I whispered in her ears.

"Yes, of course I do." Emma replied.

"That night, I knew I loved you and I could never let you go." I took a deep breath.

Emma said. "I knew I loved you, too."

"I never imagined my love for you could have grown more, but it has."

Emma shook her head in agreement. "I know, me too."

We stood in silence for several minutes, holding each other close. I buried my nose in her hair, smelling her sweet scent and relished feeling her body pressed against mine. "I'm really going to miss you over the next six weeks, but you know what would make me feel better?"

"What? Tell me. Anything . . ."

I turned her so I could look into her eyes. "I want to know that you will be my wife. Will you marry me?"

Chapter: Emma

My heart skipped a beat. "What did you say?"

Jared nervously smiled at me and repeated, "Emma, will you marry me?"

"Yes! Yes, Jared! I will marry you!"

I stood on my toes to kiss him and his strong arms pulled me close.

"I don't have a ring yet, but I'll get you one."

"That's not important." I smiled and kissed him again.

"I will though." He insisted.

We turned and watched the water cascading over the stones and a vision of Eric filled my mind. I shook him out of my memory as a tear rolled down my cheek.

"You okay?" Jared asked.

I turned to hold him close. "Yes. I couldn't be happier. Love you."

Jared smiled at me. "I love you, too."

* * *

We woke up early the next morning to get Jared ready to go to OCS. As soon as I could, I called my parents to let them know we were engaged. They were ecstatic. "He's a good man." Dad said, "I'm happy for you."

We told Mr. And Mrs. Stafford about our engagement while Mr. Stafford drove the four of us to Quantico. They were happy as well. The two hour long drive seemed to fly by as we talked about what the future held for us. When we arrived at Quantico, we watched as several families said their goodbyes. There was no pomp and circumstance. The new Marines simply grabbed their belongings, and walked away.

I tried not to cry, but it was impossible. I was going to miss Jared desperately. I gave him a last kiss goodbye and watched as he walked toward our future. The early morning sun reflected off his newly shaved head. His strong shoulders were pulled back as if ready to face what was to come. I was so proud of him. I could tell his parents were, too.

The drive home was difficult. I wished I could be alone with the range of emotions I was feeling, but because Jared's parents were there, I had to be sociable. I just wanted to curl up in a ball and cry so I could get it over with and move on with the next six weeks. I was relieved to get back to the condo, but it felt so empty without Jared. I allowed myself to cry, then wrote him a letter. After sealing the envelope, I lost myself in cleaning, attacking and disinfecting every surface, including the walls. I could tell it was going to be a long six weeks.

Chapter: Eric

IT HAD BEEN TWO YEARS since I lost Emma; That night, I suddenly awoke out of a sound sleep by the desperate pain and hurt I knew so well, from our separation long ago. Out of nowhere, tears filled my eyes and I sobbed. I wondered where in the world this came from! I was thankful my roommate was out partying again. If he would have seen me wake up sobbing . . . well . . . that would have sucked. I looked at the clock. It was only 11:32 p.m. My light was still on. I had fallen asleep at my desk, my hand still grasping a cup of coffee, my head on a pile of psychology articles I was reading for a paper I had started to write. I looked around my cluttered room, thinking that something had changed, but everything seemed in its normal chaotic order. Clothes were piled on my bed and on the floor. Dirty dishes and old pizza boxes were scattered about. Metallica and Pink Floyd posters were on the wall. Yes, everything was still the same, but something was different.

I longed to hold Emma again. My mind drifted to our very distant past. I had never heard back from Emma. I had written her a letter while I was in Anger Management Class, but she never wrote back. I never understood why, but I assumed that she wanted to move on. Deep inside, I thought so as well. Sometimes, when you love someone so much it hurts, you need to let them go, especially if fate won't let you grow together. It hurt, badly, and after years of missing her, I suddenly realized that the saying is true, "You should never give up on someone you can't go a day without thinking about."

There wasn't a day that I didn't think of her at least once. I had been with many other women since Emma, but there was always something missing. I never felt the magic that I felt with her. I wondered where she was and if she was okay.

Unsure of where these emotions suddenly came from, and tired of years of wondering, I decided that I was going to find her. I got on the internet and searched for her, but nothing came up.

I decided that in the morning, I was going to do something I should have done years before. I was going to call her home number.

Eventually, I fell into a restless sleep, excited about what the morning would bring.

* * *

"Hello?" Mrs. Fiorello answered.

"Hi, Mrs. Fiorello. It's Eric."

"Eric?" she asked in amazement.

"Yes, is Emma available?" Excitement filled me. Were those butterflies in my stomach? I haven't felt them in years.

"Um, no Eric. I'm sorry. She doesn't live here anymore."

"No?" Maybe Emma was away at college, too.

"No, she lives in a condo, with her fiancé." I thought I could hear a smirk in her mother's voice.

"Her fiancé?" I responded. I felt the light that was glowing inside of me, the light that only Emma could bring, extinguish. The flame was gone, along with the hope. I was too late.

"Yes, Eric. I'm sorry." Mrs. Fiorello's words were spoken, but the sentiment was not there.

"I see," I replied.

"Would you like me to tell her you called?"

"Yes, yes . . . I would," but then I reconsidered. "No, no . . . that's okay."

"Okay then, bye Eric!" Mrs. Fiorello spoke. Was she actually stifling a laugh?

"Wait, Mrs. Fiorello. How long has Emma been engaged?"

"Since last night, about 11:30 or so." She paused, and seemed a little concerned. "He's a really great man. I think you'd be happy for her."

"Oh, that's good . . . um . . . thanks. Bye."

I hung up the phone. A hollow, emptiness filled me. I had lost Emma forever, last night. A cold chill ran up my spine as I wondered how I knew that. I scoffed. Whatever spiritual or emotional channel we had was still open, but the door to a real relationship together had been sealed closed and we were to remain, eternally, apart. What kind of shit is that?

I punched the wall and my fist throbbed in pain. "Damn it." I growled. "Why didn't I try to find her earlier? Why did I have to be so late? Why, GOD, Why are we supposed to be apart?!?!"

That abominable voice in the back of my mind spoke. "Some things aren't meant to be." That's exactly what Emma had always said.

"Fuck. I guess not." I yelled to no one. "I guess, fucking, not."

I walked out of the door, slammed my way into the elevator and went for a run. As my feet pounded the pavement, releasing the anger inside of me, I resolved myself to the fact that it was time to let her go. *It's time to truly move on.*

And I did.

Chapter: Jared

OCS WAS OVER. I WAS tired, hungry and sore, but nothing could bring my spirits down. I was going to see Emma again.

We OCS graduates packed and ate together before we marched in formation to our graduation ceremony, performing the drills that have been permanently carved into our minds as our family and friends watched and cheered us on. My eyes scanned the crowd, searching for her. Hundreds of faces were watching us intently and smiling. Then I saw her, standing there like an angel. Her dark hair glistened in the sun, while her eyes scanned the lines of Marines, searching for me. Our eyes met and she smiled that gorgeous smile I love so much. She clenched her hands in excitement and waved. I winked. It wouldn't be long now. As soon as the graduation ceremony was over, I would hold her in my arms again.

When I finally could, I ran to Emma, threw my arms around.... She kissed me hard.

Coming up for breath, Emma asked, "You ready?"

"Ready?" I laughed. "For what?"

"To start the rest of our lives together?"

I nodded my head in agreement and laughed, "That and a few other things."

I could feel her smile when we kissed again. Our parents encircled and embraced us. "Let's go home." I said. They all laughed.

"Let's go home."

Life quickly returned to normal, and the two weeks that remained before I had to move into the dormitory at University of Virginia passed by instantaneously. There was nothing as awesome as being under my own roof with the woman I loved more than life itself. It was great to be home.

Fortunately, I had saved up a lot of money while working at Le Garde-Manger, so Emma could stay home at the condo without having to go out to work. Emma's parents had volunteered to help out with some of the mortgage payments for the months during the school year because they did not have to pay for her room and board at Towson. It was comforting to have a home with Emma there waiting for me.

Once school started and we were separated again, the weeks and the few weekends we were apart seemed like nothing compared to the six weeks at OCS. Our reunions always sparked an intense, unrelenting fire in my body. The time I spent with Emma was so passionate, so full of unending warmth and powerful tenderness that when we parted, I could feel her heat like the golden embers that survive long after the flames have died down.

Chapter: Emma

October 2003

THE THIRD WEEKEND IN OCTOBER, our senior year of college, the woods had changed from their camouflage brown and green into their dress colors, yellow, red and orange, as if to celebrate the successful completion of yet another summer.

Dad, Jared and I were walking in the crisp, autumn morning air on a wooded path through the park. The path was no longer a newly paved road, but a well-worn and beaten trail. Plants had grown through the pavement, weakening it so it crumbled under our feet. Slippery, green moss covered the damp areas of the path, and small lacy mushrooms sprouted wherever they found a suitable home.

I hadn't been to the park in years, but it looked exactly as I remembered it, just with older benches and more mature plants. Our breath escaped from our mouths like tiny ghosts, encouraging us to move on. Crows cawed in the distance and something large, probably a deer, ran through the brush, cracking sticks and rustling leaves as it ran.

"How does it feel?" Dad asked, looking at me with concern.

"Fine . . . okay . . ." I replied. I no longer had nightmares of this place. At one point, I had loved coming here. It was simply beautiful; not scary now.

"Are you sure?" My dad asked.

"Yes. It's a beautiful day. This is a beautiful place. It's over. That part of my life has been over for a long time."

My dad smiled. "You healed well."

"It took a long time, but yes."

A tear sparkled in the corner of my father's eye. "I'm glad."

Jared winked at me over my father's head and reached around to encouragingly pat me on the back.

A wave of happiness filled me. I am okay. I survived. I'm healthy, in love and very, very lucky. I let out a laugh. "I'll race you guys! Up the hill! I'll beat you both."

"You wish" Jared grinned, looking at me daringly.

"Wanna bet?" I dared back.

My dad stopped, put his hands on his knees and stooped down, as if to take a break.

"You okay?" I asked wondering why he suddenly stopped.

He looked up at me, smiled slyly, then yelled, "Go!"

My father bolted up the hill. Jared and I, laughing in surprise chased behind him. By the time I reached the top of the hill, my sneakers were slipping from the cold condensation that blanketed the ground and my heart was pounding in my head. Dad and Jared had reached the top first and we were all out of breath, laughing heartily.

"That felt good." Dad smiled as he stretched his arms toward the sky.

I sat down and the cold moisture penetrated my running shorts. Jared came to sit next to me. A huge flock of geese honked as they flew overhead. "Dad, do you remember that children's book you used to read to me? The one about the geese?"

My Dad responded, "Yeah, I...."

I heard a gasp, and then a thump. My dad was grasping his left arm and lying on the ground.

"Dad!" I ran to him. "Dad! Jared call 911."

Jared had already started dialing, but shook the phone in frustration. "I don't have a signal . . . I'll find one . . ." Jared ran off.

I cradled my father in my arms.

"Dad, are you okay? What hurts?"

He gasped, "I think . . . I think it's a heart attack."

"Oh no, Dad . . . stay with us . . ." Tears started rolling down my cheeks.

Dad tried to smile, but grimaced. "Emma, don't cry. It'll be okay," he tried to reassure me, but his voice was growing weaker.

"Dad?"

"Emma?"

"Yes?"

"Emma, I need you to know before I go . . ."

"Don't go . . . Dad stop . . ."

"I need you to know that I did it . . ."

"Dad!"

My father grabbed my arm and looked me squarely in the face, "Please stop and listen to me now, Emma . . ." Dad tried to catch his breath, but coughed. "Emma, I'm sorry I failed you. I should have protected you!"

"Dad! I'm fine . . ." I cried, "I'm fine. You never failed me!" I tried to smile, tears streaking down my face.

"Emma, I killed him. I took care of him for you."

My stomach clenched. "Oh, Daddy!" Tears burst from my eyes. I tried to catch my breath but I couldn't get the air past my throat.

"No one knows, Em. No one knows."

"Dad?"

"I love you, Emma. I am so sorry."

A long, rattling breath escaped from my dad and then his eyes stared blankly into mine.

Jared was running back to us, out of breath. "I finally found a signal. They're coming. They'll be here soon."

I pulled my father's now empty body up to my chest and looked vacantly at Jared. "It's too late. He's gone."

I never, ever went to that park again.

* * *

The last words Dad spoke haunted me. He killed my rapist and nobody knew it but me. I wondered what I gained from this knowledge, and what it meant for my dad. Where was his soul now? What am I supposed to do now that I know?

Matt's case has long been cold and I would never implicate my father, but knowing the truth tore me apart. Killing something or someone, no matter what the reason, tears at your soul. I knew this. I hurt for my father and the secret he had kept hidden for all of those years. I hope that his telling me, helped him in some way.

I longed to see Eric so I could talk to him again, feel him again. He would understand. Eric would know what to do or say. I felt guilty, but I felt that there was no way Jared would understand this or my feelings. No way at all.

I decided to keep the secret from everyone. I knew there was nothing I could do with this ungodly knowledge except understand that my father loved me and he had made this awful decision out of that love, so he could avenge my rape. This fact boiled within me night and day. I wished that he hadn't resorted to murder, but I kept asking myself, if it were my child, what would I have done?

* * *

Three days after the funeral, I began helping my mom sort through tons of paperwork. My dad had seen to it that she'd be fine once he was gone, but the paperwork was mounting and I wanted to see it through. Mom, spent her days and nights either in a state of constant drunkenness or hung over. Her doctors had also given her anxiety medication so I had no clue how functional she truly was. She had barely spoken to me since my father's death. I figured she was in as much shock as me.

As she sat on the black leather office chair, she stared at the endless piles of paper sitting in meticulous stacks on her dark cherry desk and sighed.

The white, autumn sunlight coming through the bay windows embraced her. Long pieces of her graying black hair hung haphazardly in different directions and she kept running her fingers through them, desperately trying to grasp on to something. Her eyes were puffy and swollen from crying and her cheeks were tearstained, but she still looked beautiful.

"So," she spoke, clearing her throat. "You never fully told me what happened."

"Well," I started, surprised at her sudden question, "We ran up the hill, we were laughing and having a good time and then . . ."

My mother cut me off sternly and the smell of day old alcohol enveloped me. "Yes. I know. I know that, but did Dad have anything else to say?"

"Oh . . ." my throat tightened. "Yes . . . yes he did."

She glared at me, "Well??? What did he say?"

"He told me that he was sorry and that he loved me." Tears started spilling from my eyes.

Anger shook my mother's body, "Anything else?"

Oh God, did she know? No, she didn't . . . she couldn't . . .

"No." I lied.

"Oh, I see." She glared at me with anger and spoke with disgust, "He always loved you best. His "sweet, baby girl," but you've amounted to nothing, NOTHING but a dirty little . . ." She breathed deeply to stop herself, then continued through gritted teeth, "I spend almost thirty years . . . THIRTY YEARS with the man and he doesn't tell you to tell me anything?"

I stuttered in shock. "Oh . . ." I always thought my mom was a little distant, but I never realized her disgust for me was so deep-seated. I guessed my dad had kept it hidden from me. I frantically considered what I should have said. I should have lied. I was so upset by what my father did say, I never even considered . . .

"Mom, he loved you. He loved you desperately."

"Yeah right. On his death bed, he didn't say a thing."

"He was scared and confused. It was fast. Really, really fast."

My mother stood up, puffed out her chest like she was going to attack me, but then she broke down hysterically.

"I know." She cried. "I know. I'm sorry. I'm so, so sorry."

I tried to hug her but she pushed me away. "Get the hell away from me!" She screamed as she slapped me across the face. I stumbled back and pressed my cold hand against my cheek to lesson the sting. At that moment, I realized how much my mother truly did resent me. She resented the fact that I was born and that she had to care for me. She resented the fact that I was "Daddy's little girl." She resented the fact that my rape brought me even more of my father's attention. She resented the fact that she was not there when my father died and she resented the fact that at the end, he told me he loved me but he did not say anything about her.

While the lack of words my father could have spoken to my mother created a hole in her heart, the words that were spoken created a hole in mine.

My mom defiantly looked at me. "I'm leaving. I'm going to go spend some time with my friends in Italy. I can't stand being here any longer. I don't want to see you and I don't want to see this place. Now that he's gone, I'm finally going to live a little." Her eyes pierced mine, expecting a rebut but there was nothing I wanted to say. Her mind was set on leaving, and whenever anything got tough in life, that's what she did best.

I had always suspected that she never cared much for me but now it was blatantly obvious and it hurt. For a brief moment, I wondered what was wrong with me, but then I realized that maybe it was something wrong with her. Refusing to allow her to hurt me anymore, I turned and left the house and never looked back.

From that point on, my relationship with my mother broke apart and we quickly became estranged. From that point on, in her strange, twisted mind, Dad had abandoned her for me.

Chapter: Jared

December 2003

EMMA BECAME DISTANT AFTER MR. Fiorello's death. She became withdrawn and quiet, staring at nothing for hours at a time. I would try to get her to talk to me, but she refused to respond. In fact, she didn't seem to want me around. When Emma's mother packed her bags and left for Italy, nothing felt the same anymore. One day, as we were sitting in a cold, uncomfortable silence in our living room, I asked Emma if I could take her out to dinner or the movies—anything to get her out of the house. Her empty, abandoned eyes met mine and with out a word, she left the room. I found her curled up in bed, the blankets pulled over her head. I didn't know what to do or say, but it sure looked to me like we were facing a long, cold winter.

I bought an engagement ring for Emma and planned to give it to her on Christmas. As the holidays grew closer, Emma seemed to cheer up more and more. Once or twice, I caught her smiling and for a brief moment I hoped that things were returning to normal. Each time, though, her eyes became stoic and she'd stare at the wall. Each time, my heart broke all over again.

Something had happened, beyond her father's death. It couldn't just be her mother's leaving the country; Emma hadn't been all that close to her. I just didn't know what had affected her so much that she had completely changed from joyous to despondent. I desperately wanted to know so I could help her.

One week before Christmas, a letter arrived from Emma's mother, stating that she had met a man named Leonard who was showing her the high-life: fancy dinners, expensive wines and fine jewelry. He had asked her to move in with him. Cassie informed us that times had changed and she was no longer going to live by the constraints of a family. She wanted to enjoy what was left of her life and she was going to take advantage of Leonard's invitation. She wished us a "Merry Christmas" and closed the letter, "Ciao! Cas"

Silent tears slid down Emma's face as she read the letter out loud. I internally vowed to make this the best Christmas Emma ever had—a tough venture since it was her first Christmas without her father and now her mother had really and truly abandoned her.

I decided the best way to escape this reality was to take her away from this town, our families and the memories, so it could be just the two of us, embracing the season and beginning our future life together.

I made reservations at the Little Rock Winery Bed and Breakfast, nuzzled at the foot of the Shenandoah Mountains in Virginia. It looked quaint and cozy and I envisioned us drinking wine by a fire. I planned to give Emma our engagement ring and let her know that we would begin our life again, as a solitary couple. I wanted her to realize that we didn't need anyone but us to live a secure and happy life. If some people chose to be selfish and superficial, that was their choice and we could choose otherwise.

When I told Emma my plans, she seemed excited and even gave me a hug. I held her in my arms and kissed her forehead. It felt so good to hold her again. I closed my eyes and prayed that this was going to be a changing point for us—a new beginning in a hopeful direction.

On Christmas Eve, we arrived at Little Rock at nine in the evening. The mid-Atlantic rarely had snow on Christmas, but this Christmas had turned out to be a white one. It took five hours to accomplish the three-hour drive to the winery. Cars were spinning out everywhere and my hands were tired from clenching the steering wheel as the car spun out for the final time in the unshoveled driveway at the B&B. I turned to see Emma frown and I started to doubt that this trip was a good idea.

I left Emma in the car and walked up a slight hill to the farmhouse to check in. The farmhouse loomed over the farm, its white paint peeling, but in an appealing, homey kind of way. Warm light poured from the windows and illuminated the snow along with the white Christmas lights adorning the well-pruned holly bushes along the front of the house. A man-sized folk art Santa Claus sat on the porch swing, smiling at me in holiday cheer. A large wreath hung on the door, covering the brass knocker. Unable to reach it, I banged on the old red, farmhouse door. The door opened, and I was greeted with a warm hello and laughter, the sound of "White Christmas" playing in the background. I was given the keys, some instructions and then wished a "Merry Christmas" and before I knew it, I was walking back to the car to retrieve our luggage and Emma.

I opened the trunk, pulled out our two bags then helped Emma out of the car. Our hiking boots cracked through the snow and Emma grabbed onto me as she slipped on the stairs to the cottage. She huffed and anger filled her eyes. I wondered if I should offer to take her home, but it would have been ridiculous to turn around now. It had started to snow again. The cold, bitter wind whipped at Emma's hair as I opened the door.

The warmth of the cozy room greeted us, changing my mind and quieting my doubts. I knew we were in the right place.

A blazing, hot fire romantically lit the cozy bedroom. A full sized bed covered in a ton of pillows looked inviting and artwork of wildlife and the Blue Ridge Mountains decorated the walls. A Christmas garland along the mantle of the fireplace surrounded six wrought iron candlestick holders holding red candles. A small Christmas tree decorated with white lights and animal ornaments of all kinds stood next to the couch. An open bottle of Cabernet Sauvignon, Emma's favorite, two wine glasses and a tray of chocolate covered strawberries waited on the coffee table.

I turned to look at Emma's face, which glowed in the light of the fire. Her frown had disappeared and there was a look of relief and peace in her eyes, something I had not seen in a long time.

Chapter: Emma

THE RIDE TO THE BED and Breakfast sucked and I was pissed: pissed at my Dad for dying and leaving me with a horrible burden, pissed at my mom for being a bitch and blaming me for something I had no control over then abandoning me for fine wines and jewels, pissed that I had no one to talk to about this mess, and pissed that we were out in the snow, risking life and limb to get away from it all. Everything seemed ludicrous.

Jared had checked us in, then helped me out of the car and up the stairs to the cottage, which I slipped on in the stupid snow that we haven't had on Christmas for as long as I could remember. As I waited for him to open the door, cold wind whipped my hair and bit my nose, freezing every inch of me. I felt like having a tantrum. I wanted to stomp my feet and scream like a two-year old, but all I could muster was a snort.

Jared finally opened the door and I watched as he walked inside. His back darkened as he entered the cottage, but the front of him became haloed in an orange glow. I followed him inside and closed the door. It was beautiful. A fire was gently burning. There was beautiful artwork and a cozy bed. I was surprised to see a Christmas tree and immediately noticed two of my favorite things, Cabernet Sauvignon and chocolate covered strawberries, waiting on the rustic coffee table. My eyes ran over the warm, beautiful surroundings then fell upon the man who had done this for me. My heart melted as I realized how much I truly did love Jared. He was staring at me, his freshly shaved head and face and his gorgeous blue eyes gleaming at me, angel-like in the fire's orange glow. I ran into his arms and the tears that I had repressed came to the surface and erupted from me as Jared held me close.

As the pain in me drifted away, I could feel Jared's strength and love, holding me as if he would never let me go. I knew then, how lucky I was. I had a good man. He wasn't Eric, no one could ever be, but he was Jared and that was more than enough for me.

"Jared, I'm so sorry." I said.

"It's okay, honey. I know." He replied as he stroked my hair.

"No, you don't . . ." I sighed.

"Well, maybe I don't, but I'm here."

I pulled away from him so I could look him in the eyes. "I know, and that means everything to me. I have to tell you something."

"Okay, tell me," He smiled patiently.

I told Jared everything my father had said. I watched him closely, like I did so long ago when I told him about my past, searching for any hint of distress or disgust, but there was none.

When I finished telling him, Jared shook his head in understanding and surprised me by saying, "Well, that makes sense."

Never expecting to hear this, I asked, "What do you mean by that?"

He explained, "Well, the first time I met your father, he asked me if I knew about your past."

"Yeah, and . . ." I encouraged.

"Well, I said yes and he said something like 'Emma doesn't know it, but I took care of it.' I didn't feel like I knew him well enough to ask him what he meant, and the subject never came up again."

"Oh. Wow." Was all I could respond.

"So, have you told anyone?" Jared asked.

"No, not a soul, except for you."

His eyes filled with understanding. "So that's what's been wrong? It's not me?"

"No, it was not you. It was that, and it was sort of you. I just didn't feel I could tell you."

"Oh." Jared looked upset.

Trying to lessen the blow, I said, "I'm sorry. It's just . . . um . . . that was a very difficult, horrible time in my life. I know you accepted it all, but sometimes I don't feel like you could ever really understand like . . . well, anyway, I didn't want to burden you."

Jared said, "You are never a burden. Stop."

"Okay, I'm sorry."

Jared understood my pause too well, "I know I'm not Eric. I'll never be and I've never been through what the two of you have, but that doesn't mean I can't handle it. I hope you realize that I love you and I am here."

"I know, I should've known. I'm sorry."

"No more secrets?"

I smiled, "No more secrets."

Jared pulled me to his body and held me for a bit.

I pulled away. "Do you mind if I go take a shower?"

"No, go ahead."

As I walked into the bathroom, I said, "I love you."

Jared smiled, "I love you, too."

Chapter: Jared

EMMA LEFT TO TAKE A shower. Once the bathroom door shut, I fumbled around in my bag and found the engagement ring I had hidden. I opened the box and stared at the tiny, little ring that would hopefully go on Emma's tiny, little finger. The diamond seemed large on it and glowed in the fire's light.

What Emma had just said echoed in my head, like gunfire in a canyon. I got a headache just thinking about it. I twisted the ring back and forth between my thumb and forefinger as I sat down on the couch.

It wasn't the fact that Emma's dad killed her rapist that bothered me. It was Eric. Eric had a hold on her heart. Did I fit there? Did she, could she, love me as much as she loved Eric?

I thought of the life we had together so far. It was pretty much perfect. Deep down, I knew she loved me but I was also very painfully aware that she would always love Eric. There was no changing that. He had been too important in her life for that to change.

I inhaled deeply and told myself, "But, he is gone and I am here now. I am her present and her future. He is her past and he is gone."

I heard the shower stop and a few moments later, Emma came out, wrapped in a fluffy white towel, her brown hair was damp and clean, her skin flushed pink from the heat of the shower.

I quickly stood up and hid the ring in my pocket. She looked gorgeous and I couldn't help myself from walking up to her, pulling her sweet smelling, soft body close to mine. I ran my hands over her bare back and softly embraced her. As I bent forward to kiss the curve of her neck, a startling question arose in my mind and I could feel my stomach clench. What if Eric came back?

Chapter: Emma

I WALKED OUT OF THE bathroom, wrapped in a luxurious towel and Jared greeted me with a huge hug and a kiss, melting away the remaining cold ice that had frozen my soul since my father's death.

I had told Jared what my father had confessed. He wasn't shocked and he cast no judgment. I was the luckiest girl alive. As Jared kissed me, I smiled. Jared kissed me even harder. Then he pulled away and said, "I love feeling you smile when I kiss you."

I replied, "I love it when you kiss me."

Jared unwrapped the towel from my body and it fell to the floor. He gently caressed my shoulders then ran his fingers along the curve of my breasts as I unbuttoned his pants. As they fell to the floor, he stepped out of them and quickly removed his T-shirt. He wrapped me in his arms and carried me to the bed. We became lost among the pillows and blankets as we made love for the first time in months. "We" were back and I felt whole again.

As we laid on the bed in silence, my head resting on Jared's chest, he twirled my hair around his fingers.

"I love you, Em."

"I love you, too, baby."

"I'm so happy to see you smile again." Jared said.

"Me, too. I feel much better now."

Jared gently pushed me aside and got out of bed. He went to grab his jeans. Surprised I said, "Leaving so soon?"

"No, I . . ." he walked into the bathroom with his jeans, then came back out naked and crawled back into bed.

"What was that all about?" I asked as he laid back down and pulled up the covers.

Jared pulled me back down to his chest, "Emma, I know it's Christmas Eve, but I'd like to give you your present." I lifted myself up so I could look him in the eyes.

"Now?"

"Yes, now." He smiled. "Em, before I left for OCS, I asked you to marry me," he touched a bit of my hair and then started twisting it gently. "And when I asked you, I asked you from the bottom of my heart and my soul."

Tears formed in my eyes, and I nodded my head, "Yes, I know."

Jared continued, "And you said yes."

I chuckled through the tears and said, "Yes, I know." I leaned down and lightly kissed his chest.

His face tightened and his eyes got serious for a moment, "And . . ."

I put my finger to his mouth to stop him from speaking. My eyes searched his and I said, "And I want you to know that I want to marry *you* with my entire heart and soul."

"Are you sure?"

"Yes, I couldn't be more sure of anything."

Jared's face relaxed, his chin quivered and a tear rolled down his cheek. "It's just that . . ."

"I know, I'm sorry. He was an important part of my life."

"But, what if he shows up again? What if he comes back?"

I smiled, "Well then, I would have to say, 'Eric, I'd like you to meet my husband, Jared' and the two of you would become the best of friends."

He scoffed, "Uh, I don't know about that . . . ."

"You would. You would both really like each other. Trust me. And anyway, he won't come back."

"What makes you think that?"

"Because, it's been years and years and he never has."

"So," Jared asked again, "You wouldn't go back to him if he did?"

"No, never. We were never meant to be. He is my past, my very special past, but you are my here and now, my glorious, fantastically . . ." I start to kiss his stomach, ". . . Sexy . . ." I kiss even lower, ". . . Future."

Jared groaned with pleasure then pulled me up to face him. "Then, Emma? Will you marry me?"

"Of course I'll marry you." I answered. He pulled his hand out from under the cover and slipped an engagement ring on my finger. It was simple and gorgeous, exactly what I dreamt it would be. We made love again, then snuggled next to the fire late into the night, enjoying the chocolate covered strawberries and wine.

In the midst of so much loss, we let our love back in for the most romantic Christmas ever.

* * *

On the drive home, we decided that there was little need to wait to get married, and an even smaller need to have a wedding full of pomp and circumstance. Shortly, we applied for a license and arranged a small wedding with the Justice of the Peace in downtown Annapolis. We informed our parents and closest friends that we were going to be married on December 31 and all were welcomed to join us if they so desired.

I sent my mother an email to invite her to the wedding, but she declined, stating that there was simply no way she could make it home in time from Italy. I knew that was true, but she also made a point to tell me that nothing could change her plans to celebrate New Year's Eve in Rome, not even the marriage of her daughter. I replied that I understood. Actually only very slightly disappointed, I was quite relieved that we would not be graced with her presence. I promised to send her pictures which seemed to please her.

Jared's mom and I shopped at the "White House" and found a very simple but elegant wedding dress. Jared wore his dress blues, and surrounded by poinsettias and carrying a simple red and white rose bouquet, Jared and I were married. It was beautiful.

* * *

We both graduated from college in the spring: Jared with a bachelor's degree in Computer Science and I earned a bachelor's degree in Elementary School Education with a focus on Special Education. Jared made Second Lieutenant and received orders for a staff position at Camp Lejeune. He was stationed there until September 14, 2004, when he would be transferred back to Quantico for the brand-new "Officer Basic Course" or OBC, which was a specialized training session for officers who were going to be stationed in Iraq or Afghanistan. This training would teach them how to be officers to the enlisted men during the war and taught them the ins and outs of being a Marine. Much of the information learned at OBC was not taught to the Marines until this course began. From what I could understand, this was to be the most specialized training for the officers of war. Information was scarce and Jared refused to talk about it. The entire ordeal made me very nervous.

So, my biggest fear was confirmed. I wasn't blind. I knew it was coming. My husband was a Marine. Our country was at war. I knew it was only a matter of time before he would have to go, but knowing that didn't make it any easier.

We sold the condo and packed our things into two sets. One set contained the bare minimum of what we needed to survive and it followed us to Camp Lejeune. The rest of our belongings went to storage.

The drive to Camp Lejeune was long, but we were excited for a new beginning. I had never been to that part of the country and the first thing I noticed about Camp Lejeune was that it was hot and sticky. Old brick buildings stood proud and tall and spindly pine trees dotted the horizon.

Within a short time, I had met several other Marine wives and we often met for early morning walks. I enjoyed Linda's cool, smooth attitude and though she was extremely quiet, I loved to be in her presence. Her poker-straight, black hair was always neatly pulled back into a long ponytail. A small, black tattoo saying "Om" sat at the base of her neck. Her eyes held an understanding far beyond her years. Always wearing jeans and a comfortable shirt, usually black, she was simply and elegantly herself. She was never trying to prove anything and remained quietly attentive during our walks, only speaking if she was asked to give her honest, practical advice. Linda seemed to enjoy our company, but also her time alone.

Erica was beautiful, bouncy and full of laughter. Her chocolate brown skin always smelled like sugar cookies and her smile was the brightest I've seen. Her eyes danced with excitement, and anyone in her presence just had to smile. Her personality was fun and magnetic, and we quickly became close friends.

The third woman I walked with was Suzy, and unlike Linda and Erica, I didn't quite take to her. Suzy was an excessively bubbly, fake blond who's southern drawl clicked and clanged as she constantly talked, rarely stopping for breath. Suzy was obsessed with image, constantly checking herself in the mirror, making sure her lipstick and mascara were just so, even in the middle of a morning walk. She gossiped so much, that there was no doubt in my mind, that the second she was away from the three of us, her conversations turned to our perceived downfalls. Every time Suzy was near me, I could hear my Nana's voice echoing in the back of my mind, "There's always a bad apple, Em. But, they just make you appreciate the good ones all the more." Suzy was definitely a bad apple. In fact, I soon had the opportunity to find out just how toxic she was.

* * *

The war droned on and on. Spouses came home to base, some whole, some injured, some dead. I dreaded the day Jared would leave and I shuddered whenever I saw the tears and the fear in the other husbands', wives' and children's eyes when they had to say goodbye. I tried to be sympathetic and helpful for my new friends, making them a pan of lasagna, taking them out to lunch or watching their children for a much needed break, but I often felt at a loss and didn't know what to say. War sucks. Watching your spouse leave to fight in a distant land and not knowing if they will return alive or whole again must be gut wrenching. I didn't know, firsthand, how this felt, but I knew my time was coming soon. My guess was that Jared would be deployed almost immediately after the six months of OBC training at Quantico. I prayed that the war would be over by then, but I knew that prayer would not be answered as I wanted it to be.

Erica's husband left for Iraq on June 15, 2004. That night, I arrived on her doorstep with a hot pan of lasagna, a bag of salad, a loaf of fresh Italian bread and a bottle of wine. I rang the doorbell and waited. I could hear her footsteps as she walked to the door, which creaked open as she peeked through.

"Oh, Hi Emma! I'm glad it's you." She opened the door a little more to let me in. Erica was in a maroon bathrobe that perfectly accented her flawless brown skin. Her face was tear stained but she smiled and gave me a hug. "Come on in." She said.

"How are you holding up?" I asked.

"Okay, I guess . . . have to say, my heart skipped a beat though when I heard the doorbell." She replied.

"Really, why's that?"

She laughed as a tear rolled down her cheek. "I know it's stupid. Alex isn't even in Iraq, yet, but I'm dreading that someday that doorbell will ring and it won't be someone I want to see, if you know what I mean."

I understood, and was speechless.

"You hungry?" I asked.

Erica laughed, "Aren't I always?"

"I brought you some salad and lasagna." I handed her the bags of food and followed her into the kitchen.

"You gonna join me?" She asked, a pleading look in her eyes.

"I'd love to. I didn't want you drinking that wine alone!" I grinned.

"Girl, you're the best."

Erica got out some plates and silverware while I opened up the food and wine.

"So," I asked, "when do you think you'll hear from him?"

"He'll call when he gets there. He's expected to get there late tomorrow night."

"I see." I replied as I sliced the lasagna and placed it on the red and gold edged plates. The smell of the warm tomato sauce comforted me. I started to place the salad into bowls. "Soon, I will know what it's like."

I said. "Our time will be here before we know it." Sighing, I continued, "I think Jared will be deployed next April, after OBC."

"You're probably right. It's no piece of cake, I'll tell you that." Erica responded.

"I know. I can't imagine."

"You know what makes it worse?" I could hear anger building up in Erica's voice.

"No." I answered.

"Having a bitch like Suzy tell you your husband's been sleeping with another woman two days before he leaves."

I dropped the bowl of salad I was holding. "What?" I demanded.

"No joke girl. That bitch told me Alex was sleeping with Linda."

"Linda? No, you gotta be kidding. That's impossible!" I was stunned.

"Yep, that's what she told me two days ago. But he wasn't."

I didn't know Alex too well, but I could not imagine Linda ever sleeping with another woman's husband, especially a friend's.

"He wasn't?" I urged her to continue.

"Definitely not. He doesn't even know Linda. Never met her. He's talked to her on the phone when she's called the house, but that's it."

"So, what made Suzy say something like that?"

Erica snorted, "She's a vile bitch." She shook her head as she sat down on the oak kitchen chair and placed her forehead in her hands. "You see, Linda stopped by to see me a few days ago. Alex's car was still in the parking lot, but I had driven him in my car to get his hair cut. Well, Linda knocked on the door, and thinking I was home but just didn't hear her, she let herself in like she always does. She looked for me, couldn't find me. No one was home, of course, but she stayed and waited about twenty minutes, hoping to catch me. She even had a cup of tea. Eventually, she left, and she locked the door behind her. Suzy must have seen her and thought Alex was home and thought she was screwing him. But he was with me the entire time!"

I was in shock. All I could mutter was, "Oh my God!"

Erica continued, "Before I knew it, Suzy's bangin' on my front door, demanding to see my husband. She confronts him and tells him off in front of me. Initially, I believed her and was mighty pissed, but then I realized the day she was talking about . . . . I tried to explain the misunderstanding to her, but she refused to listen to me. Kept talking over me! And now, now the whole fuckin' base thinks my husband and Linda have been screwing around behind my back."

"Oh my God! I am so sorry. If it helps at all, I never heard anything about it."

Erica caught my eyes, and she seemed relieved, "Well, that's good I guess. Most bad news travels fast . . . too fast I fear."

I groaned, "Jesus, with friends like that, who needs enemies?"

"Tell me about it. Of course, the shock of it all upset me, but I worked it out in my mind. Linda always knows the right thing to say. She's one smart cookie. Had me feeling better in no time. Alex and I are fine . . . it just made the last couple days that much harder." Erica started to cry again. I held her close and told her everything would be fine, but both of us knew we had no idea what life was going to hand us.

She pulled away, grabbed a tissue to wipe away the tears streaming down her face. Through her tear filled eyes, she smiled and said, "Well, enough of these damn old tears. Let's eat."

I stayed with Erica until late that night. I always imagined the first night would be the worse. We planned to have dinner together every Tuesday night. When I left her house, she had that big, gorgeous smile on her face and I felt that, with all she was facing, that was the best I could do.

* * *

Two mornings later, I was relaxing in bed, still glowing from an early morning twist with Jared, who had just left to go on a run. The sheets on Jared's side of the bed were still warm and I pulled them up around my head to immerse myself in his scent. I drifted in and out of blissful consciousness.

At 7:00, someone started banging loudly on the front door. I dragged myself out of bed, pulled on my pink-flowered bathrobe and quickly walked to the front door. There was more loud rapping on the door and the grape vine wreath that hung on the back of it bounced with each strong knock. I watched as several dried flowers floated off the wreath and to the floor.

"I'm coming!" I yelled, getting more and more irritated with each obnoxious knock. I threw the door open and found Suzy standing there, blonde hair standing on end, her usually perfect mascara streaming down her cheeks. She smelled of day old rum.

"Suzy!" I exclaimed, "What's going on? Why are you banging on my door like that! It's seven a.m.!"

Her shrill, southern voice carried through the apartment complex, "I'm angry! That's what I am! Angry!"

I couldn't help being condescending, "Okay, Suzy, so why are you angry?"

She collapsed dramatically against the wall, placing her palm on her forehead, "Everyone's talking about me! Everyone! Nobody likes me." Loud sobs erupted from her, echoing through the hall.

I spoke softly to her, "Come inside, Suzy. Stop making a scene." Coaxing her inside, I shut the door behind her.

Suzy continued, "I try to help. I try to help everyone. They just don't know what's best for them . . ."

"As in, you try to help by spreading bad information about certain husbands sleeping with certain friends, all in the name of friendship, only to find out that the rumors you started were based on bad information and you hurt the people you supposedly care about and now they are rightfully mad at you?"

Suzy looked at me, stunned. For once, her lips stopped moving. Then they opened and closed slowly, like a fish pulling in water, trying to think of something to say but she was rendered speechless. "I . . . I . . ."

"Don't come here crying to me." I walked toward the door and opened it. "You are your own worse enemy. If you stopped running your mouth long enough to use your ears and eyes, you wouldn't be in this trouble."

"I . . . but . . ." Suzy stuttered.

"Suzy, you almost ruined a good marriage, of two respectable people, by jumping to conclusions and spreading bad information. Next time, shut your mouth and get your information straight!"

Suzy started to whimper. "See? See? Even you turned against me! Oh the lies! The lies."

I nodded toward the door ushering her to leave, "Yes, Suzy. Your lies. Please leave."

"But I, I thought I was your friend?"

"Friends don't do the things you've done to your friends. Please leave."

"But nobody understands . . ." she faltered.

"Oh, I think everyone understands quite clearly."

I closed the door then peeked out of the curtain to see Suzy walked dejectedly to her red Camry.

"Good riddance." I thought to myself.

The base became blissfully peaceful once all the rumors stopped being spread around. It's amazing how one person with a low self-esteem can mange to cause so much upheaval in everyone else's lives.

Linda, Erica and I continued to walk together every day, and Erica joined Jared and I for dinner every Tuesday night. Erica quickly became my best friend and though I never told her about my past, I felt she knew and understood me better than anyone, except Jared. We spent every moment we could together.

Our four months at Camp Lejeune quickly ended and before we knew it, we were moving to Virginia so Jared could complete OBC training at Quantico. I continued to keep in touch with Erica and Linda. By January, Erica called to let me know Alex arrived home safely from Iraq and her relief was palpable.

The phone rang again six weeks later, as I sipped chamomile tea and watched snow flakes falling outside our apartment window.

Erica sounded very excited. "Hey girl! Guess what!"

"What?" I asked.

"I'm pregnant!" We both let out screams of excitement! This was such incredible news!

"I haven't told Alex yet."

"Really?" I asked.

"No, girl. You are the first to know!"

I was grinning ear to ear. "Wow! I'm honored! So when are you going to tell him?"

"Tonight, when he gets home. I'm going to make him a special dinner: steak, candlelight . . . the whole nine yards!"

"That's sounds so romantic!" I replied. "I can't wait to hear how it goes! How's Alex doing, anyway?"

"Okay, I guess. Iraq was really tough on him. He keeps waking up screaming . . . having nightmares or something. I keep trying to get him to talk to me about it, but he won't hear of it. Tells me I won't understand and he doesn't want to worry me with the crap he's seen."

"Oh, no. I'm so sorry to hear that." I said.

Erica sighed, "Yeah, it was bad, really bad over there. I think he's got that post-traumatic stress syndrome. I've been trying to get him to go get some help, but he won't. He drinks instead. I keep telling myself, 'girl, that man's been through a lot, so a drink now and then won't hurt anything,' but honestly, he's drinking way too much."

"Do you think you'll be able to talk him into getting help eventually?" I asked.

"I don't know. I hope so. He seems to think the guys will think he's a wimp or something. I keep telling him, it takes a real man to face his demons head on. I think he'll eventually go, hopefully sooner than later."

"I hope so, too."

"Yeah, and to think all this time I was only worried about him dying or being blown to pieces! Well, my man's home 'whole,' but not completely 'whole' if you know what I mean. This psychological stuff is bad, too, on all of us."

I tried to sound optimistic, "Well, maybe the news of the baby will cheer him up!"

"Yeah, I think so," Erica hesitated. "I hope so. Maybe it'll put a fire under his butt so he can get some help. Things have changed, girl. Things have changed."

"I'm sure the two of you can work through this. If you need to talk, I'm always here."

I could hear Erica smile, "I know, girl. Thanks! Love you!"

"Love you, too!"

* * *

I never expected a call from Erica to affect me so profoundly. First, I worried about Alex. I had heard about post-traumatic stress disorder, but I didn't really know much about it. The numbers of wounded or killed troops were reported regularly, but we never heard about this silent disease. I wondered how many veterans suffered from it and if they were getting the help they needed. I knew, first hand, how much counseling helped and hoped that the egos of these men and women didn't stand in the way of their healing.

Second, the phone call made me worry even more about Jared. I knew he would be deployed soon, probably in the upcoming spring. This prospect terrified me. My husband would be going to war and he had a good chance of being killed, being horribly maimed, and whether he was injured or not, he could suffer from post-traumatic stress disorder. Not a promising outlook, no matter what happened. I found myself crying, and resolved to face the fact that I was a wife of a Marine, and I was proud of the job he was doing. I vowed to stand by him no matter what, in sickness or in health, in good times or in bad. I loved Jared with all my heart and took my wedding vows very seriously.

Third, I started thinking about having a baby. When Erica told me she was pregnant, a little seed was planted in my mind. For a few hours, it sat there, like an annoying little pebble, but I could ignore it. Then its roots started to grow, penetrating my every thought until it blossomed into a need that consumed my mind and body. I wanted a baby. I wanted Jared's baby and I wanted it soon.

Deciding to take Erica's lead, I went to the commissary, got some steak, baking potatoes and salad. Then, I ran to the liquor store and bought some beer for Jared. When I got home, I took a shower, did my hair and make-up, put on Jared's favorite black thong and dressed for dinner. By the time he got home, dinner was served on our best plates, with my favorite red dinner napkins and candlelight. The blinds were drawn and Norah Jones was playing softly in the background.

Jared looked pleasantly surprised when he walked through the door, a smile lighted up his face. "What is all this?" he said as he pulled me close and kissed me.

I kissed his neck, smelling his warm scent and whispered in his ear. "I wanted this to be a special night."

"Okay," he grinned and kissed my cheek, "I'm all for that, but why?"

I pulled myself back so I could look into his gorgeous blue eyes. "Because I want us to make a baby, right here, right now."

My voice shook as I spoke, nervous about what his reaction would be, but once again, Jared's reaction surprised me. If he was shocked at my proposal, I saw no hint of it in his eyes. The corner of his mouth lifted in a smile as his leaned down and kissed me hard. Without saying a word, he effortlessly picked me up in his arms and carried me to our bed. As we made love, I could feel his heart and soul envelope me. Tears of happiness escaped from my eyes while dinner grew cold and the candles on the dining room table slowly burned out.

* * *

Four weeks came and went, and so did my period. I was disappointed, but Jared was really enjoying his newly assigned position as baby maker, and I have to say, I was enjoying it too. I really missed seeing Erica and Linda everyday, but our phone calls kept us all up to date. I made some new friends in the Marine Wives' Walking Club, and had grown particularly close to a woman named Jen. Jen had a friendly face, bouncing, green eyes, and bob-cut brown hair with blonde highlights. We walked everyday together, and often went out for lunch.

Jen loved studying the paranormal and was really excited about a show called "Spirit Hunters." She liked it so much that every Wednesday night she would host a "Spirit Hunters" party. A group of us would get together, have snacks and drinks and watch the newest SH episode.

"Spirit Hunters" focused primarily on disproving, or debunking, the paranormal experiences people had within their homes, often giving alternative explanations for the creaking floors, the sounds of footsteps, the mysterious smells, the dark shadows and the eerie feelings seen and felt around them. But occasionally, the team would collect evidence that there may be a haunting, and this evidence would send chills up our spines.

I loved watching the SH team work together as they scientifically explored haunted houses, historical sites, museums and prisons, and I quickly learned a lot about ghost hunting.

High EMFs or electromagnetic fields often caused people who were sensitive feel as though they were being watched, or that they had a paranormal presence around them. High EMFs could be produced by old electrical boxes and faulty electrical wiring, so once these items were repaired, the "haunted" feelings would disappear. However, sometimes a mysterious EMF spike would occur that could not be correlated to any electrical issues, and it was believed that in these cases, a spirit may be present.

I also learned about EVPs, or electronic voice phenomena. The "Spirit Hunters" team would often use digital recorders during their investigations to catch disembodied voices that could not be heard by their ears alone. They would ask a series of question in the hope that the spirit or ghost that was present would answer them. Several times, an answer was found on the digital recorders, confirming a presence in the home.

Other phenomena such as cold spots, or areas where the temperature would suddenly drop were also explored. In paranormal theory, some believed that cold spots could occur in areas where a spirit might be present. The "Spirit Hunters" also experienced battery drain, when freshly charged batteries on their equipment would suddenly lose power, on several occasions. They believed that this occurred when spirits were using energy from the environment to try to manifest themselves.

Sometimes, a ghost would make themselves known by filling the room with a scent, such as roses or cigar smoke. When this was mentioned, I often thought of the experience I had when my grandmother came to visit me and it brought tears to my eyes. I was relieved to know that others had experienced such similar things, and that my grandmother may, very well, have come to say goodbye.

I really looked forward to my Wednesday nights watching "Spirit Hunters" with the girls. It was extremely interesting, and I hoped that someday, I would have the chance to "ghost hunt" for myself.

* * *

Clover Doves

I heard from Erica regularly. I had told her we were trying to conceive a baby, and every so often she called, hoping to get some good news from me, but no news ever came.

Erica, on the other hand, was growing bigger and bigger everyday and had suffered from horrible morning sickness. I would call to check on her, and would spend hours listening to her stories of nausea, throwing up, body pains and not being able to get out of bed. A gnawing pain of sadness filled me as I listened and wondered whether I would ever be blessed with those symptoms.

Before I knew it, it was April. The crocuses were already fading and the daffodils were in full-bloom. I was sitting by a window, sketching a hyacinth and listening to the robins sing when the phone rang. It was Erica, "Girl, I've got some bad news."

My heart skipped a beat and my thoughts instantly went to her baby. "Oh no. What?" I said.

"Suzy's husband was killed by a suicide bomber outside of Baghdad."

Not expecting to hear that, I said, "Oh shit. I am so sorry to hear that. Have you seen her?"

"Yeah, I went to her house as soon as I heard." She responded.

"How'd it go?" I asked, not shocked at Erica's response. This was the Erica I loved so much. Even after all the pain Suzy had caused her, she still found it in her heart to embrace her during this difficult time. I wondered if I would have done the same if I were in her position.

Erica replied, "She was so grateful. She hugged me and cried on my shoulder. It's horrible you know . . . simply horrible."

"I can't imagine." I said and shuddered at the thought of losing Jared. I think it would kill me. "Do you think she'd mind if I called her?" I asked Erica.

"No, that would be good. She'd like that." Erica gave me her number then said, "I'm so relieved that Alex came home. You know, PTSD isn't fun, but he's here with me and I'd take that over this any day."

"How is Alex doing?"

Erica answered, "Okay, better. Finally got some help and he seems to be working through it. He's not drinking so much anymore. We'll be okay." She quickly changed the subject, "Any baby news yet?"

I sighed, "No, not yet."

"Well, keep on trying. It'll happen. You'll see." She encouraged.

I doubt it. I thought to myself.

We said our goodbyes and I hung up the phone, filled will doubt and hopelessness.

I picked up the phone and called Suzy. Though she spoke through tears, I could tell she was happy to hear from me. I said everything I could possibly think of to say, and still felt it wasn't enough. She was living our worse nightmare.

* * *

The day OBC training was over was the day Jared got his orders to Iraq. He received a six-month deployment starting on May 1, 2005. Even though he was still a Second Lieutenant, he was to command a platoon of 26 marines near Ramadi.

When Jared called to tell me, I couldn't help but cry. I tried to stay strong, but fear gripped every cell in my body. I couldn't escape it, even in my sleep. I was constantly dreaming of men in camouflage, being blown to pieces by roadside bombs and suicide bombers. I dreamed of Jared's gorgeous blue eyes desperately looking at me for one last time as a tear rolled down his horror stricken face.

I hid my fear from Jared, but its hold increased every morning when he walked out the door. I hoped that maybe I was catastrophizing. I told myself that he would be okay, but every time I watched him walk away, I feared that our days were numbered and I'd soon watch him walk away for the very last time.

Chapter: Jared

AND SO, MY TIME CAME. It had loomed over us for months. We watched other Marines come and go and now my training would culminated in a six-month deployment to Iraq. The sacrifice had to be made, but I was proud to do it. We cried, laughed, made love and hoped, passing the last days, hours and minutes we had left together. Emma put on a good front, but she was scared. I could see the fear in her gorgeous brown eyes. She tossed and turned at night and cried in her sleep. Black circles formed under her eyes, and when I came home from work, her eyes were often red and puffy.

I had to admit, I was scared too. The stories I heard about the endless assaults, the roadside bombs and suicide bombers were hard to take for even the most hardened Marine and I was new to it. Men and women were being critically wounded and killed every day. I knew OCS and OBC training had prepared me for the war, but it was still an unknown entity. I was ready to face it, to finally be inoculated with the reality of it, so I could overcome it and move on.

And, that's what I did.

* * *

On June 14, 2005, at my station in Iraq, I had just gotten off the phone with Emma, a very precious event that really didn't happen all that often. I was glad to hear her voice, but I could tell she was down. She had thought she was pregnant. She even had a positive pregnancy test, but when she went in for her six-week appointment, the nurse told her it must have been a false-positive. I tried to cheer her up, telling her

I'd be more than happy to get right back to work on this when I came home at the end of October, but she just scoffed at me.

"Don't jinx us, baby. Don't even talk about that." She said.

I told her not to worry. I would be home before she knew it, but I was just being hopeful for her sake. I had already survived two car bombings, unscathed, but I had four months left to go. Three of my men had been critically injured and one killed. The dangers we faced every day were non-relenting and savage. Although I'd never been a very religious man, I found myself praying for safety, praying for my men and praying that this war would finally end.

I told her I loved her.

She started to cry, "I love you, too."

My heart sank, "Emma, please don't cry."

"I know. I'm trying to be strong. I just miss you so much and . . ." she started to sob.

"I miss you, too, Em. If I could drop everything and come home to you right now, I would. I'll be home soon. I promise." An uneasy feeling enveloped me, as if I had just told a lie.

Her reply was a sob. We held on in silence for a few moments and she said, "I'm so terrified of losing you."

I couldn't hold the tears back, "I know. I'm scared, too. But no matter what happens, please remember that I will always love you. You are my world."

"Me, too." She cried. "I love you, too. Call me soon."

"I will." I replied as I hung up the phone, fear still gripping me.

My platoon was on checkpoint duty near an old bridge outside of Ramadi, the capital of the Anbar province, where insurgent groups regularly attacked. We had to have constant vigilance, even when we were exhausted from the hundred and ten degree heat and the constant, unrelenting sun for fourteen hours a day, that parched our bodies and scorched our skin. A long line of beat up, civilian vehicles was stopped, waiting to be inspected. The smell of exhaust filled the air. Covered in a film of sweat and dirt, I longed for a beer.

Suddenly, about twenty vehicles back, a huge bang temporarily deafened us. The sound of falling shrapnel and a cloud of billowing smoke told us that a vehicle had exploded. Two of my privates and I left our post and, M16s at the ready, ran toward the indistinguishable vehicle engulfed in flames. No corpse could be seen in the detonated car, but the smell of burning flesh permeated the air. The car bomb had demolished and set afire two cars in each direction, in the front and in the back of it. Civilians were running from the line of cars, screaming, clutching their children to their chest, sobbing. I noticed a large white bus, five vehicles in front of the detonated car, its rusty metal was flaking large pieces of white paint off its exterior. A group of three women wearing black burkas were slowly exiting the bus. Their heads were bent down, as they carefully watched their footing on the rusty steps of the bus. From a distance, they looked elderly, somehow encumbered.

As I searched for insurgents and survivors in the bombed vehicles, the crowds of civilians that had left their cars were starting to pool in three distinct areas. One group stood near the checkpoint station, another stood off in the distance to the left of the station, and a third stood off to the right. Everything was chaotic. Screams penetrated the air as women and children cried hysterically. People were bleeding, wrapping their wounded bodies with scraps of clothing, holding onto themselves in fear and pain. A man lying on the ground writhed in misery, his left side burned, tears streaming down his face. I could hear the sound of sirens rushing to the scene.

All the while, the three women in burkas moved slowly toward the screaming masses, as if in slow motion. I quickly made my way back to the checkpoint station.

"Take care of the wounded!" I commanded, "Get the supplies and move the civilians away from the line of vehicles!" I continued to survey the surroundings. The three women continued to move slowly, floating like dark, ghostly shadows above the ground. Then they divided up, one gliding toward the crowd to the left as the second glided silently to the right. The third glided straight ahead, moving toward the checkpoint station, where I now stood. The hairs on my arms and neck stood erect. This isn't right, I thought. This isn't . . .

BOOM! An explosion rang through the air. The civilians in my group and the group to the right of me screamed in terror as the men, women and children in the group to the left were silenced forever.

The burka'd woman had detonated herself as she reached the crowd of civilians. Arms, legs, hands and other unidentifiable body parts spewed across the land, blanketing the ground with blood.

BOOM! I didn't stop to look. The second woman had detonated herself. More screams. More blood. "I have to stop this!" I thought.

I ran toward the third suicide bomber, hoping to prevent her from coming any closer. I glanced behind me. The checkpoint station had emptied. The civilians had fled. I noticed three of my men closing in behind me, backing me up.

I pushed forward. My eyes met the bomber's deep brown eyes and they seemed to smile at me. They looked very familiar to me. Emma entered my mind.

"No!" I yelled lifting up my rifle. "Stand back . . . Move back!"

Her head tilted to the side and she looked at me questioningly then took a step forward.

'No!" I demanded. "No!" I pulled the trigger. Bullets penetrated her neck and her forehead. She fell to the ground.

"No . . ." I screamed as horror and confusion gripped me. "No . . ." I muttered as I moved forward. "Emma . . ." A single tear flowed out of the corner of my eye.

The woman's body lay in a heap at my feet. Emma's eyes stared back at me.

I stood there confused, my men shouting at me. "Sir! Sir! Get away from the body!"

In a daze, I turned to see one of my men running toward me shouting, "Run!"

BOOM! The third suicide bomb detonated.

* * *

My death was quick, painless. I had left my body before it was hit by the blast and watched as it exploded into hundreds of pieces.

I floated there watching the clean up, the sorrow, the pain. A private retrieved my dog tags, pulling them off of whatever was left of me. I watched as he clutched the bloody metal tags to his chest. I knew they would be returned to Emma. Oh my God, Emma . . .

A familiar voice spoke behind me. "Emma will be fine, Jared." Warmth and light radiated around me and I turned to discover Mr. Fiorello suspended in light. He continued to speak. "She'll be in good hands."

"Whose?" I asked.

"There is no need to worry yourself with earthly concerns. Please believe me, Emma will be fine. It is time for you to move on." Somehow, hearing this, I felt at peace. I looked one more time at the world I was leaving behind, the world I had lived in. I turned from it and followed Mr. Fiorello home—where I belonged.

Chapter: Emma

June 15, 2005, 8:50 a.m.

I HEARD A KNOCK ON the door.

"Be there in a minute!" I called out as I quickly pulled on my old, black, running shorts, a T-shirt and tied my sneakers. "You're early!" I exclaimed with a laugh. Jen told me that she would be there at nine to go on a walk. I was excited to have some company and exercise.

I pulled my long, brown hair up into a ponytail and looked closely at myself in the mirror. There were no puffy circles under my eyes, no swollen eyelids, no tear stains . . . nothing to signify the expanding emptiness blossoming inside of me or the tears I had shed last night. Jared's absence hadn't festered in my mind when I believed a piece of him, a product of our love, was growing inside of me, but now . . .

Knock, knock, knock. The front door pounding continued.

"I'm coming!" I called. I grabbed a bottle of water and ran up to the door. The doorknob felt unnaturally cold as I turned it, catching my attention as I opened the door. "I am so ready to go on this . . ." My sentence dropped when I realized it was not Jen who was knocking. My heart stopped, I gasped and stumbled backwards. My body started to tremble as if an earthquake was shaking my world apart.

Two Marines in crisp, dress blues, flanked a chaplain in a white frock whose stole was embroidered with a cross and purple and blue doves. The three men looked at me with sorrowful eyes.

"No . . ." I whispered. "No . . ."

Clover Doves

"Mrs. Emma Stafford?" The Marine on the left spoke softly, sadness reflected in his deep brown eyes, his face stoic. I recognized him from base, but I did not know his name.

"Yes." I replied as tears started to stream down my cheeks. *I'm asleep.* I tried to convince myself. *This is just another bad dream.*

He moved forward, his eyes penetrated mine. "I am sorry to inform you that your husband Jared was killed in action last night."

"No." I replied. "No. He's not dead. I talked to him, just last night. He's fine . . ."

The chaplain stepped forward and tried to take my hand. I pulled it away. "Emma, I know this is very shocking, horrible news, but it is true."

"No." My head shook in protest, but the truth resonated within me. A primal, guttural scream, starting from the base of my being escaped, and echoed through the halls of our apartment building. "No . . . no . . . not Jared. He's coming home!"

The chaplain stepped forward and took my hands. I crumbled into his arms, the rough, white fabric of his frock pressed against my tear-streaked face. He placed one hand on my head, the other on my back and held me close. "I am so sorry." He said. "I am so very, very sorry." Numbness spread throughout my body as grief consumed me. Silent tears flowed like a river down my cheeks. I could not speak. I could not move. I could hardly breathe.

A gasp broke the anguished silence. Jen had arrived, on-time and ready to walk. Her hands were folded against each other as if in prayer and they were pressed against her mouth. Tears streamed down her face, shock was in her eyes. Pulling away from the chaplain, I ran into her arms.

I don't remember anything else about that day, but there is one thing I know for sure. The friends I had made surrounded me with support, bringing water, food, tissues—whatever I needed. The Marine Corps watched out for their own. I was well taken care of in my greatest time of need, and though I was despondent, hollow and empty, and felt as if my world had ended, I was never alone.

Chapter: Eric

June 15, 2005, 8:53 a.m.

ALTHOUGH THE WARM, GOLDEN SAND pressed into my skin and the bright morning sun embraced me, a chill ran up my spine.

I sat up and watched as the sudden high winds whipped the distant waves, speckling the restless ocean. Immense waves began to surge to shore, violently crashing and spraying me, covering the sand with bubbly foam.

Sorrow gripped my soul. Tears welled in my eyes.

Something, somewhere had changed.

"Emma." I whispered.

Chapter: Emma

JARED WAS GONE.

He had died a hero and was buried at Arlington National Cemetery on July 4, 2005. Hundreds of people were at his funeral: other Marines, our friends, including Erica and Alex, Jared's parents, even my mother, who had lost herself in Italy for the past two years, managed to be there in remembrance. Meaningful condolences were spoken as people attempted to touch and hug me, but I graciously pulled away. I needed to stay strong. Like a spring snow embraced by the sun, any physical touch could melt my meager façade instantly.

Jared was gone.

A chaplain spoke. The twenty-one gun salute barely registered in my mind, only slightly awakening me from my fog-like state.

Jared was gone.

The American flag was ceremoniously folded and handed to me. I ran my finger along the flag's ridged seams. The fabric reminded me of Jared's running shorts: shorts he would never wear again. I kissed the flag and clutched it to my chest. I nearly collapsed, but Erica grabbed onto me before I hit the ground. I leaned into her body and she held onto me with all her strength.

Jared was gone.

There were roses and wreaths. Sobs echoed in the empty recesses of my mind. I dropped one exquisite red rose. *Only one? Surely you deserve more than that. Goodbye, my love.*

Jared was gone.

Marines in dress blues walked up to me. Each face became Jared's. Words were spoken, "Brave . . . great admiration . . . good man . . ."

Jared was gone.

I don't remember going home. I don't remember the food, the drinks, or the people that surrounded me. All I could remember was, Jared was gone.

Chapter: Eric

July 5, 2005

SUNBEAMS SNUCK THROUGH THE CRACK in the curtains, waking me up long before it was necessary. I threw back the covers and sat up in bed trying to decide what I should do with the few days I had off before I started graduate school. It was great to be back at our old house in Ellicott City. My father had been transferred back to the area so my parents had stopped renting out the place and moved back here during my senior year of college six months ago. I hadn't been home since Christmas.

In June, I had graduated from the University of Colorado with a degree in psychology and had been accepted to a doctorate program at University of Maryland. I only had a few more days before my educational responsibilities would overtake my life, so at that moment, I only had plans to relax.

I could tell my parents had already left for work. There were no clicks of my mom's high heels in the hallway, no rustlings of the Baltimore Sun, no murmurs of my parents' voices in the kitchen. Everything was absolutely quiet. I walked into the hallway and could smell a faint wisp of my mother's perfume, mixed with the sweet scent of the fresh floral arrangement she took such pride in having in the hallway. It was great to be home.

I stretched and walked back into my room to change into running clothes. I had energy to expend and thought a run up to Joe's to get breakfast would be a great way to take care of it. I opened the curtains, allowing the sun to brighten my surroundings. As I started pulling up the covers to make my bed, the soft sound of a man's footsteps echoed in the hallway behind me. I turned and called, "Dad?"

No one answered.

Shrugging it off, I finished making the bed and went to put on my old T-shirt. A chill hung in the air, and I shivered. As I turned to walk to the bathroom, I caught a reflection of a man with deep, blue eyes in the mirror. I jumped and looked behind me, but no one was there.

Sheesh, I better get to Joe's to get that coffee. I laughed to myself.

The neighborhood appeared older than it had the last time I was there. The trees and shrubbery had grown significantly, shading the streets from the sweltering sun. Echoes of my past reminded me of walking these streets lost, lonely and confused, but the successes I had had over the past few years left me feeling confident. I knew that life would lead me in the right direction if I would let it. The past was the past. But yet—a part of me wished Emma was still a part of my present.

I ran past Emma's street and considered running past her house, but I knew she and her family were long gone. My heart twinged every time I thought about it.

My stomach growled and I shook off the sudden sadness that overwhelmed me once again. I needed some coffee. I needed to get to Joe's now. I listened to the rhythm of my feet increase in an effort to get me there quicker. I felt like I was on a mission. I laughed to myself: a mission for coffee and a bagel.

The blue and white awning outside of Joe's had become worn. Dirt stained the white rows making them look gray, but the inside still looked and smelled exactly as I remembered it. The scent of fresh coffee and pastries enveloped me. The dark bricks, the oak furniture and the candles invited me to make myself comfortable, so I did.

After I ordered my coffee and bagel, I sat down at a two-person table in the back corner of the coffee shop and grabbed a newspaper laying on the empty table beside me, a current edition of our town paper, "The Crier."

I gasped as I unfolded the paper to see on the front page, a large picture of Emma at Arlington National Cemetery, holding a folded American flag, looking despondent at a coffin being lowered into the ground. Mrs. Fiorello was next to her, dabbing her eyes with a tissue. Other people surrounding her, but none that I recognized.

The article was titled "Local Hero, Killed in Iraq." The caption under the half-page picture stated, "Mrs. Emma Fiorello-Stafford, widow of Second Lieutenant Jared Stafford, laid her husband to rest at Arlington National Cemetery on July 4, 2005."

I took a quick sip of coffee and read on. Jared had been killed on June 16, 2005, while valiantly protecting civilians from a suicide bomber outside of Ramadi. Chills ran up my spine when I looked at Jared's photograph. The blue eyes staring at me were the same eyes I had just seen reflected in the mirror at my house.

* * *

Confusion gripped me and I felt a sudden urge to run home. I pitched my bagel and coffee into the garbage and hurried out the door. A voice in the back of my mind told me I needed to find Emma. She needed me and I could not let her be alone.

My heartbeat echoed in my head as my feet pounded the sidewalk. My mind began to overflow with understanding. "This was it," I thought. "This was why I've been feeling so much pain and anguish lately. Emma's hurting, bad, and she needs me."

My legs picked up speed as I turned the corner to pass Stewart's Hardware. The parking lot was empty except for a young mother holding her child next to a blue sedan. A dark, burly man had just walked up to her and they seemed to be arguing. Though I could not hear the words being spoken, I could tell that he was demanding something. I watched as the curly, brunette grasped her little girl to her side and stumbled backwards, trying to get away from the aggressive man. Something wasn't right. Instinct took over and I ran toward the woman.

The voices became louder, "Sir, it's just a diaper bag."

"Give it to me then." He growled.

The woman threw the bag toward the man and it hit the pavement, its contents spilling all over the ground. He smiled wickedly. "Now, that wasn't so bad, was it?" He bent down and started collecting the items on the ground, shoveling them back into the bag.

"Stop." I yelled. "That stuff's not yours. Give it back."

He turned toward me, surprise and anger in his eyes. "What did you say?" he demanded taking a couple steps toward me as the mother backed quickly away, hiding behind the car.

"Give her her stuff back." I repeated.

He snarled as he reached into the pocket of his saggy, dirt stained jeans. A flash of silver glinted in the sunlight.

"No!" the mother's scream echoed through the town walls as a gun shot rang in my ears.

Part 3
The Beginning

Chapter: Emma

July 23, 2007

LIFE WENT ON. IT ALWAYS does. Even when you feel your life has come to an end, the world keeps spinning and you're still on it. Eventually, you begin to live again. You noticed the small insignificant things in life that had gone by unnoticed for so long: a single, purple violet hidden in the summer grass, a ladybug, waiting in ambush on the stem of a rose, a bluebird, puffing its chest as it sings for a mate.

It had been two summers since Jared was killed in Iraq. I was still alone, but I didn't feel lonely. During the day, friends and work kept me from dwelling on what could easily tear me apart. My life had not been easy, but I was determined not to let it pull me down. Several months after Jared died, I had moved back to Ellicott City and had gotten a job at Ellicott City Elementary School, working with special needs children. I lost myself in books, refreshing my memory of all I had learned in college and developed the skills to enable my autistic students to slowly open up and express themselves. Receiving a hard-earned smile, hearing a giggle or feeling the warmth of a child's hand suddenly grasping mine brought happiness to a part of me that had grown distant and cold after years of pain and heartache.

I had bought a small one-story cottage that overlooked an overgrown garden that, at one time, must have been gorgeous. The garden surrounded an ancient willow tree, whose branches seemed pulled against their will toward the earth. I spent my free hours in the garden, slowly weeding and pruning the plants, losing myself in its inner beauty. The garden healed me. It allowed me to feel emotions when I needed to, and to work out my angst when it engulfed me.

During my first summer in the garden, I would sit on the same rock every night: the one with the striations from millions of years of pressure. It always held the warmth of the summer sun, long after the sun had begun to set. I would take my flip-flops off and place my feet carefully on the ground, now and again feeling a prick from a wooden shard or a thorn, but I didn't care. At that time, no physical pain could hurt me as much as the emotional pain I felt from losing Jared.

Cold tears would run down my cheek and I would feel desperately alone. Taking a deep breath I would scan the ground around me, trying to find something, anything to focus my mind on. One day, I noticed tiny bird's nest fungus, camouflaged in the mulch, that popped up during the previous night's rain. They had already dried to a crisp in the mid-afternoon sun, their tiny black eggs ready to explode into life once touched by rain again.

Another time, I spotted a hidden patch of purple clover. I can still feel the stem snap between my fingers as I picked the largest blossom. I had never really looked at a clover before. The large purple flower actually consisted of many tiny flowers, elegantly placed together. Each little flower had one large purple petal, and in front of it, a small set of petals shaped exactly like a dove. Each dove looked as though it was trying to escape the grasp of the flower, straining to reach the stars up above, a place where I too longed to be.

The cold winter holidays were always the worse. Each year friends would invite me over or stop by, momentarily making me forget the pain, but once the gifts were given and the warmth of the goodbye hugs dissipated into the frigid winter air, I would feel very much alone. Crawling into a cold and empty bed on Christmas Eve was the worst. Memories of the time I had spent with Jared would tear me apart. I had stopped celebrating New Year's completely, refusing to acknowledge the passing of another wedding anniversary without my husband.

Time continued to pass me by, slowly ebbing like the tide, floating along like a feather on a light summer breeze. Now, almost two years later, the emptiness that gripped my soul had finally started to release its grasp and happier feelings replaced the sadness and grief that had permeated every cell for so long.

However, any happiness I felt was also clouded by guilt—guilt stemming from something I could not control: my dreams. For the past several months, I had felt so much comfort and peace when I slept. Dreams filled my nights, but these dreams were of Eric, not Jared. Eric was holding me in the dazzling, white light that comforted me so long ago. His strong arms wrapped around me, sheltering me with his strength, and the sweet smell of his skin relaxed me. These dreams transported me to another place and time, and the comfort they brought filled my soul. I longed to be in Eric's arms again. I knew, in my mind, that this didn't lessen the feelings I had for Jared, but I still felt guilty: So guilty, my stomach hurt, so guilty I found myself unable to eat and so guilty I was losing a ton of weight.

The beginning of our story started late one summer evening—one that began like all the rest. As with most evenings, I wandered around my backyard to pass the time. I pulled buckets of weeds, enjoying the musty scent of the dirt and mulch mix with the strong floral scent of the lilacs and roses that constantly bloomed. Soft, moist dirt pressed into my bare knees and covered my hands and fingernails, a tangible evidence of my closeness with the earth. The birds' songs and the sound of the willow tree blowing in the wind brought harmony to the environment. That evening, I found a miniscule, black toad in the rock garden and another single violet, tilting its tiny face toward the sun. It was a humid summer night. The thick haze was settling close to the ground as dusk quickly darkened the sky. I watched as bats began chasing the mosquitoes swarming in the evening light. Then several mosquitoes found me, so I decided to go inside and take a shower.

Slipping into a cool nightgown, I grabbed a cold glass of ice tea and sat down in my favorite rocking chair to reread "Persuasion" by Jane Austen.

The rocking chair sat next to a large bay window that overlooked the garden. Moths were bouncing off the screen trying to reach my reading light. The sun had almost completely set, but still a soft blue light shone behind the trees along the western horizon. A light breeze played a soft lullaby on the wind chimes while the face of the full moon shined brilliantly above.

I looked out the window into the moonlit garden, watching the leaves of the willow tree whisper sweet nothings to the stars above. My mind wandered to another time. A familiar smell filled the room and enveloped me. I turned expecting to see Eric, but no one was there. The smell, the warm sweet smell of his skin was inescapable. I called out. "Is that you?" but there was no reply. My eyes searched the darkness. Nothing was there. I thought to myself, "It can't be; he's not dead. At least I don't think he is . . ." I turned and looked back out at the garden.

I remembered the last time my room filled with the smell of someone I loved. It was after my grandmother had died. I remembered the feeling of peace that enveloped me as her smell permeated the room, inescapable.

I felt that peace now, but there was an underlying sense of confusion. The warm, familiar scent was definitely Eric's, not Jared's. I had dreamt about him for weeks now and I knew his scent well.

Eric couldn't be dead, could he?

Guilt washed over me as I shook my head in disgust.

Why am I dreaming of Eric? Why is it Eric's smell that is haunting me? Jared's dead. Not Eric. Jared should be in my dreams. I should be longing for Jared's touch. It should be Jared's smell in my room.

A cold tear slid down my cheek.

Jared's gone and he'll never come back. He never came back.

The strong, seductive smell of a man permeated my every sense.
Confused, I began to wonder. *Maybe this is Jared?* I turned around and my eyes searched the dark room for a sign.

"Jared, is that you?"

Still no response, only the soft whispers of the willow tree blowing in the breeze outside and the bugs tapping against the window.

I watched the clouds wisp past the full moon and more tears fell. I shivered as a cool breeze blew across my neck. Then I felt the cold hard pressure of a hand caressing my back.

I jumped out of the rocker and turned to look behind me. No one was there. My body shook from cold and fear.

I called out, "Who's there?"

The strong scent that permeated the room suddenly got more intense. It was so strong that I could barely breathe. Then, its intensity quickly subsided and it disappeared completely. Whatever it was, whoever it was—gone.

I turned off my reading light and jumped into my bed. Pulling the covers up around me, I tried to shake the chill that had reached my bones. My eyes scanned the room, looking for any explanations to the many questions swirling in my brain.

There were no answers.

My senses were on overdrive. I jumped at every little noise but my mind could explain every one of them. Crack! That was the house cooling in the night. Rumble! That was only the ice maker . . . As the night wore on, I started to think I had been imagining things. My mind continued to race.

Maybe there wasn't really a smell in my room. Maybe I imagined a hand caressing my back. Maybe it was all just a weird daydream caused by my own guilty wishes and desires. Maybe, Jared had finally come to say goodbye.

Realizing that it could have been Jared coming to say goodbye, I spoke out loud, "Jared, if that was you, I love you and I miss you."

As soon the words left my mouth, footsteps echoed above me in the attic. I sat up straight in bed, my body shaking uncontrollably. "Jared?" I called out.

Something slid along the floor above me. Terrified, I crawled under my blankets and listened closely to the noises above.

"Jared? Is that you?"

I was answered with silence. Hidden under the blankets, I listened in the darkness for what seemed like hours, but no more noises came.

The chill I felt continued to embrace my body. No matter how hard I tried, I couldn't get warm. Eventually, I fell into a restless sleep, hidden deep beneath my covers.

*   *   *

The next morning, I awoke drenched in sweat but I was still shaking uncontrollably from a chill. My stomach churned and I ran to the bathroom barely making it there to reexamine last night's dinner.

The room spun as I blindly searched for a thermometer in the bathroom drawers. Finding one, I stuck it in my mouth and sunk down to the floor. The cold white tiles chilled me even more, but I could not move. The thermometer beeped. My temperature was 103.1.

That explains it. I wasn't going crazy. I was getting sick and hallucinating from the fever.

Breathing a sigh of relief, I closed my eyes and fell asleep on the floor.

*   *   *

Hours later, the sound of birds singing woke me up, and I was surprised at my surroundings. I found myself curled up on the soft, blue bathroom rug with a towel on top of me for warmth. I could hardly remembered walking to the bathroom, much less putting a towel on top of myself, but that's where I was.

My chills were gone. The fever had broken, but my stomach was still painful and I still felt nauseous. I pulled myself off the floor and went to the kitchen to make a cup of hot tea. Sitting down in my wicker rocking chair, I could feel the warmth of the sun shining through the window soothe my aching body. I watched robins searching for earthworms in the backyard. The sunlight glistened on their black wings and along the crest of their head.

The tea had settled my restless stomach. I closed my eyes as I listened to the birds continue to sing. It was so peaceful. The rhythmic motion of the rocker and the warmth of the sun lulled me back to sleep.

A soft voice behind me whispered, "Emma."

I jumped and turned to look, but no one was there. Chills ran up my spine.

"Another fever setting in," I thought to myself. *"I've got to get to the doctors."* I reached for the phone.

I dialed my doctor's office and a friendly voice greeted me.

"Dr. Stephen's office, this is Amy speaking, how can I help you?"

"Hi, this is Emma Stafford," my voice croaked, "I'm sick and I would like to come in today."

Amy replied, "Please hold, I don't know that we have any appointments available today."

The phone clicked as I was put on hold and music filled my ear. "Everything I Do" by Bryan Adams was playing and my groggy mind drifted to Eric again. I could feel his body pressed against mine as we danced at homecoming, his voice singing every word softly in my ear.

"Emma?" Amy's voice interrupted my day dream.

"Yes?" I replied.

"You're in luck. A 9:45 appointment just opened up. Can you make it in?"

Surprised I could be seen so soon, I answered, "Yes, I'll be there."

* * *

The jovial lines on Dr. Stephen's face overlay the lines clearly etched by the years of care and fulfillment, that he received treating thousands of patients. He had found his calling, and the positive effect it had on his life radiated from him. His wavy blond hair was neatly disheveled and streaked with gray. His blue eyes twinkled. I wondered if Jared would have one day looked like this if he had survived. "Hello, Emma! I haven't seen you in a while! What's been going on?" He smiled as he reached into his perfectly pressed white coat for a pen to take notes.

"I've been really sick," I replied. "I've been nauseous a lot. My stomach hurts and now I have a fever."

"When did it start?" Dr. Stephen's asked as his flipped through the papers in my file.

"I'm not really sure. It's been awhile, gradually getting worse over the past couple months. I thought I was just having trouble dealing with Jared's death, but now I think it might be more."

"Hmmm . . ." he responded, as he finished looking over my file. "How are you doing now, emotionally?"

"A lot better." I responded, truthfully.

"Good. Well, you have lost over 20 pounds since we last saw you over a year ago. Have you been dieting?"

"No." I shook my head, "No, I just didn't feel like eating. My stomach hurts a lot, and I get nauseous really easily so . . . ."

"How long has this been going on, again?"

"Months, but now it's different, I have a fever."

A look of concern flashed across Dr. Stephen's face and he moved toward the exam table that I had been sitting on. "I see. Please lay back on the table and let me have a look."

Dr. Stephen pressed on my stomach. I winced in pain.

"Did that hurt?" He asked.

"Yeah." I responded, relieved he wasn't pressing on my abdomen any more.

"Okay, Emma. You need to have a CT Scan of your abdomen. I'm a little concerned about the prolonged pain and lack of appetite and I want to get a good picture of what is going on in there. Until the results come in, eat a bland diet and keep yourself hydrated. Drink water, caffeine-free tea and get plenty of rest. Your fever seems to be gone, but if it comes back take 600 mg of ibuprofen. It will help. I'll have Susan call the radiology department and have her set up an appointment for you, STAT."

When he finished, I said, "Thanks, Dr. Stephen."

"No problem," he responded, playfully punching me on the shoulder. "But next time you feel this sick or painful for so long, come in sooner, okay?"

"I will," I smiled.

Coincidentally, radiology had a cancellation as well, and I was able to get the CT scan done within the hour. By the time I had gotten home from both appointments, I was exhausted and crawled into bed. I slept soundly through the rest of the day and through the night, only awakening because the early morning sun streamed directly onto my face.

Fortunately, my fever was still gone, but my stomach still ached horribly and I still felt nauseous. I fixed a cup of tea and grabbed a banana, to try to eat some breakfast.

At 9:00, the phone rang.

A woman's soft voice spoke quietly on the other line, "Hello, may I please speak with Mrs. Emma Stafford?"

"Yes, this is Emma." I replied.

"Hi, Emma, this is Susan at Dr. Stephen's office. We have received the results of your test and we would like to meet with you later today."

My heart skipped a beat, and my mind started to race with the possibilities.

"Okay, what time?" my voice shook as I asked.

"Is 3:00 convenient for you?"

"Yes, I can be there at 3:00."

"Okay, We'll see you then." She responded sweetly and hung up the phone.

I hung up my phone and slowly sank down onto the cold hardwood floor. "This can't be good" I spoke out loud. "If the results were fine, they wouldn't ask to see me, right?"

But no one answered. I was alone. Jared had been killed. I had no kids. My father was dead, and my mom was in Italy. I felt hollow inside and my head throbbed from the silence and emptiness that surrounded me. I was unequivocally, desperately alone and now terrified about my health.

"Emma." A voice whispered behind me.

Startled, I jumped up and looked around. This time I had no fever. I had clearly heard my name.

"Who's there?" I demanded.

But there was no response.

* * *

I arrived at Dr. Stephen's office thirty minutes early. My fingers felt bony and cold, as I clasped my hands nervously in my lap, waiting. Outdated magazines were stacked in precarious piles on the side tables that sat among the rows of chairs that held patients anxiously waiting for their appointments. Dr. Stephen briefly stepped into the waiting room, as he quietly directed a medical assistant to her next managerial task. When he glanced around the room, his gaze met mine and the corners of his mouth lifted in an apologetic smile. He turned and left the room.

"Great." I said under my breath.

Time crept by until my name was finally called. I was ushered into Dr. Stephen's office where he was standing behind his dark cherry desk, waiting for me. He greeted me with a smile and gestured toward a chair. "Hi, Emma. Have a seat."

My eyes followed him as he slowly walked around his desk to close the dark wooden door behind me. His strong shoulders lifted then relaxed as he released an audible sigh before returning to his desk to take a seat.

Dr. Stephen faced me, his startling blues eyes boring into mine. "Emma, your test results have come back and I am sorry to say I have some bad news. You have a tumor on your pancreas and multiple masses in your liver. We won't know for sure until we have a biopsy, but it is most likely pancreatic cancer."

I must have been holding my breath because I suddenly found myself gasping for air and all I could mutter was "Oh."

"We need to start treatment immediately. First we need to have a surgical consult with Dr. Payden to confirm whether it is cancer or not. Then an oncologist will start an aggressive treatment with chemotherapy and radiation."

"I . . . I have cancer?" I interrupted.

Dr. Stephen head nodded slowly up and down. "Most likely, Emma. I am so sorry. Please know that we have a fantastic team that can help you fight this and we are going to do everything we can to prolong your life for the longest time possible."

I bit my lip, "Prolong my life? I can beat this, right?"

"We can hope. It looks like metastatic, stage four pancreatic cancer right now. We need to do more testing and treatments to know exactly what we are facing."

"Stage four?" I asked. "I *can* beat this."

Dr. Stephen's face hardened and his voice became almost robotic, "There is a four percent survival rate for five years if it is, in fact, stage four pancreatic cancer." The lines on his face softened as he continued, "We are all going to do everything we can, to the best of our abilities, to beat this. We have a wonderful team of doctors."

I sunk into my chair trying to grasp my new reality. I never felt more alone than I did at that moment. I had no one with me. No shoulder to cry on. No one to tell me it was going to be okay. I was facing the biggest challenge of my life, alone. I was in shock and at a loss for words, "But . . . I . . ."

"Emma, do you have someone I can call for you? Someone who can be here for you right now?"

"Um . . . I don't know." I couldn't think. I stuttered. "I . . . I have some friends but . . . . um . . . . No, no one to call right now." I didn't want to burden my friends with this. Not yet. Not now. I continued, "Right now, I need to deal with this alone."

As soon as these words escaped my mouth, a cool breeze kissed my neck and a cold hand grasped my shoulder, but I didn't jump until I heard the words, "You will not be alone," whispered in my ear.

* * *

I left Dr. Stephen's office shaken to the core, but for the moment, I felt strangely at peace. I kept envisioning Eric holding me in the light, and I desperately held on to that image. I decided that if I had to face my own death, it was okay to focus on whatever brought me comfort, and the vision of Eric did. I released the guilt inside me.

When I got home, I made a cup of tea, and sat at the kitchen table in silence, trying to grasp what was to come. The hum of the refrigerator vibrated in my ear as I stared at my distorted reflection in the toaster. "It looks like I have cancer, stage-four cancer," I thought. "I can fight, but the chance of me surviving is small." I tried to diminish the fear that gripped me. I really didn't want to die alone. I considered calling my mother, but what could she do. She was still in Italy, on her fourth or fifth boyfriend, sleeping her way to the most wealthy lifestyle she could obtain. She wouldn't leave that for me. She'd already shown she was more than willing to abandon me repeatedly. Why would she come back to help me die from cancer? It would be too tough for her fragile soul.

I sighed and a cold tear rolled down me cheek. I continued to think, "And Jared is gone. Erica and Alex were just transferred to Quantico. I'm not close enough to my friends around here to really burden them with something like this, and Jared's parents . . . no . . . the pain they've been through is too much. I could never ask them."

A vision of Eric kept flashing in my mind, and his name escaped my lips, "Eric."

A feeling in the pit of my stomach pulled me to the attic stairs. I got up from the kitchen table and slowly climbed the cramped staircase hidden in the back of the pantry to the small, dusty upstairs storage area of the cottage. When I reached the floor of the attic, I stubbed my toe on a musty, cardboard box that was sitting at the top of the stairs. "What the hell?" I cried out loud, more startled than hurt. I knew I hadn't put the box there. In fact, I hadn't seen this box for years.

I kicked the box out of the way with my other foot, and the top of it opened, revealing piles of old pictures and letters inside. Curiosity pulled me to the box, so I picked it up and carried it to the middle of the room to sit under the single, cobweb covered light bulb lighting the area. Piles of old, musty boxes, Jared's old CD collection, discarded clothes and an old, broken radio and T.V. set surrounded me. I searched through the box, and as I dug deeper and deeper into it, I found myself watching a slideshow of my life in reverse. There were pictures of Jared and I on our wedding day, pictures of our college graduations, pictures of us hanging out with Erica and Alex. Then there were pictures of Jared and I at the community college with Judy and pictures of Beth and I at our high school graduation. Beth looked beautiful. I stared at her picture and wondered where she was now and if she was happy. As I dug deeper into the box, my breath suddenly stopped. A picture of

Eric stared up at me. My heart, too, stopped briefly and tears started to flow. The love I had ignored and pushed away for so many years flourished in my heart and I ached to be near Eric again. I could still feel the magic I felt when I looked into his eyes. I could still feel the piercing pain of our breakup. I had never stopped loving him. It had taken everything within me to move on without him and I had. I never regretted my life with Jared, but there was no way I could love anyone like I loved Eric.

I looked into the box again and found the picture Eric gave me when he came home from the beach the week before homecoming. Inside a heart drawn in the sand at the beach it read, "I love you, Pumpkin," and on the back of the photograph in faded black ink read the words "I miss you, Emma. There is never a moment that you aren't in my heart or on my mind. Love forever, Eric."

I whispered out loud, "Eric, do you remember me? Do you still feel the love we had like I do?"

Knowing I spoke only to the bursting boxes and the cluttered mess that surrounded me, I put my head in my hands and sobbed, "I hope you know how much I have always loved you!"

My crying ceased as a cool breeze blew across my neck. Behind me, I heard a click and then a static buzz that sounded like someone tuning a radio. I stood up to look behind me and watched as the tuner on the unplugged, broken radio spun by itself, the spinning metal on the knobs reflecting the light, searching through the radio stations.

The tuner stopped abruptly and Skid Row's "I Remember You" burst from the speakers. The sudden noise made me jump and I fell to the floor. I recognized it instantly. It was one of Eric's favorite songs.

My body shook violently from the sudden coldness I felt in the attic, along with the shock of the music playing from the broken radio. Immediately after the song ended, the radio turned off and the room filled with warmth again.

My voice quivered, "Eric?" I pulled myself up from the floor, straining my ears, hoping to hear a reply. No reply ever came.

I didn't leave the attic for hours. I sifted through the boxes, throwing away old junk, figuring if I was going to die, someone had to go through this mess, and it might as well be me. Honestly, I was also hoping to find an answer to the mysterious radio incident and was secretly praying that something else would happen. I wondered who was trying to contact me. Everything pointed to Eric, but was it Jared? Regardless, believing someone was with me and that someone was trying to reach me, took the pang of loneliness away. Unfortunately, the attic remained quiet.

By evening I was exhausted: My arms and back ached from moving boxes back and forth, my knees felt bruised from pressing into the hard floor for so long and my mind was tired from the racing thoughts that continuously streamed through my head. I begrudgingly admitted to myself that I had probably done too much in my condition. After grabbing a plain bagel and a banana to eat, I crawled into bed and quickly fell into a restless sleep. Visions of Eric began to fill my dreams when I was suddenly awoken by a soft voice whispering in my ear, "Emma."

Sitting up quickly, I turned on the light. No one was in my room. I flipped the switch and the room filled with darkness again. As I snuggled back down into my covers and drifted back to sleep, I was suddenly disturbed by the feeling that someone was sitting at the end of my bed. I jumped up and turned the light on again.

My heart pounded and the hairs on the back of my neck stood erect as I stared at the imprint at the end of my bed. The icy air that surrounded me, combined with the sheer terror I suddenly felt, caused my body to shake violently. I stared at the foot of my bed, refusing to blink. Nausea overwhelmed me. The air felt charged with cold electricity.

Slowly, a shapeless black mist spiraled in the area where a person should have been at the end of my bed.

"Who are you?" I asked, terrified I'd receive a response.

No response could be heard.

"Why are you here?" I asked, my voice shaking as violently as my body. My clenched hand moved forward to feel the blackness in front of me. My hand felt as though it had just entered a freezer. I opened my hand stretching my fingers in the mist, which began to spiral more rapidly, causing a cold breeze to encircle my hand. Then the mist suddenly disappeared, the imprint lifted, and warm air surged around my hand. Whatever it was, was gone.

As the chill receded, warmth hugged my body. My nerves stopped firing and exhilaration filled me. "That was incredible," I thought. It was just like those "Spirit Hunters" shows I had watched with Jen, but better!

Spirit Hunters! Realization hit me. EVPs, electric voice phenomena! I realized that if I had some sort of recorder, it may pick up a voice I cannot hear, and if I was lucky, that voice may let me know who it is and why they are here! I ran to my bedroom closet, spilling out the contents of old boxes looking for Jared's old digital recorder. I hoped and prayed it wasn't in storage. I emptied box after box with no luck. Then I heard a thump in the attic. My bare feet grew cold as I ran through the house turning on every light in every room as I ran to the attic. When I reached the top of the stairs, another box was placed haphazardly in the middle of the doorway. My eyes searched the surroundings as a cold breeze brushed gently against my skin, sending chills up my spine. I scanned the air, looking for another black mist, but found none.

I dropped to my knees, my hands shaking as I opened the box. There, on top of everything, was Jared's digital recorder.

"Thank you." I whispered, my eyes still searching the room. I pushed myself up and ran to the kitchen to grab some fresh AAA batteries. Once I put them in, I ran back to my bedroom, crawled into the bed and pulled the covers up around me.

I pressed the record button. A red light appeared. The digital recorder was recording. "Hi!" My voice rattled. "Who are you?" I asked.

Cold air seeped into my room, dropping the temperature by several degrees and I shivered. I waited for a reply, then asked, "Why are you here?"

I watched in amazement as a depression formed at the end of my bed. My heart pounded loudly in my ears. I shuddered in fear and excitement. I knew whatever it was, whoever it was, was not here to hurt me. It was here to help.

I looked down to make sure the digital recorder was on. The red light had gone out. I pressed record again but the light did not come on. The recorder was dead. Maybe it was battery drain, I chuckled to myself, just like on Spirit Hunters! I had learned that there was a theory that ghosts or spirits could drain the energy out of electronic devices when they were trying to manifest themselves. Perhaps this was happening now.

"Hold on" I spoke out loud. "I need to get more batteries." I ran back to the kitchen, grabbed a couple more batteries, but my shaking hands kept dropping them as I tried to replace them in the recorder. Once I had finally managed to get them in, I pressed record to make sure it was working. It was. I ran back to my room, hesitating at the door before I walked in. The air in my room had chilled so much it felt like I was walking into a deep cave. I took a deep breath and walked inside.

"Hello?" I called out. I looked at the end of my bed. The depression was gone, but the temperature in the room made it clear that I was not alone. I looked at the digital recorder. The light was still on. I continued, "Um, this is a digital recorder. In theory, if you say something, I may be able to hear what you say on this machine."

"Who are you?" I sat and waited.

"Why are you here?" My ears could not detect any answer or noise.

"Jared, is this you?" I asked, my voice cracked as tears filled my eyes.

"If so, I love you and I miss you."

The cold air seemed to swirl around me. "Is there something you want to tell me?"

Still, no audible answers could be heard.

I turned off the recorder and rewound it. Immediately after it stopped, I turned up the volume and hit play.

Static crackled as I listened to my own voice, "Who are you?" More static, but no detectable answer.

Then, my recorded voice asked, "Why are you here?" As I listened to myself sitting in silence, I heard on the recorder a strong, low whisper that sounded like, "You." I stopped and rewound it. Sure enough, I clearly heard, "You." I continued to listen. "Jared is this you?" Silence followed. There was no response. "If so, I love you and I miss you." The coldness in the room seemed to deepen as the recorder played on. I found myself shaking even harder, not from fear, but from the cold. In fact, I found myself feeling strangely at peace.

"Is there something you want to tell me?" My voice echoed. Even though the volume was as high as it could go, I put the speaker up to my ear. Static crinkled, but within it, a low male voice responded, "Call your mom. Call Erica."

I gasped and pressed record again. The red power light glowed. "You want me to call my mom and Erica?" I asked the empty cold room.

I sat for a moment then pressed stop and rewind. I listened to my recorded voice, "You want me to call my mom and Erica?"

Static rattled; then the disembodied voice spoke, "You are not alone."

A sudden burst of warm air hit my body, chasing away the cold chill that had oppressed me. The room suddenly felt light and airy. The "ghost" was gone, but his sudden absence left me feeling uneasy. The peace I felt inside of me when he was present was comforting, but the words spoken comforted me even more. Apparently, I was not alone as I had feared. Someone was here watching over me, but who? Jared was dead, Dad was dead, but it was Eric's face that kept coming to me. Was Eric dead, too?

Whoever it was, he wanted me to call my mom and Erica. He didn't want me facing cancer alone.

I picked up the phone and dialed my mother's number. It had been months since the last time we spoke. She picked up the phone on the second ring. "Hello?" She answered, her voice heavy with sleep.

"Mom?" I said, cracking from the sudden surge of emotion within me.

She sounded startled, "Emma? What's wrong?"

"Mom, I need you. I have cancer."

Chapter: Cassie

CANCER. MY BABY HAS CANCER.

These words reverberated in my mind, a haunting echo as the intensity of its meaning tore a hole in my heart.

As soon as I hung up the phone, I headed for the liquor cabinet. I poured some scotch, and swallowed the entire glass before collapsing to the floor. "Why?" I cried, "Why?"

Images of Emma's short life flashed in my mind. Christ, it had not been easy: First the rape, then her abortion, then her father went and died on us, then Jared went and got himself killed. Now stage four pancreatic cancer? What the bloody hell! I pulled myself up from the Persian carpet, feeling the silk of my nightgown cling to my body. I walked over to my dressing mirror and looked into my own, black, empty eyes.

"Cursed." I said aloud as I poured another glass full of scotch and drank it down. "Yes, Emma is cursed." Hot tears fell. "Cursed from birth . . . and to have a mother like me."

I threw the empty scotch glass across the room and watch as it shattered into a thousand pieces.

My bedroom door slammed open and Frederick ran in, a look of shock in his amber eyes, his salt and pepper hair disheveled. "Kassi! Vat ees tse matter?" Vat ees se meeneeng off dis?" his heavily accented voice demanded.

Fred's eyes were ablaze as he took in the shattered crystal lying on the floor. I noticed his blue jeans and white T-shirt were speckled in paint. He must have been working again.

I poured another glass of scotch and downed it, then crumpled to my knees and cried, "My baby has cancer. Emma has cancer."

His eyes softened, "Ach, shooley dis ees kurrable! Zey arr not SO far behind in Amerrika, or?"

"No, Frederick. It's stage four pancreatic cancer. It doesn't look good." I couldn't look at him. Regret filled me, unraveling my resolve to maintain that the lifestyle I had chosen was right. "How? I can't believe I . . . . How could I abandon her for all these years? Now she may die and I . . . ." The reality of the last eight years gripped me. Emma needed me after the rape and after the abortion, but I wasn't there, not really, and I unintentionally spread the news of the abortion. I had tried to avoid her at all cost: I couldn't stand the pain in her eyes. I had wanted it to disappear and go away, but it didn't. I stood and silently watched as her pain had slowly torn her soul apart.

James had grown distant as well and he had become obsessed with finding the rapist. Strangely, once the rapist was found dead, James grew even more distant from all of us. I always wondered if he was upset that he didn't get to kill the bastard himself. Something preoccupied him. Something, but what?

Then he went and died in Emma's arms, leaving me alone, with no final words of love . . . but he made sure Emma knew he cared about her. That bastard. After over 20 years of being together, he only managed to tell his daughter that he loved her. I resented Emma for many reasons but I hated her for that.

But it wasn't her fault, was it? No, but I ran. Ran away to find a new life. Italy captivated me: the art, the architecture, the wine and the men. Oh, I could play the men. I could get everything I ever wanted or needed: fine homes, jewelry, the best clothes, food and wine. I found a world I could escape to, a world I could be happy in. I easily forgot about my girl, a woman really, she could take care of herself by then. I had hated being a mother. I knew from the moment I conceived Emma that I wouldn't be a good one, and I wasn't.

But Emma stayed strong and moved on, going to college and marrying that hunk of a man, Jared. But Jared's hero complex got the most of him and he got himself blown up, leaving poor Emma the victim again. Oh, poor Emma . . .

"God, listen to myself! I'm horrid." I cried out loud. "I've been a horrible mother!" I had forgotten that Frederick was behind me and his voice made me jump.

"Vell, I do not know zat zat ees so chorible," Fred said, "but you can visit cher now und do vat ees possible to, er, 'make up' mit cher."

"Yes, yes I could." I considered this, but I was frightened.

Frederick placed his hand on my shoulder. The wrinkles around his eyes smiled reassuringly as he encouraged me to go home. "Talk wit her. Make peace wit her. Show her dat you have some sympathy, or, er, support for her. Eet ees not yet tsoo late." He paused then continued, "You I vill miss. I vill . . . but you must do so, as I said." His hand patted my back, emphasizing each word.

Frederick booked the earliest flight for me that he could for Saturday morning and made reservations to have me picked up at the airport. I had a couple day's time to pack my belongings and take care of ending my life in Italy. I planned to stay with Emma indefinitely. I had no idea how I would handle my child being so ill and very possibly dying, but I became resolved to be there, trying to be the strong, attentive and caring mother she had always deserved.

As I started to empty my drawers into my suitcases, my mind explored the past. I realized how miserably I had failed every other time Emma needed me. I had crumbled internally every time I watched her struggle with the pain. I clearly remembered drinking excessively and running from the house every time she needed me to be a parent. I couldn't handle it. Then that loser Eric showed up. Oh, how I resented Eric. He would stay with her and hold her and talk to her. Eric subtly let me know that I disgusted him. He despised me. I could see by the look in his eyes how he felt . . . like I was a failure as a mother. But now I knew—he was right.

I started to sift through the clothes hanging in my closet and wondered what ever happened to Eric. "He's probably some burned out bum somewhere," I snorted to myself.

"Well, I'll be the one there for her now." I smiled, "It's the least I can do."

My chest clenched and my heart started pounding rapidly. I went to the medicine cabinet and swallowed some anxiety drugs then lay down on my silk comforter.

"Yes," I thought as I drifted into an intoxicated slumber, "Yes, it's the least I can do."

Chapter: Erica

I'LL NEVER FORGET THE CALL. It was just after breakfast on a Wednesday morning. I was cleaning off the oatmeal Henry had smeared all over his little face when the phone rang.

"Hello?" I answered.

Emma's voice sounded weak and empty on the other end. "Hey, girl. I really need you right now. You have a minute?"

"Of course, Hon. What's up?"

Emma sighed, "Oh, girl . . . I've got cancer."

The phone dropped out of my hand and I scooped it off of the floor as I released Henry from his high chair. "Please tell me I heard you wrong." I replied. "You did not just tell me that you have cancer, right?"

Emma laughed weakly, "Yeah, I wish. I have cancer. Pancreatic cancer."

"Is that bad?" I asked, not wanting the answer.

"Well, for me it is. I'm going to fight it, hard, but I might not have that much time left. I hate to ask you this, but could you come see me for a couple days? I could really use some company."

"I'm on my way. Let me take care of a few things. Is Friday okay?"

"Yeah, that would be great."

"I'll get Henry's grandparents to watch him a few days. They'll love spending time with him."

Emma replied, "Thank you so much, Erica."

I tried to stay strong, but I could feel my voice crack. An ugly cry was coming on. "I'll be there, girl. Soon. Love you."

"Love you, too!"

When I hung up the phone, tears burst from my eyes. How in the hell could Emma have cancer, after all she had been through already? I pulled myself together and called Alex to let him know what was going on. Then I arranged for Alex's parents to watch Henry while Alex was at work. They were more than happy to do it.

I walked over to Henry, picked him up and held him close, immersing myself in the sweet smell of his skin. I placed him on my hip and started to pack my things. He strained to get down to go play with his toys, but I didn't want to let him go. Life suddenly seemed too short and too fragile to me. Henry struggled against me as he said, "Momo." I hugged him close to my chest, one more time, treasuring the feel of his soft breath against my neck. When I finally let him down to go play, I silently prayed that I could protect him from all the pain life can bring.

Chapter: Emma

It was Wednesday. I had called Mom and Erica like my protector suggested, and both were on their way. Erica would be driving up from Quantico, and would arrive on Friday, and Mom would be flying in on Saturday. I was not going to be alone.

I decided to spend my day in the garden. I wanted to feel the dirt between my fingers, smell the earth and feel alive. Ironically, I felt better than I had for quite some time—maybe because I finally knew the cause of this latest pain; maybe because I didn't feel alone. Whatever it was, I treasured feeling whole, complete and alive, even though I knew this feeling would be fleeting.

The humid, flower-scented, summer air filled my lungs and the hot summer sun warmed my back. I knelt down and started to pull up the purple clover that had started to spread beyond the border of my garden. Suddenly, a cold chill ran up my spine and I felt as if someone was watching me. Instinct made me turn and look at the bay window that overlooked the garden, but no one was standing there. My eyes scanned the window, searching for a black mist, but there was none to be found. I looked beyond the window, and noticed my wicker rocking chair was slowly rocking back and forth as if someone was sitting in it. I stood up to face it head on, and it stopped. I smiled, shook off the chills and allowed the sun to warm me again. "I'm glad I'm not alone." I thought to myself and I turned to start weeding again.

I lost myself in the mulch, the dirt, the flowers and the bird songs. Before I knew it, hours had passed. Resting, I sat against the western side of the willow tree's trunk, bathing in the warm, blinding brightness that shined through the hanging willow branches. The bright light and warmth of my skin, reminded me of my dreams of Eric and I smiled to myself. I rested my eyes and enjoyed feeling alive. When I slowly reopened them, I jumped. A semitransparent outline of a man stood right in front of me. My heart missed a beat, and my mouth could hardly form the words that wanted to escape, "Jared, is that you?"

A cool breeze kissed my face as the cloudy image shading bits of the sunlight moved closer. I pushed myself up into a crouch to see who it was.

Once he was close enough for me to see his face, I didn't want to blink, fearing that he would disappear.

I never expected to see a ghost of my past standing before me, but there he stood, transparent, strong and beautiful. He was older than I had remembered him: the contours of his face had matured and he had a five o'clock shadow. His gorgeous eyes took my breath away. I had dreamed of looking into those intense, brown eyes, the ones staring into mine at that moment. His semitransparent body glowed in the light and he wore a pair of jeans and a black T-shirt. One hand laid casually at his side and the other was stuck in the front pocket of his jeans.

"Eric!" I gasped.

Eric smiled, "Hey, Pumpkin."

I stood transfixed, looking at the ghostly shadow of the man I had always loved with my entire heart and soul.

"I don't understand," I started, "have you . . . are you . . ."

"I had to find you, Emma. Once I knew what was to happen, I knew I couldn't let you be alone."

I continued to stutter, "But you . . . are you . . . what?" I was confused. All the signs pointed to Eric, but I still believed the spirit had been Jared's. I couldn't believe Eric had died, too.

Eric stepped closer, pushing another cold breeze through me.

I stepped back, "You're the ghost? You're dead?"

"Yes, I died, but as you can see, I'm still very much here." Eric chuckled and his smile melted me.

I stared at him in disbelief, "How, when did you die?"

"The day after Jared's funeral, I had seen your picture on the front page of 'The Crier.' I was running back home so I could come find you when a petty thief shot me. And . . . well . . . it doesn't matter. I'm here now."

"Oh my God." I replied, "Where's Jared? Have you seen Jared?"

Eric nodded his head. "Yes, I have seen him. He knows I'm here . . ."

"Well, where is he?"

The intensity of the look Eric gave me made me turn away. He answered hesitantly, "He'll be coming, later."

"Oh." I shivered as questions filled my mind.

"So, um, how come I can see you now?"

Eric chuckled again as he took another step forward, "It's hard to do this appearing stuff. I had never done it before, so it took me awhile to get the hang of it. I really don't know how long I'll last this time." I watched as he lifted up his arms and hands and moved them back and forth in front of himself, studying his own body, with a look of amazement in his eyes.

I raised my eyebrows and found myself laughing. "Okay . . ."

Eric tried to explain, "I have to pull energy from the environment around me to appear and so I can speak loud enough for you to hear. I kept making the mistake of only coming at night, when there is little electricity being used and no solar energy."

I thought about the battery drain I had experienced. The lack of more energy must have allowed him to appear only as a mist.

"It's frustrating," Eric continued, "kind of like trying to drive a stick shift with the emergency brake on. No matter how perfectly I tried to shift, something was holding me back, and wouldn't let my body change gears, but instead of a brake, it was a lack of energy and me not knowing how to channel it."

I smiled and shook my head. Even in death, Eric was still all about cars.

Eric took another step closer and he stared at me. His eyes became serious and he bit his lip. "God, Emma. I've missed you so much."

"I've missed you, too." A tear rolled down my cheek.

Eric's face searched mine, "Can I try to hold you?"

I nodded my head and he came toward me. I stood completely still as he wrapped his arms around me. The hairs on my body stood on end as a cool electricity surrounded me. Eric's body felt like a pillow of cold air as it pressed against mine. I carefully placed my hands and head on his chest, aware that they could travel right through his being if I pressed too hard. He wrapped me in his arms and sighed. Although I felt chilled to the bones, I felt more at peace than I had in years. I may have thought I remembered how it felt to be near Eric, but I had forgotten the intensity of the bond we had between us. Another tear rolled down my cheek.

Eric slowly pulled away and he carefully tried to wipe the tear with his semitransparent fingers, but he couldn't touch it.

He shook his head and smiled, "Oh, well." He cupped my chin in his hands and said, "We did it though."

"Did what?" I asked.

"We succeeded so well in this life that we've earned being together in our next one."

I stepped back to look at him, "What?" I asked in amazement. "What do you mean?"

Eric answered, "Well, you know how you always had that feeling that we were not meant to be together?"

I nodded.

"You were right, about this lifetime anyway, and that was entirely my fault." Eric looked away and continued, "Apparently, I hadn't been choosing the right paths in my past lives. I kept taking the easy way out, doing drugs, alcohol, never facing the problems head on, to better myself and the people around me. Our souls have not been together for many lifetimes, but we were brought together in this one. Being with you made me remember how things could be and when I lost you, something deep inside of me refused to let me fail again. I know it sounds crazy, but a voice inside of me kept encouraging, "If you make the right decisions in this lifetime, you can be with your twin flame in the next." Well, I knew you had to be my twin flame, and believing in the truth of that voice, I began making better choices. We were brought together, then separated in this lifetime, so a part of us, deep down inside would remember what we were working for: to be together again. We both had to overcome our failings, independently, and we did."

I was confused, "Twin flame? What's that? I thought we were soul mates?"

Eric smiled. "No, Jared's your soul mate. Well, one of them at least. I'm your twin flame. Our souls are independent, yet one—a mirror image of each other. You are my yin, I am your yang."

Eric stepped toward me again, and reached out to touch my hand, a cold pillow of air wrapping around it. "While I lived, there was not one day I didn't think about you. I love you so much." He stopped to look at me again. I couldn't speak a word.

He continued, "I got over all my addictions, got through college, and had planned to become a psychologist, before I got killed."

The words Eric spoke were almost too much to comprehend. We stood in silence and thoughts and questions ran through my mind. So, they are true: life after death and reincarnation. I had thought so, but now here was 'living' proof. I chuckled. Wow.

Then I realized, Eric saw what he had to overcome, but what about me. What was it that I had to overcome? I remembered thinking I had killed myself in a previous lifetime. Did I? Why weren't Eric and I together for so many lifetimes? What did we do wrong? I always thought we were soul mates, but twin flames? What did that mean and where were we going from here? And Jared? How did Jared fit in all of this? I loved him so much, too. It made sense that he was my soul mate, but wait? *What?* Things had gotten even more complicated.

I turned to face Eric. I didn't know where to begin. "Whew! I have so many questions! So, what was I supposed to accomplish?"

I noticed Eric's image begin to flicker before me, and the outlines of his body started to fade into the sunlight. He answered, "So much . . . . you . . ." his mouth still moved, but I couldn't hear the words he spoke.

"Eric?" I called out. The pillow of cold air that had wrapped around my hand was replaced by warmth as Eric's ghost faded away. I could not hear a word he said, but could read his lips before he disappeared completely. They said, "I love you."

I longed to see Eric again but he didn't appear anymore that day. That evening, I worked frantically to clean my house before the biopsy that would occur the following morning. As I prepared for my mom and Erica's arrival, I wondered if the energy Eric had expended on his appearance rendered him incapable of appearing again, and if so, for how long. I constantly glanced over my shoulder, hoping to catch a glimpse of a moving shadow, or feel a cold breeze. I changed the sheets in the guest rooms, thoroughly cleaned the bathrooms and removed the clutter that had accumulated on every horizontal surface. By 8:00 that evening, the house was immaculate and smelled of bleach and Pine-sol. I collapsed in an exhausted heap on my bed.

* * *

The next morning, I found myself lying on a rough, white stretcher, in the interventional radiology recovery area at Mercy Medical Center. I was wearing only a bright pink hospital gown, a pair of underwear and a pair of white socks and was waiting to receive an ultrasound guided liver biopsy. The blue-paisley patterned curtains that enclosed me danced in the wake of the multitude of nurses and doctors that walked by. I watched anxiously as a technician slid my records into a plastic holder at the nurses station. A clock ticked loudly in the hallway. Footsteps and voices continued to ebb and wane, as I desperately waited for someone to come talk to me. Finally, a squat little man named Dr. Young entered the room. Although small in stature, he had a very domineering presence—his jet black hair meticulously in place, his glasses and shoes well-shined and his hands perfectly manicured. His demeanor made one feel as though he was in control of the world. Considering my life was at stake, this didn't bother me one bit.

Dr. Young talked me through the procedure, preparing me for what was to come. I tried my best to listen, but fear gripped me. Two words, biopsy and cancer, echoed in the cavernous regions of my brain. My body broke out in a cold sweat and my field of vision turned white. Dr. Young's voice grew distant as I repeatedly came close to a total black out, but each time I came close to passing out, a cool breeze would kiss my forehead, bringing me back from the tunnel of light my unconscious brain kept pulling me to. Eric was with me, and knowing he was present helped me stay strong through the entire procedure.

Once the biopsy was complete, I took my time getting dressed, hailed a taxi and made my way home. My abdomen throbbed in pain and I was exhausted from the entire ordeal. When I got home, I grabbed a tall glass of ice tea and curled up on the couch. In a tired daze, I found my eyes searching the room for a black mist, but there was none.

A sigh escaped my lips. "Eric?" I whispered softly. Feeling stronger and a little more brave, I called out again, this time more loudly, "Eric?"

A cool breeze blew across me. Realizing that Eric would need energy to appear, I got up and turned on every light and appliance I could, hoping it would help. Light bounced off every gleaming surface as the room hummed with electricity.

My painful and exhausted body suddenly felt exhilarated as I saw a black shadow start to form in front of me. I watched as a small area of swirling black mist slowly grew and expanded until the shadowy outline of Eric's body stood before me. His shadow flickered in the light, forming and disappearing before my eyes.

I urged him on, "Come on, Eric. You can do it." The lights in the room began to flicker as his shadow grew stronger, and soon I could see the details of his face.

"Hey! I knew you could do it" I winked at him as I slowly pulled myself off the couch. Pain from the biopsy made me wince. "Thanks for coming to the hospital today."

Eric smiled weakly at me and he reached out to grab my hand. The cold grasped my hand and quickly spread through me.

Eric's form seemed weaker than it had the day before and when he spoke, I could barely hear his words. "How are you?" he whispered.

"Okay." I replied, and even in the midst of all my abdominal pain and all the fear I felt as I waited for the biopsy results, I honestly meant it.

"Good." He smiled. "Your mom and Erica will be here soon?"

"Yeah, Erica tomorrow. Mom, Saturday."

"Good." He answered again.

We sat down on the couch. Eric continued to hold my hand.

I turned toward him and said, "So, I guess my results are bad, huh?"

Eric looked shocked at my question. His eyes met mine briefly, then he turned to look away. He didn't say anything.

I pressed on, "That's why you're here, right?"

Eric's eyes turned back to mine as he replied, "Yeah, more or less. It's complicated."

"Explain it to me then." I demanded.

He hesitated, then answered, "Well, like I was saying before, you and I had a lot we could potentially accomplish in this lifetime. Well, we did. In fact, the elders told me we far exceeded their expectations this time and that's why I was allowed to come back to you," Eric paused as he looked down at his body, "like this."

"What do you mean by all that?" I asked. "Please tell me, I have so many questions."

"Like what?" he asked. I watched him closely as his shadowy form seemed to grow stronger before me.

"First, why are you really back here, like this. Why didn't you just move on?"

Eric smiled at me, and reached up to touch my cheek. "The most basic reason is that you are my flame and until you join me and we choose our next paths in life, I wasn't going to move on. We've been separated for too long now. I didn't want to move on without you if it meant we'd spend another lifetime apart. I was told that you and I were free to choose to live our next life together, and there was no way I would give that up for anything. I've missed you too much.

"Furthermore, I didn't want you to be alone in death. You've been through too much to die alone. I asked the elders and they said your collective consciousness had grown enough to grasp my appearance, so they allowed me to come."

"So that means . . . I'm dying?" I whispered.

Eric looked away suddenly and bit the inside of his cheeks. He looked guilty as if he had said something he wasn't supposed to.

I changed the subject, "The elders? Who are the elders?" My mind drifted back seeing Eric in the light, surrounded by the other ghostly figures after I was raped. "Were they the other figures standing with you in the light?"

Eric responded, "No, those figures were your soul family."

"Soul family?"

"Yes, our soul family. All of us work together, changing roles from one life time to the next, helping one another remember exactly who we are."

"And that is?"

"A part of the universe, a part of God." Eric answered.

I bit my lip and sat in silence, trying to grasp all that he said. I then asked the question that had confused me since I first saw the vision, so long ago, "The day I was raped, did I die? And why were you there waiting for me in the light if you weren't dead?"

Eric chuckled. "You don't miss a thing, do you? That must be why the elders thought you were conscious enough to receive this information now, in your human form." Eric reached for my other hand and pulled me close. Cold air pressed all around me as I laid my head on what should have been his chest.

"Okay," Eric hesitated before he started, "here it goes. No, you didn't die. Sometimes when your body or your mind are in so much pain, your soul can temporarily leave it. Most of the time, the soul hovers and watches what is happening to its earthly body, but your soul left and instinctively returned home, where it knew you'd feel safe."

As Eric continued, he seemed to struggle with the words. "Each one of our souls is made up of a certain frequency of energy. Your energy is a mirror image of mine, as we are twin flames. There are 'positive' and 'negative' portions of all energy, just like electrons, which are negative, and protons, which are positive. Well, the negative portion of our energy, and in saying this I in no way mean it is bad or inherently evil," Eric paused and looked at me to make sure I was following along. I nodded to encourage him to continue, "Well, our negative portion is the part of us that reincarnates into human form. The 'positive' portion of us, resides in the original source, waiting for our 'negative' portion to flow back to it, so the two halves, can once again, create a whole. The combined total of all of our energies makes up the entire energy of the universe. We are a part of it and it is us. All of it, is 'God' and we are all a part of God.

Our combined energy seeks to grow larger and more beautiful, so it remembers how to be all that there is: encompassing all things good and all things bad. Reincarnation allows us to experience all that exists and to grow from it, making our souls grow more beautiful—more suitably a part of God—from one lifetime to the next. So, since our energy is divided, when your soul or 'negative' energy escaped your earthly body, it went back to the source, where the 'positive' portion of our entire soul family always lives. You were attracted to my energy, because we are twin flames, and you drew my positive energy into the form you'd recognize—me, as Eric, and I held you in my arms. I know you clearly remember this."

"I do," I stuttered, shocked at the intensity and the power of the words Eric was speaking. Tears leaked from my eyes, "That vision has brought me peace for so long."

"I know." Eric pulled me closer.

"So, who are the others in our family?" I asked.

"I can't share that with you now. You'll recognize them soon enough."

I thought for a moment then asked, "So, your energy transformed into 'Eric.' Does that mean 'Eric" is not usually your true form?"

"No, our image changes from lifetime to lifetime. When a soul is ready to move on, it may not remember or recognize exactly what is happening right after death. So to help the newly released soul, the soul family tends to transform into the shapes of people recognizable from the most recent life time, in order to support a comfortable transition. After the mind-based amnesia lifts and the spiritual memory returns, we resume our true form of pure energy. If a very advanced soul leaves its earthly body, that soul may be met by others in their true form, but some advanced souls are not met at all. They remember instantly where to go, and don't need any assistance for the transition."

"Wow, that's incredible."

Eric agreed, "It's beautiful."

I pressed my head into the cold pillow that was now his silent chest and reached up to run my fingers along the ice cold contours of his face. "So," I hesitated, "you mentioned I've accomplished all I needed to so we can be together again."

He pulled my hand away from his cheek and held it to his chest as he looked at me. "And more." Eric's eyes smiled.

"So, what did I have to accomplish?"

Eric sighed. He looked as tired as I felt. "In the simplest form, survival. You had committed suicide during your last lifetime, so you had to live through all that pain again, without succumbing to it."

When Eric spoke these words, I jumped up and began to pace the room, "I knew it. I KNEW it. I heard a voice in my head speaking, "Not this time. Not this time." I wondered if it meant.... And, wow, it did."

"Yeah," Eric said nonchalantly, "that was the universe talking to you. The collective conscious speaks to everyone, but only some of us are in-tuned enough to listen."

I looked at Eric amazed. This news was huge to me, but he was nonchalant about it.

"So, why did I kill myself before?"

"Well, you were raped and got pregnant from the attack. It was during a time when rapes were well hidden and women were sometimes made to feel responsible for the attack. Unwanted pregnancies in unwed mothers were also more than frowned upon. You were embarrassed and rather than shame your family, you slit your wrist."

I felt a twinge in my left wrist as I thought about my pasts, both of them. I could still remember the touch of the cold razor blade as it slit through my skin. I squirmed in discomfort.

"Okay, so I get why I had to face all that again in this lifetime and overcome it, but why did I have to face the rape and unwanted pregnancy in the first place?"

Eric laughed nervously and averted his eyes from mine. "You leave no stones unturned, do you?" He got up and walked to the window. It was obvious he wasn't going to answer this one.

I frowned and bit my lip, "Well, inquiring minds do want to know."

"You'll understand and remember all that once you cross over."

"Oh, okay." I responded, then we both sat back down on the couch. The hairs on the back of my neck stood on end. Crossed over, I thought to myself. Here I am, casually speaking with a ghost about my own death. If I told anyone, they'd think I'm nuts. Maybe I am. I turned away from Eric and secretly pinched myself to see if it was all a dream. It wasn't. That pinch felt very real.

Eric spoke, as if reading my mind, "It's real. This is all real."

"How'd you do that?"

"We're twins. I can read you and feel your emotions. You're just like an open book to me. Even when I was alive and across the country from you, I could still feel your strongest emotions."

"Really?" Guilt engulfed me. I hadn't felt Eric since we broke up and he left town. I glanced away from him, wondering if he knew. "Like what?" I asked.

"The night you and Jared got engaged, I had fallen asleep at my desk. I woke up with a start at 11:32, engulfed by the terrible pain of losing you again. I woke up sobbing. You know, I had moved on, been with quite a few girls after we broke up, but I knew the pain of losing you well, and had been suppressing it for a long time. That night . . . it just . . . ." Eric shook his head. "It was bad."

Eric grabbed my hand as he continued, "I realized how much you meant to me, and that I needed to find you. Early the next morning, I called your house, hoping . . ."

"You called me?" I interrupted.

"Yeah, I called your parent's house. Your mom answered the phone."

"She never told me that!"

"Well, I asked her not to. Anyway, your mom answered and told me that you no longer lived there, and that you had just gotten engaged the night before." Anger flashed in Eric's eyes. I had seen that look before. He was pissed at my mother.

"What exactly did she say?"

"Exactly what I told you. It's what she didn't say. I could tell she liked informing me that you had abandoned me." He glared angrily, losing himself in thought. I knew Eric never liked my mother and apparently this hadn't change, even in death.

"Needless to say, my heart broke into a million pieces. You'll never know how much I regretted waiting so long."

I didn't say it, but I completely understood.

Eric went on, "And then, I think I felt your pain the morning you were told that Jared was killed. I clearly remember the day. It was June 15, 2005, at 8:53 in the morning. I was sitting on a beach and became overcome with a sorrow I couldn't explain. I couldn't figure it out. Your name kept echoing in my mind."

My mouth dropped open, "You've got to be kidding. That's exactly when I found out."

He smiled briefly and nodded at me. "Yeah, I figured that out once I read the article on Jared's funeral."

I stood up and walked to the window, and found myself entranced by the willow branches waving in the wind. I lost myself in thought. I wondered why I never had an experience like these. Why didn't I ever feel Eric's emotions? I figured that Eric was already aware that I hadn't felt him, so I decided to ask. I needed to know the truth.

I whispered in shame, "Why didn't I feel you?"

I heard light footsteps as Eric walked up and stood behind me. I could feel his cold body press against mine as he wrapped his arms around me. Eric whispered softly in my ear. "Because nothing serious or emotional ever happened to me, except my death, and that was the day after Jared's funeral. I'm sure you were so emotionally distraught, there was no way you could distinguish the horrible feelings you had."

Relief filled me. A hot tear rolled down my cheek. I turned to look at him. "You're tired," he said as he ran his fingers through my hair. It felt like the cold caress of a soft winter breeze. "You need to go to bed."

"No," I insisted, "please stay."

"No." He took my face in his hands and gently kissed my forehead. His lips felt like ice against my skin and a shiver ran through me. "I love you, Emma."

He backed away as I answered, "I love you, too," and I watched as he faded from view. The lights that had dimmed in his presence suddenly glowed brightly again.

Chapter: Emma

ERICA ARRIVED AT 10:00 THE next morning. Her usually bright and cheerful face looked sullen and tears had just been streaking down those lovely checks just before I answered the door. As soon as she saw me, she dropped her bags and ran into my arms, bursting into tears. I hadn't expected this, and started to cry, too.

"God damn, girl, you've gotten skinny!" Erica tried to sound cheerful through her tears.

"I always said I wanted to lose a little weight." I replied.

Erica pulled back and looked reproachfully at me, then we both burst out laughing. We laughed until we started to cry again.

"This fucking sucks!" Erica yelled.

"Tell me about it . . ." I grabbed her purse and duffle bag and led her into the house. I showed her the guest room and placed her two bags on the bed.

"House looks good," She said.

"Thanks, I cleaned it up before my biopsy."

"So, any news yet?" Erica asked.

"No. No news 'til Monday, but as far as the docs are concerned, it's a done deal." I bit my lip and looked away.

Erica looked at me and shook her head. "Stage, fucking four, fucking pancreatic cancer. You couldn't come down with a better cancer than that?"

I shook my head and laughed, "Well, if I knew I'd have my choice . . ."

"SHUT UP!" Erica laughed and hugged me again. Tears started rolling down her cheeks again, "I'm sorry."

"No, hon. Don't be sorry." I replied. "Hey, we gotta keep trying to laugh through this, okay? If not, we might just cry ourselves to death."

Erica glared at me, those chocolate brown eyes boring deep into my soul. "Well, I'm not gonna let you die." She shook her head as she walked over to the bed and opened her baby blue duffle bag. "Not if I can help it."

"Want some tea?" I asked as she started to sort through her things.

"Yeah," She replied as she pulled out a huge pile of books from her bag. The pile was so huge that there couldn't have been much room in her bag for anything else.

I was stunned. "Erica? Didn't you pack any clothes?"

"Clothes? Who needs clothes? You need chemo, radiation and a good diet. Says so in these books and we're gonna cure you!"

I couldn't help but chuckle. "Where in the world did you get all those books?"

"Bookstore. The American Cancer Society put them out. I've been reading everything I can and we are gonna make you better."

I smiled. Erica was such an optimistic, joyful, caring person. Even in the midst of a crisis, even when there seemed to be little to be happy and hopeful for, she could spread happiness and hope. She was an angel to me. I grinned with the realization that she must be a part of my soul family.

"What're you smiling at?" She asked looking at me as if I'd suddenly become someone else.

"Books? Research? Thanks girl." I said, sincerely meaning it. "You know, I only found out a couple days ago, and it isn't confirmed yet . . ." We turned and walked toward the kitchen. I grabbed a kettle, filled it with water and put it on the stove and grabbed a box of tea out of the cabinet.

Erica looked at me in exasperation. "Well, like you said, the doctors think it's a done deal, right? And girl, you need to have a plan." My eyebrows lifted at her and I smiled as she continued. "There's no time to waste if we're gonna beat this thing."

I dropped the tea bags on the counter and walked over to hug her. "You're the best, you know."

She replied, "No, you are, and we're not gonna lose you."

When I pulled away and walked to the cupboard to get the tea cups, my heart sank in my chest. I wondered how I could have asked Erica to come here and face this with me? How selfish was that?

I shook my head in disgust as I gently set the cups on the kitchen table and continued to lose myself in thought. I knew I was going to die. My time had come. My guardian angel had already arrived. He was the one who asked me to call Erica and my mom. Why?

I wondered if I could explain any of this to Erica. Would she believe me? Could she handle it? I wasn't even sure yet that I could handle it all.

I watched as Erica opened the book called "Quick Facts: Pancreatic Cancer" and sat down at the table. She started to speak, "It says here . . ."

"Erica?" I interrupted.

"Yeah, hon?" She replied.

I took a deep breath and slowly walked to the table. I pulled out a chair and sat down.

"I'm dying," I whispered. The tea kettle started to whistle behind me, but Erica's eyes stayed on mine, even as I got up to get the teakettle.

She pleaded, "I know you think that, but there's a chance."

I carefully poured hot water into the tea cups, and watched as the hot steam dissipated in the air. I placed a tea bag into each cup.

"Erica," I said as strongly as I could as I handed her a cup of tea and sat down across the table from her, "My time has come. I will be moving on."

Her eyes swelled with tears and she shook her head, "No . . . no . . ."

I grabbed her hand. "It's okay. I'm okay with it. I know I won't be alone."

Tears flowed down her cheeks. She seemed to understand. "Jared?" she asked.

I nodded my head, "Yes, and Eric."

"Eric?" Her eyes grew wide. "Who's Eric?"

"Someone very special from my past. He's here."

Erica's eyebrows jumped up a couple inches on her forehead and she looked around the room. She turned back toward me and said, "Okay, girl, has the cancer already spread to your brain, 'cause if it has, we're screwed."

I giggled, "Oh, Erica. I am so sorry." I grew serious and looked down at the table, "I should have never asked you to come here."

Guilt washed over me for dragging Erica away from her family and for mentioning my 'visitor' in passing. I knew people would think I'd gone crazy.

Erica's voice cut through my rambling mind, "Don't be silly, girl. I want to be here. I wouldn't want to be anywhere else except, maybe . . . at a hot, sandy beach, under a brilliant blue sky, holding an ice-cold Bahama-mama with you and no cancer . . . . Yeah, that'd be nice."

I nodded my head, "Yeah, it would be."

"So, you're telling me you're not gonna fight this thing?" Erica's voice broke and her lips quivered.

"No. I'm gonna fight it with everything I've got, but it probably won't make a difference."

She looked at me with resolve, "We'll see about that."

"Yeah," I said, playing with the handle of my tea cup and looking away, "We'll see about that."

"So, your mom's coming tomorrow?"

"Yeah, she'll be here sometime in the late afternoon." I sighed.

"You okay with that?" Erica asked. "I know you haven't really seen her in years."

The only time Erica had met my mother was at Jared's funeral where she had managed to look down her nose at everyone there.

"As okay as I can be." I responded.

"Well, if there is anything I can do to help out the two of you, let me know."

"Okay." I replied. "I will," wondering again why I had brought Erica into all this. Could she deal with my mother along with everything else? Her family? My cancer? Then I remembered that Eric had told me to call her. I had to trust that he knew what needed to be done.

I had never shared my past with Erica and knew it was too late to do so now. I just prayed that my mother would be able to act like a mature adult, and if I was really lucky, maybe she would even act like a real mother. I certainly didn't get my hopes up.

For the rest of the day, we talked and explored my garden, where we sat under the willow tree, listening to the breeze blow through it's long branches and admiring the sun filtering through it's leaves.

I showed her where the tiny toads hid, and how if you looked closely at the purple clovers, the miniature flowers actually looked like doves, taking off in flight.

By evening I was exhausted and turned in early. Eric never made an appearance, but I was sure that he was glad that Erica was here. I certainly was glad that she had come.

Chapter: Cassie

IT FELT AS THOUGH I had flown around the entire world, rather than across the Atlantic. First class was as comfortable as it could have been: I had room to stretch, but not nearly as much as I'd like, the chintzy fabric on the seats wasn't nearly as soft and comfortable as it should have been and the complimentary drinks not nearly strong enough. Thank god I had my Xanax.

A tall, gorgeous limo driver greeted me at the luggage claim. Frederick knew exactly what I liked. The driver's brilliant blue eyes were accented by his dark skin and hair and his black suit hung perfectly on his sculpted body. It took everything in me to keep my hands off him. *He'd be good in bed,* I thought. *Perhaps Emma . . .*

Reality hit me and I frowned. *Oh yeah, Emma . . .* How easily the drugs and alcohol made me forget the reason I was on this trip. How I preferred being in a blissful stupor.

I crawled through the open limo door and grabbed a complimentary water to chug down another pill. Calmness successfully restored, I watched as the unfamiliar landscape passed me by. It amazed me how much the environment could change in a few years' time.

An hour passed before the limo stopped in front of a little one story bungalow. It was quaint, but no where close to what I had been used to. Certainly good enough for Emma, though.

The gorgeous limo driver opened my door and took my arm as he assisted me up the gray, shale stone walkway to the front door. I watched as he stacked my luggage on the porch, imagining how it would feel to grab his tight butt. When he was through, I sauntered up to him and coyly slipped him a fifty sending him on his way. He thanked my profusely.

 I sighed and waved as I watched him climb back into the limo and drive away. I wished I could escape this nightmare with him. We could have so much fun. "So long, gorgeous." I whispered.

 I turned toward the door and felt panic rise within me. I fumbled through my Coach bag for more pills and swallowed them dry. I found my sterling silver compact, checked my hair, powdered my glistening cheeks and refreshed my lip stick before ringing the doorbell.

 I listened as Emma's footsteps approached the door.

Chapter: Erica

EMMA WAS IN THE RESTROOM when the doorbell rang, so I answered the door for her. There stood Emma's mother, not at all what I had expected, but on the other hand, her appearance did fit the bill.

Ms. Fiorello was everything Emma was not: fake and haughty. It was clear that I was in the presence of a first-class bitch. Her dark brown and unnaturally highlighted hair was pulled back into a perfect French-knot. Her stretched skin, high cheekbones, perfect nose and Double D chest spoke loudly of plastic surgery and her make-up looked as if it were done by a professional. Ms. Fiorello's eyes, at least the part that hadn't been pulled back with her cheeks, were shaped exactly like Emma's but they lacked any expression or soul. They were glazed, as if she was on drugs. Ms. Fiorello's red tailored suit was obviously expensive. The strand of pearls on her neck and those that decorated her ears must have been real. Her four-inch heels made her stand close to six feet tall and as she stood proud with perfect stature, she looked down her nose at me.

Her surprised, but icy, gaze penetrated mine and her nose wrinkled before she spoke, "Oh, and who are you?" A strong smell of alcohol escaped her painted lips and I found myself engulfed in an unbecoming mixture of day old perfume and rum.

I straightened my shoulders and squarely looked her in the eyes. "I'm Erica, Emma's friend." I replied, attempting to smile under her intense scrutiny.

Her eyes scanned over me. I could tell she was not impressed with my appearance. I must have looked uncouth in my jean shorts and tank top, but hell, I wasn't here to impress anyone. I was here for Emma.

Ms. Fiorello's penciled-in eyebrows lifted when she finally placed my face, "Yessss . . . oh . . . yessss. I remember you. You were at Jared's funeral; am I correct?"

"Yes," I answered, "yes, I was there. Come in." Ms. Fiorello's heels clicked across the hardwood floor as she marched into the cottage leaving all eight of the Christian Dior suitcases stacked on the porch.

"So, where is my Emma?" she asked, her voice as smooth and cold as ice.

"She's in the rest room." I grunted as I lifted some of her luggage to carry into the house. Each suitcase was as heavy as a boulder, far exceeding the airline maximum of fifty pounds. It looked like Ms. Fiorello planned to stay awhile, and my gut told me that might not be a good thing.

The toilet flushed and water splashed in the sink before the bathroom door opened with a flourish. Emma stopped cold when she saw her mother. "Wow, Mom. You look incredible!" she said, clearly shocked at her mother's appearance.

Ms. Fiorello, shaken by Emma's emaciated and pale condition stuttered, "Yes, well . . . Frederick treats me well. And you, you look . . ."

Emma smiled demurely, and flipped her hair as she finished her mother's sentence, "Incredibly gorgeous for a person who may die within the year."

A chuckle escaped my lips and I nodded my head. Emma's incredible sense of humor and acceptance of the situation amazed me.

An intense look filled her mother's eyes, "How dare you joke about such a horrific thing!"

Emma scoffed, "Well, it's not like I have a choice whether I have cancer or not, but I do have a choice about whether I'm going to spend my days laughing or crying, and I chose laughter."

"Humph," grunted her mother. "A new outlook on things, I see. I've seen you cry more than twenty women."

A cold look passed through Emma's eyes as she replied, "And you—you've run away more than a hundred cowards could. I've found that facing my pain and my mistakes makes me stronger. Running makes you weak." Emma's nose sniffed the air, "And addicted."

"Okay!" I butted in, laughing nervously as I tried to break the tension in the room, "So how was the trip, Ms. Fiorello?"

Ms. Fiorello's stiff face didn't move as her lips smiled and her eyes remained hateful. "Fine. Is it, Erica?" she sneered. "Just fine."

I shivered at the look in Ms. Fiorello's eyes and noticed that the room suddenly grew cold. I glanced at Emma and was shocked to see her smiling as if she had just received the greatest gift. When I turned back to face Ms. Fiorello, I was surprised to see her shivering and visibly shaken. "Did you hear that?" she asked.

"Hear what?" I replied, looking back and forth between Emma and Ms. Fiorello. Emma was still smiling. Ms. Fiorello looked disturbed, "That voice, saying . . . . oh never-mind. I must be hearing things." She shook it off.

I hadn't heard a thing. Must be the drugs, I thought.

"Okay . . . um, well," I continued, "I'm glad to hear the trip was fine." I raised my eyebrows at Emma hoping she would give me a clue as to what was going on, but she just kept smiling. I bent over to pick up two of Ms. Fiorello's suitcases. "Let me show you into your room."

"Thank you," she replied, glancing anxiously around the room and then at the ceiling. She quickly followed me out of the room, refusing to carry a thing.

Ms. Fiorello remained in the second guest room as I carried in all of her luggage. Once I was done, I shut the door behind me, leaving her staring at herself in the mirror. I was surprised to see tears slowly starting to leak from the corners of her eyes. *So, the crazy, selfish bitch actually has feelings,* I thought to myself.

When I walked back into the living room, the hairs on the back of my neck stood on end again, and Emma was still standing there, grinning.

"What the hell was all that about and why in the hell did you ask that bitch to come here? She's evil!" I demanded.

Emma looked at me, her eyes shining brightly, "'Cause Eric told me to."

"Eric? Who the hell is this Eric?" I asked, completely confused and dumb struck.

"He's the one who just told mom not to fuck up again. This was her chance to make it right."

"What?" I looked incredulously at Emma.

She pointed to the green armchair and said, "He's right there, don't you see him?"

My eyes followed Emma's pointed finger to the armchair but I didn't see a damn thing. "Girl, you need to sit down. The stress from that bitch is already getting to you." I grabbed her arm and led her to the couch, noticing that her smile never faded and her eyes remained glued to the empty armchair.

"I'm fine, Erica, really," Emma exclaimed.

I shivered. Something was definitely not right. I searched Emma's face, but there was nothing there but sheer happiness. Her smile was freaking me out. Footsteps echoed on the hardwood floor behind and I jumped at the sound. I turned to see Ms. Fiorello walking into the room. Her appearance made me gasp. She had put on a pair of blue jeans and an extra-large, pink sweat shirt. She had taken out the tight French-knot and her long hair fell just below her shoulders. Her eyes were swollen and her perfect make-up had disappeared, apparently wiped away by the tissues that had wiped her tears. I was staring at an older, healthier version of my best friend. She took my breath away.

Gingerly, Ms. Fiorello walked further into the room, the elite, condescending air that had surrounded her completely dissolved. She meekly sat on the couch next to Emma, and pulled her into her arms. She softly spoke, "I am so sorry, baby. I am so very, very sorry."

Suddenly, the room filled with warmth, as if the summer sun, once hidden behind the clouds, suddenly made it's appearance again. I instantly stopped shivering. I didn't understand what had changed or what had happened, but whatever it was, was good.

All three of us burst into tears.

Chapter: Emma

Eric's presence had made short work of Mom's bitter attitude. When she arrived, I could sense him enter the room, but I couldn't see him. The air rapidly chilled and the hairs stood up on the back of my neck. His disembodied voice whispered the words, "Don't fuck up this time. This is your chance to make it right." I wondered if my mother had heard it, and quickly turned toward her to see her eyes suddenly grow large as they darted around the room searching for the source of the voice. Her body began shaking violently. The expression on her face was priceless. I couldn't help but smile.

I knew Eric had finally spoken the words he wanted to speak to her so long ago. He hated how my mother abandoned me throughout my life, and he wasn't going to let her get away with it now. I wondered if this was some sort of goal she needed to accomplish in this lifetime and if it was Eric's job to help her try to overcome her faults. I decided I'd ask Eric later. Regardless, it affected her, bringing her back to reality and a little closer to earth. By the time, Eric's presence had completely left the room, many things had changed for the better. He was, no doubt, my guardian angel.

The rest of the weekend passed quickly. Erica, Mom and I curled up on the couch, watching chick-flicks, and talking about everything and anything that didn't involve cancer. Erica had confided in me that she was nervous about going home to her family on Monday, leaving me alone with my mother, but her worry seemed to dissolve as we spent more time together. Erica was starting to appreciate my mother a little more, and I was, too. I couldn't remember the last time we spent time like this together, mother, daughter and friends. If it hadn't been for the circumstances, it would have been a dream come true.

A follow-up appointment with Dr. Reynolds was scheduled on Monday at 9:30 a.m. to discuss the results of my liver biopsy. Erica and my mother planned to join me for the appointment after which Erica would return to Quantico to be with Alex and Henry for the week. She was hoping to come back the following weekend.

The silence of the car ride to the hospital was disturbed only by the sound of the traffic in the city. I focused on the sounds of the engines running, anxious horns blowing and the sudden gusts of bus exhaust, determined not to allow my mind to explore the different possibilities of what I was about to hear.

Once we arrived at the hospital, I focused on the sounds of the elevator dinging at each floor, our footsteps echoing off the barren walls, clipboards smacking the registration desks and the soft murmur of patients anxiously discussing their symptoms as they waited for their appointments.

Then my name was called.

Mom, Erica and I quickly glanced at each other, then they followed me into the office, where we were asked to sit at a brown, circular table. I sat between Erica and my Mom, and we waited. I listened to the ticking of the clock.

Dr. Reynolds came in accompanied by a nurse in pink scrubs. He was wearing a white oxford shirt and tan slacks. His sleeves were rolled up, giving him a casual appearance. His dark brown skin glowed in the lamp light, and his eyes looked weary and kind. The nurse's blonde hair was streaked with silver and pulled into a loose bun. Her hazel eyes were friendly and looked deeply into mine. Something about her seemed very familiar.

The doctor set my file down on the table, placed some film up on the light box then sat down to face me. "Hello, Emma," he said as he reached out to take my hand. I wondered how he knew I was Emma. Perhaps it was because I looked like death warmed over. He shook my hand gently, then introduced himself to my mother and Erica. "Hello, I am Dr. Reynolds, I am an oncologist and I will be working on Emma's case." He pointed to Elizabeth, who shook each of our hands in turn. "This is Elizabeth, one of our oncology nurses."

Dr. Reynolds motioned Elizabeth to take a seat across from me.

The doctor continued, "Emma, I am sorry to tell you that the results from your liver biopsy have shown that the tumors are, in fact, cancerous." Dr. Reynolds turned on the light so we could view the cat scan of my abdomen. "The cancer started in your pancreas, and has metastasized to your liver and abdominal cavity. It appears that you have three large tumors and four smaller ones in your liver and several in your abdominal cavity." He pointed to each of tumors that were raiding my body. I could feel my mother's body shaking as she silently cried in the seat beside me. Erica had grabbed my hand and refused to let it go. I evaded their glances and was gripped by a sudden feeling of free-falling. My stomach suddenly felt as if it was in my throat, and I felt helplessly out of control.

Dr. Reynolds continued, "You have Stage four-B pancreatic cancer, or metastatic pancreatic cancer. Unfortunately, the cancer you have is not removable by surgery. It is extremely hard to cure and quite difficult to control, so, I suggest starting chemotherapy immediately to try to reduce the size and number of tumors. We should be able to prolong your survival. For the next six weeks, you will receive an intense chemotherapy regimen. It is to be hoped that by the end of this time, we will see a decrease in the size and number of the tumors"

"And if we don't?" I whispered.

"There is a small chance that there will be little or no change. If this is the case, there will be very little we can do. During this time, we will also be focusing on reducing the pain that you feel and making sure you maintain your nutrition."

I sighed, "So what is the prognosis with treatment?"

"If the treatment is successful, studies have shown that you can survive one to two years and will experience an improved quality of life during that time."

"If not?" I asked.

"If you receive treatment and it is not successful, you can expect up to three to six months of good life. If you choose not to receive chemotherapy at all, you will have approximately three more good months left, with appropriate nutrition and pain control."

"Choose not to receive chemotherapy?" My mother exclaimed, "Why would you even suggest such a thing!"

Elizabeth spoke, "Metastatic pancreatic cancer is one of the most difficult, aggressive cancers there are. Some patients come to terms with the meaning of this, and choose not to suffer through the side-effects that chemotherapy involves. In most cases, chemotherapy only extends your life by three months. Those patients who choose to let the disease take its own course, feel that they are creating a better quality of life for themselves, even though the quantity in days may be a shorter."

"Well, Emma will fight this with everything she's got!" My mother insisted as her eyes desperately searched mine. "Right, Emma? You tell them."

This was the first time, since my diagnosis was confirmed, that I looked into my mother's eyes. She was terrified. Fear radiated from her. Fear was something I no longer felt. I knew exactly what was waiting for me once it was time to cross over. I was not scared of death, but I had to admit, I was scared of pain. A small part of me also felt I was too young to have to face death, but knowing that the two men I loved with all my heart had already crossed over and were waiting for me made me even less upset about it.

I did, however, feel sad for those I would leave behind, especially my mother. I was not sure that she'd be able to handle my death well. So I made my decision. I would try chemotherapy for one reason, and one reason alone. I knew death was inevitable at this point: Eric was here for a reason. However, if I could prolong my life, to give my mother and me more time to work things out, I would give it a try. At least she would see that I would fight any battle I had to face, even if it was useless. Erica grabbed my shoulder from behind me and her voice shook as she spoke, "I'm sure Emma will choose what is right for her."

Her words brought me comfort.

I turned to face the doctor and the nurse and said, "I would like to try the six weeks of chemotherapy. If that treatment fails to provide any promising results, I will then allow the disease to takes its course."

"I think that's a very wise decision." Dr. Reynolds stated. "Elizabeth, will you get her set up for treatment?"

"Yes," Elizabeth smiled at me.

She arranged to have my chemo start at 8:30 the next morning. Mom seemed more than eager to get the drugs flowing through my veins, even demanding to know why chemo couldn't be started immediately. Elizabeth politely informed her that she had to get some paperwork in order. "Paperwork!" Mom screeched, "My daughter's life is at risk. We shouldn't have to wait for paperwork!" I patted her shoulder, guided her back down into her chair, and said, "Tomorrow, is soon enough." My mother glared at me, rolled her eyes, crossed her arms and huffed. I turned to Erica, who was rolling her eyes at my mother, and I couldn't help but smile. I was so happy to know that both of them were there, and even though my mother was being overbearing, it was comforting to know that she genuinely cared.

Mom planned to sit with me during every treatment and kept repeating that she would be there for everything. "I'm gonna take care of you, baby. You're in good hands," she would say as she patted my hand. These words seemed strange coming from her mouth, and years before, I would have never believed her, but I believed her now. Something had changed. I could see it in her eyes.

Elizabeth gave my mother several books and pamphlets explaining all aspects of chemotherapy, including the care I should receive with the side effects and what foods and nutrients I should eat. Elizabeth gave us a lengthy summary, but I found myself drifting, unable to listen closely to all her advice. Fortunately, Mom and Erica listened closely and took notes.

Erica left shortly after she dropped us home after the appointment. I hated to see her go, but Alex and Henry needed her. "You hang in there, girl! I'll see you Friday night!" she said. She gave me a huge bear hug and whispered, "And if that woman turns into a psycho bitch again, you call me." I laughed and watched as she drove away, thankful that she had already arranged to come back the following weekend. I became a little nervous about being alone with my mother for so long, already looking forward to Erica's welcome presence at the weekend.

I was also hoping to see Eric again, and found myself looking for black mist every time I entered a room. He was nowhere to be seen and I was really starting to miss him. He had not been present since the night he spoke to my mother and I found the last words he spoke continuously echoing in my mind. They really seemed to hit a chord with her and she became more of a mother than she had been in a long time. I was thankful for every positive interaction we had, hoping the past was behind us, and that we would continue to grow closer.

Chapter: Cassie

EMMA'S CHEMO WAS TO START the next morning. I tried to insist that they start immediately, but to no avail. After saying goodbye to Erica and seeing Emma settle on the couch for a nap, I ran to the grocery store to get all the supplies we would need for the rest of the week. Chemo was not going to be easy, and I wanted to make sure we were well prepared to deal with her symptoms and to keep her energy and nutrition up.

Once I got home, I disinfected everything I could get my hands on. Emma's resistance was going to be compromised, and she was not going to catch a bug on my watch. I wanted to make sure she had every chance to beat this thing. It felt wonderful to be an active part of her life again, wonderful to have an opportunity to be a mother to her. I prayed that my hard work would pay off and I wouldn't lose my baby. She was way too young to die.

Watching Emma face this mountainous challenge was eye-opening. Her demeanor was calm and she seemed at one with herself and her possible death, something I could never relate to. Death terrified me. I lost my belief in a god or an afterlife long before. I had seen enough suffering in the world to realize that god didn't exist; a real god would never allow the pain that so many experience in their lives. I thought about the poor, the starving, the sick, and the lonely, convincing myself that a true god would never allow that misery.

To me, life was a one-time deal: you get what you get, so you might as well make the most of it. When you died, it was over. Once Emma's father was gone, I became determined to make the most of my life: see the world and experience all the luxuries and magnificence life had to offer. It was fun. I could never get enough of the gorgeous men, the unlimited money, the sprawling mansions, the designer clothes, the fine wine and the ample supply of drugs.

But now, in retrospect, looking at Emma made me realize that my choices were so unsatisfying in the long run. I never cared about other people the way Emma did. Hell, I didn't even care about my own daughter. I could never understand why Emma educated herself to teach and work with special needs children. I never gave a crap about anything like that and couldn't relate to anyone who did. However, that's what Emma decided to do and I'm sure she made some sort of difference. In the midst of turmoil and tragedy, Emma always seemed to see a better future. Maybe that's why Emma liked working with the children so much. Their entire future was in front of them. It was a blank slate and she could be a positive influence on their lives.

I don't know what changed my attitude, but I did know it started the first night I arrived at Emma's, when I heard that bizarre, familiar voice in my head. I could still hear it echo in the recesses of my mind, "Don't fuck up again. This is your chance to make it right." The moment I heard it, my mind instantly turned to Eric. The voice was smooth and silky like his and a vision of him formed in my mind. I wondered where he was, relieved that he was not with Emma now. Eric hated me and could see right through me. He knew what a bad mother I was. He saw it first hand. I was thankful he wasn't actually there, but where had that voice come from?

Eventually, I passed it off as a drug-induced hallucination, but the message stuck with me. The words that were spoken, whether imaginary or real, were words I needed to hear. Stark reality hit me, when I realized that this could be the last chance I had to prove to Emma that I could be a good mother, and damn it, this time I was not going to fail. So that night I dumped all my Xanax down the toilet, and refused to take a drink. I thought going cold-turkey would be hard, but it wasn't. I had a few head-aches and a bit of the jitters, but Emma became my incentive to live, and for the first time in years, I started to feel alive. Once the initial withdrawal symptoms passed, I felt better than I had in my entire life.

I had really enjoyed spending time with Emma and Erica, and was looking forward to seeing Erica again on the weekend. I was hoping the week would go well without her, and I was sure that it would, as long as I stayed strong. I also believed that if I finally succeeded at being a good mother, maybe, just maybe, my baby wouldn't die. If there was a god . . . if . . . surely if I worked really hard to change, he wouldn't punish me by taking my baby. No god would do that.

Chapter: Emma

LATE THAT NIGHT, I WOKE up chilled to the bone. I quickly turned on my bedside lamp and searched the room for a shadow. I felt someone sit on the end of my bed, but there was no person and no black mist.

"Eric?" I called as I jumped out of bed and turned on every light and appliance in my room.

I watched as Eric's mist suddenly appeared and swirled, his image slowly forming in front of my eyes. "I didn't mean to wake you," Eric smiled, "but I'm happy you're up."

I walked over and sat down beside him on the end of the bed. "I've missed you." I said, taking his cold, misty hand in mine. "Thanks for having that talk with my mom. It seems to have profoundly changed her."

He scoffed and looked away, "Good. She has changed a bit, but I'm not done with her yet." He looked back into my eyes, "How are you feeling?"

"Okay," I replied. "Nervous."

"So, you decided to go with the chemo, huh?" Eric asked.

"Yeah. I thought it was the right thing to do. I know it won't, well . . . I don't think it's gonna work; that's why you're here, right?"

I searched Eric's eyes, but he wasn't going to answer me. I continued, "Well, I decided that my current life was worth at least one fight. I figured it might give me more time with Erica and my mom, and it would show them that life was worth fighting for and that I wouldn't give up too easily."

Eric placed his hand under my chin. "No, the Emma I know, would never give up easily." He suddenly seemed distant and he looked away. His eyes spoke concern.

"What's wrong?" I asked. He shook his head. He was not going to answer me. "I'm not scared, you know." I said as I placed my hands on his icy chin and turned his face back toward mine. I looked him deeply in the eyes.

"Not scared of what?" Eric asked.

"Of dying. I'm ready to die, whenever my time comes. I'll willingly go, especially knowing that you're here, waiting for me."

The faint lines around his eyes lifted briefly in a smile, but then he looked grave. "I know that's how you feel. That's not what I'm worried about."

"Then what are you worried about?" I demanded.

His reply was simple and precise, "Your death."

"What?" I exclaimed. "That doesn't make any sense." Anger started to rise within me. Why was he being so cryptic about my death? Why couldn't he just admit I was going to die and that he was here to take me home? Was that so hard? It all seemed so obvious. What could I be missing?

He looked at me, and as if he had read my mind, he stated, "I am here because you're dying."

Although I wasn't surprised, I gasped at his sudden honesty.

Eric continued, "It's just that, the fight in front of you is a tough one. My death, Jared's death—both were quick." He pulled me toward him, and held my head against his pillow-soft, ice cold chest. "Cancer sucks. Cancer sucks real bad."

Tears leaked from my eyes as fear enveloped me. *Pain,* I realized, *I was going to face pain.*

"I can do it." I said with resolve. "I'll take everything the doctors give me. They can manage the pain. I'll be fine."

Eric smiled at me reassuringly, "I know. I just hate having to watch you go through it."

I couldn't help but smile at him, "I hope you know that your being here makes it easier."

Eric bent over and his cold lips pressed against my forehead. He didn't reply.

* * *

The next morning I woke up exhausted from my late night visit with Eric. I fell asleep in the car as my mother drove me to the hospital for my first chemo session and my feet dragged as I followed Elizabeth into a room lined with brown leather chairs and IV poles. Elizabeth expertly placed an IV needle into my arm and hooked me up to a bag of clear poison that would course through my veins to kill off cancer cells residing in my body. I hoped it wouldn't kill off too many white blood cells as well. I really didn't want to have to cope with infections too.

My mother sat down in the chair next to me and pretended to read a book. From time to time, I'd catch her eyes darting nervously from the IV bag to me, then to the IV bag again. Whenever she knew I'd caught her wandering, worried eyes, she'd quickly turn a page of her book, smile supportively at me, then pretend to start reading again. This cycle repeated itself so many times that I closed my eyes for the final two hours of treatment, relieving her from having to hide her obvious feelings of anxiety and allowing myself to rest.

Nausea enveloped me when I was finally able to stand to go home. Elizabeth gave my mother a bottle of anti-emetics to help reduce the nausea and vomiting, and suggested that I sleep for the rest of the day and only consume flat ginger-ale soda and crackers until we knew how my body was going to respond to the treatment.

It didn't respond well. I quickly memorized every last curve and line of the toilet and my throat burned in pain. Relief came only during sleep, when a cool, invisible hand pressed lovingly against my forehead then held my hand.

Chapter: Erica

I GOT TO EMMA'S HOUSE at 5:15 Friday evening. Cassie greeted me with a smile when she let me in the house. A pot of homemade chicken noodle soup was simmering on the stove and the house reeked of fresh disinfectant. Cassie had far exceeded my expectations for motherly caretaking of Emma and I was thrilled to see it.

"Hey, Cas! How's our Emma doing?" I said as I gave her a brief hug.

"She's hanging in there. Had her second batch of chemo yesterday so she's feeling pretty nasty right now. Go see her. She's in her room. She'll be happy to see you."

I tiptoed to Emma's room and stopped at her door. Knocking softly, I called out,

"Emma? Can I come in?"

Her weak voice answered, "Hey, girl. Yeah, come in."

The room was ice cold and dark. The curtains were drawn and the ceiling fan was spinning so fast it looked as though it would fly off its base at any moment. Emma had hidden under all the covers. I walked up to her bed but stopped and audibly gasped when I saw her face. Her pale white skin looked incandescent in the darkness. Her eyes had sunken and developed dark rings around them. Her pale lips had cracked. She looked more weak than I had ever seen her. If she were to lie still and pretend to stop breathing, she'd look dead.

I sat down next to her on the bed and ran the back of my hand across her ice cold cheek. "You cold, Hon?"

"No." She smiled at me, "Just right." Emma's smile reached her eyes, convincing me she spoke the truth and again I was amazed at her strength.

"Okay then." I patted her hand and we sat in silence. I gently wrapped my fingers around hers, desperately searching my mind for something appropriate to say, but fear gripped me. Emma looked horrible. Until now, I had pushed the severity of the situation behind me, but the wrath of cancer was staring me directly in the face and I was rendered speechless. But I resolved not to become spineless in its presence. I would not fall to my knees, and quake in fear. I would face it down for Emma, no matter how bad it got. I whispered, "You know, I love you, girl."

"I love you, too." She responded, then coughed.

"Can I get you a drink or something?"

"Sure, that would be good. How are Henry and Alex?"

As I got up and walked toward the door, I said, "They're fine. Henry's getting big."

"I bet he is." Emma began to cough again.

"Let me go get you a drink."

I walked into the kitchen and found Cassie sitting at the table reading a Cosmo magazine. She smiled at me. "I'm so glad you're here."

"Me, too." I replied. "Emma needs a drink. Has she been able to keep anything down? She looks dehydrated."

"Only flat soda." Cassie answered as she got out of her chair and opened the fridge. "Here's an open can."

"Thanks." I grabbed the can and poured it into a cup of fresh ice. "She looks horrible." I mumbled.

Cassie shook her head as she sat back down at the kitchen table, "Yeah, I know. The side-effects are really bad."

"You're not kidding." I responded. I turned to walk back to Emma's room when Cassie called out, "Hey Erica, do you mind if I go to the store to pick up a few things?"

"No, go ahead! Take a break! That's what I'm here for!"

The corners of Cassie's mouth turned up in a smile and she said, "Thanks." She grabbed her purse and Emma's car keys and walked out the door. As I watched her leave, I noticed how much older she looked. Her perfectly colored hair was now streaked with a few strands of silver and there were deep circles around her eyes which exaggerated the once hidden fine lines on her face. If this much physical change could be seen on the outside, I wondered how she was doing within. Cancer sucked for everyone involved.

When I walked back into Emma's room, I noticed it seemed considerably warmer. Emma had pulled herself up to a sitting position and had turned on a light. The blankets were no longer up around her chin, but lying down below her waist. Emma's collar and shoulder bones protruded through her tank top, making her look like a dressed up skeleton. But her color seemed to be coming back. I handed her the glass of flat soda. "Drink up, girl. We need to get some fluids in you. Need something to eat?"

"No, I'm fine for now." She smiled.

I shook my head in disbelief. I wondered how she could possibly find the strength to keep on smiling as I mustered up my own emotional strength and smiled back at her, "Okay, so tell me what's going on? How are you feeling?"

She laughed and took a drink, "Like shit," she responded.

"That bad, huh?"

"Yeah, it sucks. This is it. If chemo doesn't work this time, I'm not going through it again. I'd rather live out my days feeling anything other than this."

"I understand." I replied, even though I didn't. What else could I say? I had no idea what it was like to be in her position. "Whatever you decide, Hon. It's your body."

"Your damn right it is," she laughed as she looked down at the skeleton she had become, "and a sexy one at that."

We both laughed.

"So, how are things going with your mom?" I asked.

"Great. Really, really well." Emma answered. "She's a nervous wreck at chemo, but she's there and it's comforting to know it."

"I'm so relieved you have her. I'd hate to think of you dealing with this all alone!" I shuddered at the thought.

"I know. I'm blessed. I'm so happy that Eric insisted that I call you both."

My heart stopped, I raised my eyebrows and looked at her wide-eyed. "Eric, the ghost, right?" I honestly thought this was behind us. She hadn't mentioned the ghost since the night her mother arrived.

I had figured the whole ghost thing was some weird psychological response she was using to deal with the shock of it all. "He told you to call us?"

"Yeah, I thought I told you." She gave me a serious look. Emma wasn't joking. She truly believed this guy was here. Maybe she wasn't as well off as she seemed.

I responded, "I don't remember, maybe . . . Are you sure you really see this guy?"

"Yeah, I'm sure. I know it's hard to believe, but he's here."

"Is he here, now?" I asked as I looked around the room.

"No, not right now. You're here. He usually goes away when someone else is here to watch me." She laughed, "I guess he needs a break, too."

"Oh, okay." I said, averting my eyes from hers.

"You might be able to tell when he's here," she explained, "the room gets really cold and sometimes, if he's trying to form, you can see a mist. He needs energy to form, so if the lights are on, they'll flicker."

I didn't know what to say, "So, um . . . it was cold in here when I first arrived. Was he here then?"

"Yes."

"And it gets warm again after he leaves?"

Emma nodded her head, "Yeah."

"Are you sure you're feeling okay?" I asked. All of this seemed crazy. It was hard enough to watch Emma fight for her life. I didn't want to watch my best friend lose her mind as well.

"No, I told you I feel like shit, but that doesn't mean I'm not experiencing what I say I am."

I laughed nervously, "Okay, okay. Ask him to tell you something I would know, but you wouldn't, okay? Once he does, let me know, then we'll talk about this a little bit more."

"Okay," Emma laughed, "I'm sure he'll enjoy that. I'll let you know when I find out anything."

I nodded my head and laughed tentatively.

That night Cassie returned with the supplies she needed for the rest of the week and served us fresh bread with her homemade soup. It was fantastic. We enjoyed each other's company, laughing at almost anything. Emma kept all of our spirits up, joking even while we watched her nausea come and go. By the end of the weekend, she was able to keep some food down and she seemed phenomenally stronger by the time I left on Sunday. I hugged her goodbye, promising to be back the following weekend. Emma stood on the porch and waved goodbye until I disappeared around the corner.

As I drove away, I thought about Emma and how well she seemed to be handling this ordeal, but then my mind turned to thoughts of Eric, the ghost. I shook my head sadly and prayed out loud, "Dear god, please don't let Emma lose her mind. I know she's in a desperate position, but please give her the strength of mind she needs to overcome this."

Suddenly, the air in the car grew ice cold. I could see my breath and the hairs stood on the back of my neck. "Eric?" I called out, grasping the steering wheel in panic. There was no reply. I looked in the rear view mirror and saw a swirl of black mist. I slammed on the brakes and pulled over to the side of the road. When I turned around to look again, the mist was gone. Suddenly, a warm gust of air filled the car and the creepy, cold feeling that had enveloped me a moment ago, disappeared. I didn't know what to think.

When I arrived home, I called Emma to let her know I had gotten home safely. She was happy to hear from me. As I was about to say goodbye, Emma said, "Oh, by the way Erica, Eric told me about your prayer in the car. I am definitely not losing my mind. On the contrary, with you, my mom and Eric at my side, I will have the strength of mind to get through this ordeal, one way or another."

Chapter: Emma

MY HAIR STARTED FALLING OUT three weeks into chemo. It was the Saturday after my sixth treatment. Early that morning, I was kneeling and staring blankly into the toilet, waiting for my throat to burn with vomit again. I gagged, but nothing came. I stood up and another wave of nausea consumed me. I grasped the cold, hard sink to steady myself. The wave ebbed and as I slowly opened my eyes, they focused on the white marbled sink I so desperately clung to. Long, fine strands of hair covered the sink and the counter. I gasped and quickly ran my fingers through my hair. When my fingers escaped its tangled grasp, they were covered in hundreds of strands of hair. "Erica?" I called out. "Erica!"

The bathroom door opened abruptly. Erica stood there in a lightweight lavender bathrobe frowning in concern. "What's wrong, Hon?"

"My hair." Tears burst from my eyes and I almost wiped them with the hair I was holding, but stopped myself. Instead, I held up my hand entangled by strands of dark hair and with the other pointed to the sink. "It's falling out."

Erica rushed forward and held me in her arms. All the resolve I had in me melted into a raging river of tears. It may seem petty, or vain, but seeing pieces of me, pieces of who I am and who I became, separating from my body and lying all over the bathroom sink filled me with a desperation about my fate that I had never felt before. The control I had felt became nonexistent. The cancer inside me smiled as it revealed its silent, evil plan to tear through my body, slowly nipping and mutilating it, piece by piece. It mocked my chemotherapy, laughing at its feeble attempts to kill off the metastatic cancer that raged throughout my body, while it inadvertently killed off healthy cells weakening me further.

It wasn't that I was scared of death. I was scared of dying. I knew what awaited me, but before I could go home, I had to watch and feel my body slowly die in the process. Eric was right, a quick death, like his and Jared's, would have been far more preferable. I almost began to resent the unfairness of it, but my anger subsided in a desperate wave of fear. The thought of unbearable pain petrified me. I didn't want to think about what was happening. I didn't want to watch what was happening and I didn't want to feel it either.

Erica continued to hold me as I cried desperately in her arms. The room turned icy cold, and all the lights dimmed. Erica and I quickly pulled away from each other and shivered as our breaths formed clouds of mist in front of us. Our eyes scanned the room, looking for a visible sign of Eric. Then, a soft, male voice spoke, "It's time for a haircut." I heard Erica gasp, then felt a pair of ice cold lips press against my cheek. Before I knew it, the cold air dissipated and warmth surrounded us again.

Erica gasped for breath, "Damn, girl! Was that Eric?"

My fingers caressed where the cold lips had kissed my cheek and I looked at her blankly, completely confused by what had happened. "No." I answered, my lips quivering, "No, that was Jared."

* * *

"Oh my god, girl! You are not telling me you have two ghosts haunting you now?"

I closed the toilet seat and sat down, putting my head in my hands. "I don't know. I don't understand."

"Well, shit. I heard that one. There was definitely someone or something here. How do you know it was Jared?"

"Because it wasn't Eric. It didn't feel or sound like Eric, and . . . the haircut . . ." I couldn't complete the sentence. My mind traveled back to the day I shaved Jared's head. He was letting me know that he would be taking care of me now. "Oh my god." I shook my head. "Both of them, here. It's too much."

Clover Doves

I felt faint, and gently allowed my body to lie down on the floor. The cold, hard tiles pressing against my body seemed to bring me back from the edge.

I looked up at Erica, who stood there, visibly shaken, but smiling, "That is so freakin' cool." She laughed. "Do you know how lucky you are?"

"Yeah, real lucky," I scoffed, still lying on the floor, looking up at Erica's face. "I'm dying and I have dead men lining up to take me home. Do you think they'll fight it out?" I laughed nervously, pulling myself up to a seated position. It was hard to imagine Jared and Eric, together, here in my house, dead, yet very much alive. Can that be good? How will that work out?

Erica interrupted my train of thought, "Well, girl, I don't know about that, but listen. You—and me, for that matter, now know, without a shadow of a doubt, that there is a life after death and you have loved ones, waiting for you."

"Yeah, but . . ." I started.

Erica's eyes read mine. She suddenly seemed full of confidence and understanding, something I desperately lacked. "There is no doubt in my mind that it'll be fine between Eric and Jared. They both loved you, and they are here for you. They wouldn't come here to make it any harder than it already is."

"I know, but . . ."

"But nothing. You're in good hands, girl!"

"Do you think Jared knows that Eric and I are twin flames? I hope it doesn't hurt him."

"Huh," Erica thought for a moment, "well, maybe Jared's a soul mate. That's gotta count for something! The two of you were too close to be anything less."

I considered that, but was still uneasy, "Yeah, I guess. Eric said he was. He said we're all a part of a soul family and we work together through our lives to accomplish whatever it is we need to do."

Erica looked at me, her eyes wide in amazement, "Wow, does stuff like that really happen?"

I nodded and shrugged my shoulders, "Well, that's what Eric told me a while ago."

"Do you think I'm part of your family, too?" Erica's eyes bore into mine.

I laughed, "I have no idea, but you could be." I did feel as though I had known Erica forever, and forever could have been longer than I ever imagined.

We sat in contemplative silence for a few moments, then Erica said, "So?"

"So what?" I asked.

"So, you want a haircut?"

I smiled, and ran my hand one more time through the long brown hair that was falling off my head. Erica was right, I was lucky: I may have cancer, I may feel sick from chemo and maybe I'm losing my hair and I may be dying, but at least I knew where I would go after I died—and I knew who was there waiting for me.

I stood up and looked at myself in the mirror. I looked dreadful. It was apparent that I had little control over my illness, but I did still have some control over my life, and I wasn't going to stand around watching my hair fall out. I let my long, brown hair fall gently around my face then pulled it back, pretending to put it in a pony tail, something I would probably never do again. I sighed, "Yeah, I'll go get the trimmer."

* * *

After my head was shaved, I took a warm shower and spent some much needed time alone in my room. I paced the floor while my mind ensnared every sense with confusion and fear. My stomach tied in a knot, my chest felt tight and I could feel and hear my heartbeat pounding in my brain. I was desperate for clarity. I longed to understand. I needed Eric.

I couldn't comprehend all that had happened, that was still happening, and felt overwhelmed. Physically, I still felt awful. I had watched my hair falling out, then I had it all shaved off—after a surprise visit from Jared. Jared. Eric had told me that he would come later. But Eric had averted his eyes from mine when he said it. I couldn't distinguish whether this was from jealousy or if he meant that Jared would show up when it was time for me to cross over. Had my time arrived?

Clover Doves

My stomach churned. Acid burned my throat. I felt like I was going to be sick again. Suddenly, the room grew ice cold, immediately relieving the nausea I felt.

A black mist swirled beside me. I watched as the tiny vortexes formed into the shape of a man. I wondered whether it would be Eric or Jared. I was terrified to see Jared again. Guilt overwhelmed me. I knew he must know my feelings for Eric and I had no way to explain myself. In all honesty, I loved Jared, too, with a love different from the love I felt for Eric, but it was love nonetheless.

My mind desperately searched for the words to say if Jared was forming before me. An audible sigh escaped my lips when Eric's face appeared.

"Hey, Pumpkin!" he smiled instantly running his cold hand across my bald head. "Look at you!"

"Yeah, lovely aren't I?" I whispered, embarrassed, looking away.

"Huh . . . lovely wasn't the word I was thinking of." Eric stated.

I turned to look at him, surprised at the anger quickly rising inside of me.

Then he said, "Gorgeous is more like it."

My anger subsided as fast as it came and I couldn't help but smile. Eric always knew the right words to say.

"Jared was here." I blurted as I sat down on my bed.

"Yeah, I know." Eric answered.

"I didn't think he would be here so soon."

Eric walked away and looked out of my bedroom window. "What do you mean?"

"Well," I explained, "when you told me he'd come later, I thought you meant, well . . . it would be time for me to . . ." My sentence dropped as I watched Eric shake his head in amazement and chuckle softly.

"You're too slick for your own good."

I gasped, "Oh my god, is it time already?" My stomach began to reflexively clench in fear.

Eric walked back to the bed, took my hand in his and looked me deeply in the eyes. He couldn't hide the smile behind them.

"Are you ready?" he asked.

"Now? Ready?"

"Yeah," Eric sat down on the bed, gazing deeply in my eyes and my mind filled with the memory of him by the pond, asking me to marry him. "Are you ready to come plan our next life together? I hate to say it, but I can't wait. I've missed you so much."

The fear I felt vanished and my heart melted. There was nothing I wanted more than to be with Eric again. "Can I just say 'yes' and come with you now? I would do it in a minute."

"No," Eric chuckled, happy to hear my response. "We still have one more job to do."

"What job?"

"You'll see, sooner than later . . ." Eric was being cryptic again.

"I hate it when you're so secretive!" I pulled away and wrapped my arms tightly around my knees.

Eric reached out and gently put icy fingers around my wrists, pulling me toward him, "I know it's frustrating, but life has to play out the way it is meant to."

Knowing that pressing any further would get me nowhere, I changed the subject, "Eric, what about Jared? I'm worried about him. I do love him, but . . ."

Eric interrupted me, "You have nothing to worry about. He loves you, too, and knows, quite clearly how we feel about each other."

"Really?" I clenched my teeth, "Is he upset?"

"No. He supports our love completely. To tell you the truth, he even understood it as a human. You know," Eric hesitated, "he has a twin soul as well."

Jealousy bit me, just briefly before relief flooded over me. "Really, who?"

"You don't know her in this lifetime, but you will recognize her soon enough."

There it was again. I was knocking on death's door. "So, it's soon?" I asked.

"Soon enough." Eric placed his hand on my cheek and rubbed his thumb along my protruding cheek bone. "Now it's time for you to rest." Eric gently laid me down. His cold lips caressed mine before he disappeared quickly.

My freshly shaved head felt cold and exposed as it pressed against the cold, clean sheets on my bed. The comfort of Eric's visit lulled me to sleep, but I was suddenly awakened as my mom yawned and stretched her way into the room. She stopped dead in her tracks when she saw me, pallid and bald, on the bed before her. She clasped her hands to her mouth, her eyes wide in obvious horror as she stumbled for the right words to say. I turned away, surprised to be embarrassed and shocked at her reaction to the "new" me. Superficial beauty had always meant the world to my mother, something I, clearly, no longer had. Anger filled me and I wondered if she really had changed or learned anything at all.

Erica walked in, smiling and fresh from her morning shower, but her demeanor quickly changed when she saw the look of horror on my mother's face. Reining in her feelings, she began to explain what had happened in an overdone bubbly voice that hardly camouflaged what she truly felt. "Oh, Cass. Relax! It's no big deal, Hon! You knew this was gonna happen. That's what chemo does to you! Emma's hair was falling out all over the place, and she chose to chop it all off rather than watch it happen. I think she looks beautiful! Sinead O'Connor, watch out!"

Erica's laugh covered the anger that radiated from her soul, and tears started to stream down my mother's face. My mother's resolve was breaking before our very eyes. I had seen this look before. I wondered how long it would take her to run.

Chapter: Cassie

THERE SHE LAY, PALE, SKELETAL and bald, a wispy apparition of what my daughter had once been, now a ghastly, cover-girl for cancer. Horror engulfed me. What was the point of all this hell? Why were we here, to live, to waste away, to die? Life and beauty were fleeting, and then what? Death, a cold, empty void, nothing? I decided it was time for me to leave. I could no longer face the horror I had seen and had yet to see. There was no point in staying. After Emma was gone, she'd be dead and wouldn't care or know whether I had been there or not. So why, then, should I stay and watch Emma slowly die? I could be doing something else. I should enjoy my life while I still could! This was all too horrible, too ghastly to deal with. I had done my best, and that was all I could do. Yes, it was time to get away.

I heard Erica's voice echoing in the background, explaining about the hair, but I didn't listen or care. Tears started to leak from the corners of my eyes as I looked at Emma, my baby, my little girl, for the last time. I didn't speak a word as I slowly backed toward the door of the bedroom. That's when Emma turned and looked at me.

Chills ran up my spine. The hairs on the back of my neck and my arms stood on end as Emma's eyes bore into mine. I watched as she used all her strength to pull herself up into a seated position. As if she had read my mind, Emma said, "You're gonna run, aren't you."

"Uh . . ." I stumbled back toward the door, shocked that she would confront me like this. What could I possibly say?

"Why is this so hard for you?" Emma demanded. "Why is it so hard for you to be a mother when the going gets tough?"

I couldn't respond, "I, uh . . . I'm . . ."

"You are not going to run. Not this time." Emma shouted. "You cannot leave me here, alone." Emma started to cry and spoke through clenched teeth. "How can you be so cruel? Do you answer to no one?"

Erica stared at me with disgust and shook her head as the room grew colder.

My tongue was tied and my chin rattled from the cold. I took another step backward toward the door and jumped when a strong, ice cold wind slammed it shut behind me. I swung around, but no one was there. Fear overcame me.

"What the hell!" I exclaimed, turning back toward Emma and Erica.

Erica stifled a laugh and Emma smiled and looked as though she had finally solved a puzzle she didn't understand.

"What the hell is going on?" I demanded. Another cold breeze blew through my hair.

"Mom," Emma smiled as she spoke softly, "it's Eric."

"What? That's preposterous! Eric's not here." I looked frantically around the room. I would have seen him if he had arrived.

"Yes, he is." Emma shook her head. "You just can't see him."

My eyes searched the room. I looked in every corner and even went to look in the open closet. The room continued to grow colder and colder, but still we three were the only ones there with the furniture. "Why can't I see him? It's not like he's a ghost or anything. There's no such thing!"

"Yes, there is." Erica stated matter-of-factly. I looked from her to Emma, who was nodding her head in agreement.

"But, Eric's not dead, is he? Don't you mean Jared?"

"No, I mean Eric. Jared has been here, too, but," she waved her hands, circling them in the empty air around her, "this is Eric."

I scoffed. Emma was clearly losing her mind. I shook my head, "No, no. You're losing it. And Erica, you shouldn't support this nonsense. There is no life after death. When we die, we die and it's over."

A hard cold gust blew across me as Emma softly stated, "No, that's not true."

I was speechless, "So, prove it to me then."

Emma looked deeply at me, a glint of anger and defiance passed through her eyes. "One of the first times Eric spoke to me, he told me that he had called your house to find me the morning after Jared and I got engaged."

I swallowed hard. No one knew about that. Not even Emma's father. I glanced around the room again, suddenly expecting Eric's face to jump out at me. I still saw nothing.

Emma growled, "You knew how much I cared about Eric! Why didn't you tell me?"

I stuttered, "He told me not to . . . and, uh, I didn't want it to . . ."

"To mess up what I had with Jared." Emma completed my sentence. I nodded my head, but that wasn't the only reason. I hated Eric: hated him for calling me on my choices. I never wanted to see him again and I certainly didn't want Emma anywhere near him.

Emma exhaled loudly, ran her hand across her bald head, and said, "I don't regret the life I had with Jared. He was a good man and I loved him, too, but . . ."

"Didn't you say Jared is here, too?" I interrupted.

"Yes, they are both here to take me home."

My hands dropped to my side. I whispered, "They are here to take you home?"

"Yes, to help me cross over, when I die."

I crumpled to my knees and sobbed hysterically into my hands. How could Emma even speak those words? Erica came over, placed her arms around me and said, "Girl, I know. I didn't believe it either, but they ARE here. I never thought I'd believe in such a thing, but I am convinced."

Erica pulled me to my feet and we both turned to look at Emma who sat proud and strong on her bed. I could see that she was truly at one with the future she soon had to face.

I shook my head in amazement. I didn't know what to believe. Something bizarre was occurring within the confines of this home, but what? I thought of the voice I had heard when I first arrived. Was that Eric? Could there really be a life beyond what we were experiencing now? I thought of the cold air that had mysteriously surrounded us and Emma's knowledge of Eric's phone call so long ago. There was no logical way to explain it.

My faith, or lack of faith, had been shaken. Maybe I did have to answer to someone or something outside of myself. Who or what, I did not know. What I did realize—I had to answer to my daughter, and in the end, that was enough right there. I walked over to her bed and pulled her into my arms. I was not going to leave her. Not this time.

Chapter: Erica

THE FINAL TWO WEEKS OF chemo left Emma's body weak and tired, but her spirit remained strong. She exuded a peace and understanding that none of us could fathom. Emma's smile could still light up the room, even when sadness and fear enveloped our souls. I could only assume that her strength came from her unwavering faith and the time she spent with Eric.

Cassie and I accompanied her to her post-chemo cat scan follow-up when she found out that the tumors had not responded to treatment at all and had actually grown.

Unlike her mother, Emma shed no tears, but nodded with understanding at the certain death sentence she had received. I understood that she had already known it was her time, and had come to terms with it over the past couple months.

As the doctor explained her options, a cold breeze blew against the back of our necks. I watched as Emma placed her hand softly on her own shoulder and patted it, as if someone else's hand were there holding it tight. I could only conclude that it was Eric.

Emma refused any further treatment, but did ask for pain management. Her medication was regularly increased as her abdomen grew more and more painful in the last few weeks. Eventually, hospice was called in and helped us prepare her home for what was to come. Emma did not want to die in the hospital. As time progressed and the pain grew more intense, Emma became so drugged that she was no longer conscious.

The last words she spoke to me were, "Girl, I love you."—three days before she died.

Cassie and I remained at Emma's side until the end. The last three days were the most difficult for Cassie because she desperately wanted to talk to her baby one more time; however, the amount of drugs Emma needed at the end put her in a drug-induced coma, so she never woke up or spoke again. I truly expected Cassie would abandon us as the anger and grief boiled inside her, but to my surprise, she never left Emma's side. Cassie's atheistic belief wavered, and she began to have faith in something beyond herself, even in life beyond death. I could see the change in her every time Eric came in. His presence would fill the room causing Emma to smile, even in her unconscious state. No one, not even Cassie, could deny Eric's presence or the happiness he brought Emma. At the sight of her daughter's smile, tears of happiness would fill Cassie's eyes and she'd whisper, "Thank you" to the frigid air that surrounded us. I prayed that these experiences enriched Cassie's life as they had enriched mine. My faith became unshakable. I knew, beyond a reasonable doubt, that there was life beyond what we knew, and that soul mates were real, whether we found them in this lifetime or not.

When Emma finally went home, Cassie and I were both at her side, holding her hands. As her life's light escaped her earth-bound body, her jaw softly opened, relaxing the muscles in her face. The corners of her lips curled into a smile

Cassie and I both released our pent-up tears, but they were not only tears of sorrow at our loss, but also tears of joy. We knew that Emma went home, to the love and care of those she had loved—continued to love—enveloped in light, love and peace.

Epilogue: Emma

MY DEATH FILLED ME WITH a sense of freedom I could have never imagined. Like a caged dove suddenly released from bondage, I shakily spread my wings, floundering at first, but then, my soul instantly homed into his open arms.

Eric pulled me close and held me tight. Instead of black mist, he was drenched in a stark white light streaked with the lightest of blue. He looked beautiful. Eric no longer felt like an ice cold pillow of air, but like the warm, strong man I remembered.

We spoke no words. Nothing needed saying. Our eyes met as our hands clasped together. All the truths we knew and felt flowed through the energy that pulsed between us. Nothing but love surrounded us. We were finally together again.

Another presence appeared, pulling my gaze from Eric's. Jared's bright blue eyes smiled at me, welcoming me home. He walked toward us and wrapped his arm around Eric and me. I felt nothing uncomfortable: no jealousy, hurt or betrayal—only love. All absolute truth was known and all was accepted. Jared kissed my cheek, smiled at Eric, then handed me a bouquet of purple clovers. As he turned to leave, he winked at me. I watched as he waved goodbye, his form melting into the bright white light.

Eric smiled as he took my hand. We followed in Jared's footsteps. It was time to enter the light and go home. It was time to see my soul family again.

About the Author

COURTNEY FILIGENZI IS THE AWARD-WINNING author of "Let My Colors Out." She graduated with honors from Towson University in 1998 with a major in biology and a minor in chemistry. She also studied sociology, death and dying and parenting. Courtney lives in Woodstock, Maryland with her husband and two sons.